# ESCAPE TO HAVANA

**Also by Nick Wilkshire**
*Thin Ice*

**Coming in 2017**
*Moscow Code: A Foreign Affairs Mystery Book 2*

# ESCAPE TO HAVANA

## A Foreign Affairs
## Mystery

## NICK WILKSHIRE

**DUNDURN**
TORONTO

Image credits: "Super Car Cuba" © Rog01
Printer: Webcom

Library and Archives Canada Cataloguing in Publication

Wilkshire, Nick, 1968-, author
            Escape *to* Havana / Nick Wilkshire.

(A foreign affairs mystery)
Issued in print and electronic formats.
ISBN 978-1-4597-3448-7 (paperback).--ISBN 978-1-4597-3449-4 (pdf).-- ISBN 978-1-4597-3450-0 (epub)

      I. Title.

PS8645.I44E83 2016        C813'.6        C2016-901310-3
                                          C2016-901311-1


1   2   3   4   5   20   19   18   17   16

   Conseil des Arts   Canada Council         ONTARIO ARTS COUNCIL
du Canada   for the Arts                                                        CONSEIL DES ARTS DE L'ONTARIO
                                                                               an Ontario government agency
                                                                               un organisme du gouvernement de l'Ontario

We acknowledge the support of the **Canada Council for the Arts** and the **Ontario Arts Council** for our publishing program. We also acknowledge the financial support of the **Government of Ontario**, through the **Ontario Book Publishing Tax Credit** and the **Ontario Media Development Corporation**, and the **Government of Canada**.

Care has been taken to trace the ownership of copyright material used in this book. The author and the publisher welcome any information enabling them to rectify any references or credits in subsequent editions.

— *J. Kirk Howard, President*

VISIT US AT

dundurn.com | @dundurnpress | dundurnpress | dundurnpress

Dundurn
3 Church Street, Suite 500
Toronto, Ontario, Canada
M5E 1M2

For Kate — I wish you a life full of adventure

# PROLOGUE

## December 2014

If Charlie Hillier had known what that evening held in store, he might have done things differently. He wasn't one for melodrama, but he could have made a hell of a speech, flown into a rage, or maybe even broken something. Even a different outfit, which wouldn't have changed anything, would at least have allowed him to say he had done *something* to mark the end of his former life.

As it was, he had barely given a thought to his usual uniform of dark suit, white shirt, and red tie when he dressed that morning. The tie was more burgundy than red, with dots small enough not to offend his conservative nature. The charcoal V-neck had been a last minute flourish, regrettable now that he was standing in the drawing room of the Swedish ambassador's residence, simmering in the collective warmth of more than a hundred guests. They stood eating and drinking in clusters, all sheltered from a late December wind that whipped the snow against the frosted panes of the Rockcliffe mansion that had been decorated with just enough red, green, and gold to reflect the season without looking like a holiday store window. The competing scents of gingerbread and mulled wine added to the festive atmosphere, as did the spirited chatter that rose above the soft chamber music playing in the background.

Charlie stood at the edge of a knot of guests, half listening to the bow-tied man at its centre, but more concerned with the time as he checked his watch again and loosened his tie. He and his wife had been there for hours already, despite his hope for an early exit, which Charlie had been sure to mention to her several times on the short drive over from Foreign Affairs headquarters on Sussex Drive. She had seemed agreeable enough, and even mentioned feeling fatigued herself after a long day at the office. But Charlie had been to enough of these functions with her over the years to know better. Whereas he was content to put in an uncomfortable hour or two of face time and call it a night, Sharon LeClair-Hillier was a born networker. There was always one more peer to share the latest gossip with or an interesting new acquaintance to make from the up-and-coming set, and Charlie always seemed to find himself standing in an open doorway at the end of these occasions, like a department store security guard waiting for the last straggling shopper to leave at the end of a day-long sale.

But tonight wasn't Sharon's fault. They had been well on their way to the front door twice, only to be derailed by one encounter after another. First, it was the Swedish trade attaché who they had first met a week earlier at the British High Commissioner's reception. Charlie couldn't resist internally assigning him the moniker of "Swedish Meatball" at the time, and nothing in tonight's encounter changed his initial impression of Lars Whatshisface. The attaché was young and freshly posted, but surely the Swedish government's outgoing briefing should have given him a better grasp of Canada's economic fundamentals. He could perhaps be forgiven for not knowing about Canada's wealth of medical isotopes, but softwood lumber? As for Lars's claim of being a former Olympic biathlete, Charlie interpreted it as a transparent plea for attention, and an attempt to compensate for some shortcoming; possibly intellectual, possibly farther south. Poor Lars's actual experience, Charlie had thought, looking up at the young Swede as he boasted to Sharon, was probably limited to waxing skis for the real athletes.

They had barely extricated themselves from the tiresome Lars when Charlie had found himself face to face with his former director and, as the two men paused to talk shop, Sharon had slipped off and attached herself to the Swedish ambassador's entourage. The last time Charlie saw her, she was in conversation with the Swedish number two, which meant she had a shot at the host himself and wasn't going anywhere for the foreseeable future. That was almost an hour ago.

Charlie dabbed at his forehead with a paper napkin and finished the glass of wine in his hand. He had lost count after four, and the cumulative effect of the warmth, wine, and hors d'oeuvres was contributing to a fatigue that was becoming oppressive. He wasn't sure how much alcohol Sharon had consumed, but judging by her bubbly demeanour, he knew they would be leaving her Volvo overnight. At least they had nothing on tomorrow morning, he thought, glancing out at the fat flakes of snow falling outside the living room window. They would sleep late; maybe have a little early-morning romp to work off the hangover and put some steam on their frost-rimmed bedroom window before the short ride over from New Edinburgh in his Honda. On the way back, they might stop off at that new brunch place Sharon had been talking about. It was a recipe for the perfect lazy Saturday morning, and as he stood there, he could almost taste the eggs Benedict.

A distant crash of glassware brought Charlie out of his reverie and, as he loosened his tie another inch, he tried to focus on the nearby conversation. The distinguished-looking man at its centre was an architect, describing the various challenges he had faced in updating the structure of the heritage house in which they all now stood. Charlie was about to head off in search of his wife when he heard the man mention the secret passageways that had been uncovered when they started the refurbishment. Sensing the wave of skepticism among the huddled group, the architect gave an enthusiastic wave.

"I'll show you, if you don't believe me."

He set off with his audience, an intrigued Charlie included, trailing behind him and led them out into the foyer and down the main hallway, following the curve of the staircase toward the rear of the house. He paused at a little alcove just to the right of the entrance to the kitchen. As his followers assembled in a pack around him, he placed his hand on a segment of wall panelling at the back of the alcove. With a theatrical flourish, he pressed on the wall and pulled his hand free, allowing a door-sized segment to pop open as he turned to his audience.

"Through here."

The architect paused at the widened eyes of the gathered crowd, and sensed the vacuum created by their collective intake of breath — puzzling, since he had yet to reveal the door to the passageway that lay at the rear of the closet. He turned to follow the stares and saw two half-naked figures, frozen in horror and entwined at the waist, standing side-on in the little closet. Lars's big paws were buried in the flesh of the woman's buttocks, his pants around his ankles. Her blouse and skirt had converged in a rumpled tangle around her midsection, and most of one breast, including a partially erect nipple, protruded over the top of a lacy bra. The minimalist, lace-trimmed triangle forming the other half of the set was dangling from her left foot, and if Charlie had any trouble recognizing her — there *was* an unfamiliar glow in her cheek — there was no mistaking the lingerie he had bought for her on their brief trip to Manhattan just a few weeks before.

Spotting her husband standing at the back of the gawking crowd, Sharon LeClair-Hillier's guilty expression faded and her eyes narrowed as she addressed him in the tone she reserved for those rare occasions when he left the toilet seat up or forgot to put out the garbage.

"Will you close the *goddamned* door!"

# CHAPTER 1

As the shuddering eased and the plane punched through the last of the thunderclouds, Charlie's heart rate returned to normal and he relaxed his white-knuckled grip on the armrests. Gone were the images conjured by his anxious brain of the sudden malfunction or explosion that would send all three hundred passengers hurtling to a certain and gruesome death, as was the accompanying soundtrack of screams and pleas of mercy to various higher beings. He knew that takeoffs and landings were when most of the trouble happened, so he was technically halfway home. The window was still streaked with the rain that had hammered the tarmac at Ottawa International Airport, but the scene beyond it now was pure tranquility. The soothing, azure horizon above a landscape of cotton candy was enough to make him forget the turmoil of the last six months, if only for a moment. The ping of the seatbelt sign, followed by a muffled announcement from the flight deck, brought him back to reality. In a few hours he would be landing, and staying, in Havana. What an odd reality it was.

He glanced over the empty seat next to him at his fellow passengers across the aisle, lost in sleep, reading, or conversation. The couple immediately adjacent seemed headed for a holiday and Charlie, envious of their apparent insouciance as his own stomach clenched, tried to imagine himself in their place. His gaze lingered on the woman, particularly the familiar way her hair was piled up on the back of her head. It wasn't until he noticed her companion's curious glance that he realized he was staring, and he was grateful for the interruption of the coffee cart.

Charlie kept his eyes on the clouds for a while, as he sipped his coffee and tried to convince himself once more why it made sense for him, the same Charlie Hillier who had spent the past fifteen years pushing paper from the comfort of his climate-controlled office in Ottawa, to be embarking on a three-year posting to Havana. The fact that heat and humidity disagreed with him would have to go on the negative side of the ledger, as would his general appreciation of creature comforts, like a regular supply of hot water or electricity. His never having been on posting wasn't really a plus either, and the rudimentary Spanish he had struggled to learn over the past six weeks wasn't going to be much help.

In fact, the Cuban posting's only real asset was its distance from Ottawa. It wasn't as far as Ulan Bator — his only other choice of posting on such short notice — but a Caribbean island, albeit embargoed and under communist dictatorship, had to be better than the frozen Mongolian steppe. Charlie would rather sweat, eat dry chicken and beans, and suffer through the occasional power outage than freeze to death on a diet of horse-kebabs. And while Havana was only a few hours away by plane, it was foreign and isolated enough that it seemed much farther removed from Ottawa; maybe even far enough for him to move on with his life. Maybe.

In some ways, he wasn't sure he would ever recover from the shock of that awful December night. It was bad enough finding out his wife was having an affair, but to discover

— along with a dozen other aghast partygoers — her wrapped around the Swedish Meatball in a broom closet was more than he felt he deserved. What Charlie hadn't realized at the time was that one of the people in the crowd worked in Sharon's division, and it hadn't taken long for vivid descriptions of the illicit holiday hump to begin floating through the halls of the Lester B. Pearson Building, where he also worked. In the weeks that followed, he had felt cloaked in humiliation from the moment he set foot in the office, an embarrassment that was heightened every time he rounded a corner or walked into a room and noticed a sharp hush, a dropping of eyes, and a not-so-subtle shift to some hastily improvised conversation.

And things had been no better at home. Far from being repentant, Sharon seemed to think *he* was somehow to blame for all the fuss, disappearing in a teary huff every time he tried to discuss their situation. They spent an awkward holiday season under the same roof, barely communicating other than to engage in an occasional skirmish. Then, one evening in mid-January, they were sharing a rare moment on the sofa together, an after-dinner coffee in hand, when she told him it was over. It had been a calm discussion, and in retrospect he couldn't remember why, or even if, he had agreed to be the one to leave, but he was gone the next day. And so, after fifteen years of what he thought was a happy marriage, he was on his own again. Well, not exactly alone. He had his older brother back East, annoyingly successful and the head of the perfect nuclear family, to remind Charlie what a failure he was. Not that he had offered anything but kind words and support on Charlie's brief trip home in the aftermath of the breakup. His parents had said all the right things, too, of course, but it didn't change the disappointment he had seen in their eyes. He had cut the trip short in the end, blaming an imaginary flare-up at the office, and hurried back to Ottawa. But if he was hoping for some anonymity to recover, it had never materialized.

Taking the passport out of his shirt pocket, he fingered the blank visa pages. In almost two decades with Foreign Affairs, he had never left Canada for work, and had always felt more than a little envious of his better-travelled colleagues (that is to say, all of them) and their stories of adventure at the far reaches of the planet, whether it was their participation in some treaty negotiation or multilateral convention of global import or the subsequent night off at the Bolshoi, or weekend on safari. Charlie assured them all that he was quite happy keeping his chair warm while slurping the stale coffee at HQ. He had repeated this mantra so often in passing up one opportunity after another that he had almost come to believe it himself. Eventually, it became moot, as the opportunities dwindled and he settled into obscurity at the lower end of headquarters middle management. That Sharon's inability to leave her aging mother, who still lived two streets away, was what really kept them both in Ottawa had never bothered him before. It seemed a small price for maintaining a happy marriage, even though the old bag had given him nothing but grief since the first day they met, having made it clear from the outset that he wasn't worthy of her daughter, and never would be. It occurred to him recently that perhaps he should have listened to her. In fact, in light of recent events, there were a lot of choices that he was revisiting, wondering what he had been thinking at the time.

Charlie put his mother-in-law's wrinkled scowl out of his mind and flipped to the photo page of his passport, drawing a sharp intake of breath at the axe murderer staring back at him and remembering the day it was taken all too well. He had just received a courier package from his soon-to-be ex-wife's lawyer containing their settlement agreement, his feverish first read of which revealed that it was the documentary equivalent of an unanaesthetized castration. Tucking the wretched document in his desk drawer, he had wandered the halls like an automaton, ending up at the official photo section twenty minutes late for his pre-arranged appointment. And while smiling was strictly forbidden for passport photos, he couldn't help wondering what the photographer must have been thinking as he took the picture of a man whose misery was so obvious.

Flipping the passport shut on the hideous photo, he felt a distinct surge of pleasure as he looked at the burgundy front cover, and the gold lettering under the coat of arms: *Diplomatic Passport*. He had his long-time friend and former colleague, Winston Gardiner, to thank for that. He was the one who had engineered Charlie's reincarnation, once it became clear that he could no longer stay in Ottawa.

Unlike Charlie, Gardiner had planned his career carefully, and had joined the executive cadre some time ago. But Charlie hadn't realized the scope of Gardiner's new directorship when they met over lunch early in February, or the power it afforded him to navigate the quagmire that was the departmental human resources system. By the end of their lunch, Gardiner had devised a plan for his new protégé's assignment abroad in a fraction of the time it would normally take, in part because of a cyclical shortage of personnel available for foreign postings. The only tricky part, given the fast-approaching posting deadline, was location. Two or three years in Ouagadougou might not offer the restorative experience that Charlie had in mind. Then again, Paris or London was out of the question on such short notice, especially for someone coming from outside the established pool of candidates. But there was an opening in Havana.

As he stared at the passport, pride gave way to self-doubt, as he tried to imagine himself in his new role as Charlie Hillier, diplomat. Surely, even Gardiner's pull couldn't save him when the Department discovered that a middle-aged desk jockey with no relevant experience had been sent to Havana? He imagined the Canadian ambassador placing an angry call to Ottawa, demanding Charlie's immediate recall after their first meeting. With his stomach bubbling with anxiety, he slid the passport back into his pocket and looked out the window for solace.

"Immigration cards." Charlie looked up as the flight attend-ant thrust a four-by-six card at him. Forcing himself to examine the Spanish side of the form, he was pleased he was able to decipher most of the instructions. He had struggled for years to upgrade his high-school French to a working level, and he had felt some of the old angst returning during those first Spanish lessons. It didn't help that his class of six included a cocky young trade officer headed to Madrid, who had the galling habit of chuckling every time Charlie tried to spit out a sentence. His neck muscles tensed as he remembered the time — not long after his passport photo was taken, as he recalled — that he had been singled out for the third person singular of *comer*, and the overwhelming urge he had felt to pounce over the table and beat the smirking little bastard to death with his Spanish reader.

Selecting a pen from his briefcase, Charlie began to fill in the form. He checked the dates on his entry visa and saw that it expired before the end of his posting. He would have to remember to fix *that*, he thought, as he filled in the date and set the form down on the tray. He stared at it for a moment, as he wondered what the consequences of an expired visa were in Cuba. But as he looked back at the passport, he drew strength from its title. Jail was for regular people; he was a diplomat, now. Though it was true that most of his job was administrative in nature, not at all what most people would associate with actual diplomacy or the cucumber sandwich set, there was no denying the fact that he would be carrying out his duties as an accredited diplomat. No Cuban customs agent was going to throw Charlie Hillier, the *diplomat*, into some stinking, rat-infested Caribbean Gulag, at least not without some pause.

Charlie had been briefed on his Vienna Convention rights, and the dos and don'ts of a posting in Cuba, so he had nothing to worry about, certainly not the fact that he was headed to a job he knew little about, in a place he had never been, and where he knew no one. In fact, considering the events of the past few months, those were all pros. And anyway, Foreign Affairs had sent hundreds of its people to Cuba over the years and, of those, how many had run into a problem? Well, Charlie recalled, there was that one guy who had been thrown off a cliff, but that was years ago, and anyway, he had asked for it by sleeping with some political honcho's wife. Besides, he was pretty sure the guy had survived, and the government disability benefits were first-rate.

Tucking the immigration form and passport back into his pocket, Charlie reclined his seat and closed his eyes, intent on focusing on the new life waiting for him below the clouds, rather than the one he was leaving behind. Lulled by the steady hum of the engines as the plane continued its progress south, he was soon dozing.

# CHAPTER 2

Charlie stood at the baggage carousel, shifting his weight
from one foot to the other and sweating. He stared at the
black rubber flaps at the end of the conveyor belt, beyond the
same three bags that had been completing their forlorn circuit
for the past fifteen minutes, and willed his luggage to appear.
Checking his watch, he was alarmed to see that he had been
standing there for almost an hour, and it was only the sight
of a dozen other passengers seemingly in the same boat —
some of whom Charlie recognized from his flight — that kept
him from panicking. Besides, he told himself, what were the
chances of actually getting any satisfaction at the lost baggage
counter in this place, if there was one? The arrivals terminal
stank of stale sweat and cigarette smoke and felt like a steam
bath. He drummed his fingers on the handle of his empty
cart and watched the same three bags disappear through the
flaps again, wondering why they hadn't been claimed. He was
imagining their owners being beaten in a nearby interrogation cell, their screams muffled by soundproof walls, when
he spotted one of his suitcases. His elation turned to surprise,
then horror, as his second bag came into view, its zipper half
undone and the contents spewing out of the sides.

He heaved the intact suitcase onto his cart and then
went about hurriedly stuffing his clothes back into the

second case as he chased it along the conveyor belt. Setting it down on the cart, he caught sight of a pair of his underwear making its way lazily along the conveyor belt and he muttered excuses as he cut in front of a young couple to retrieve the errant boxers. Putting his suitcase back together and loading it on top of the other one, he noticed it felt distinctly lighter than when he had checked it in Ottawa. He soon understood why, as he opened the top of the bag and looked inside. The majority of his clothes seemed to be there, but the two plastic bags he had stuffed with Aspirin, deodorant, toothpaste, and other toiletries were gone. He had heard of the shortage of these goods for the average Cuban, and had resolved to do his part by bringing in what he could. Now, they were in the hands of some unscrupulous baggage handler on the other side of those flaps, along with the twelve-pack of new briefs he had picked up for himself at Costco the day before.

As he waited for his third and final bag, Charlie silently fumed over the injustice and considered whether his diplomatic privileges extended to his toiletries, or his underwear. The lawyer in him started framing the argument: *These undergarments are subject to the privileges and immunities of the Vienna Convention, and their seizure represents a clear violation of Article ...*

But he had never been any good at litigation, and it didn't take long for his resolve to weaken. Theft was theft, though, and he was still pondering the idea of a formal complaint when his last bag appeared intact and he loaded it onto his cart. He looked around for someone official and saw two policemen, or maybe they were soldiers, standing near the exit. One of them was smoking a cigarette directly under what looked like a NO SMOKING sign, and as he tossed the butt to the floor and crushed it with the heel of his boot, he looked straight at Charlie. It wasn't a particularly friendly look, and suddenly Ottawa seemed far away, indeed.

Opting to raise the matter later, preferably from the safety of his new office at the Canadian embassy, Charlie set off for the exit under the now disinterested gaze of the two cops. He manoeuvred his laden cart out of the inferno into the slightly cooler air of the main terminal. He scanned the sparse crowd and was relieved to see a bored-looking man holding a sign bearing a Canadian flag. As he approached, he made out the name under the flag: CHARLES HALLER.

Close enough.

"Hi, I'm Charlie," he said, extending his hand as the man holding the sign perked up.

"Carlos. Welcome to Cuba." He shook Charlie's hand and took control of the cart. "You have a good flight?"

"Yes, thanks." He didn't feel now was the time to raise the baggage-looting incident, so he followed Carlos out through the main doors instead, ignoring the shouted offers of cigars, taxis, and more cigars. Outside, a warm breeze seemed to welcome him to his new home and put him in a much more positive frame of mind. This was more like it.

"We here," Carlos said as he stopped the cart behind a well-travelled GMC van.

"This one?" Charlie was eyeing the dented bumper as Carlos began loading the bags into the back.

"I take you to the embassy?" Carlos asked, as they climbed into the front and the engine roared to life.

"The hotel, actually," Charlie replied, rummaging through his briefcase for the name. He was to stay in a hotel while they finalized the arrangements for his government-supplied house. He would drop by the embassy later, but first he needed to take a shower and do a quick inventory of his things to make sure nothing vital was missing. "The Meliá Habana," he said, as he retrieved the email with his reservation information.

"So, you been to Habana before?" Carlos asked, as he pulled away from the curb.

"No, this is my first time. I'm really looking forward to it."

"I go to Ottawa five years ago. Is cold!"

Charlie laughed. "You were there in winter?"

"*Si, Febrero.*"

"Oh yeah, it can get pretty cold in February in Ottawa. I can't say I'll miss it this year," he added, looking out the window as they turned onto what looked like the main road into Havana. Apart from the odd palm tree, the landscape to either side of the highway was sparse, the grass a dirty brown.

He continued to take in his surroundings as Carlos chatted on, changing lanes to escape the cloud of black smoke pouring from the back of a farm truck. As they passed it, Charlie noticed its wooden box was filled with workers, and he exchanged a brief look with an elderly farmhand, his sun-weathered face wrinkling into a smile as Carlos sped by. Charlie was no mechanic, but the truck had to be forty years old and its wooden sides seemed to be held in place by a web of rope and wire. It looked like it belonged in a museum, not on the road with a dozen people bouncing around in the back. Suddenly, the embassy vehicle made sense to him, as he imagined how he might be perceived passing this relic in a gleaming Volvo or Bimmer. He couldn't help wondering whether this apparent disparity was what anyone had envisioned back in the days of *la Revolución*. Then again, Charlie thought, as the rickety old truck and its black, noxious trail disappeared into the side-view mirror, the old man in the back was the one smiling.

Charlie sat in the reception area of the Canadian embassy, looking at a painting on the far wall, trying to decide whether the harbour was in Nova Scotia or Newfoundland. He felt refreshed after a quick shower and change of clothes at the hotel, and he was looking forward to seeing where he would be working for the next three years. From the outside, the converted villa on 70th Avenue didn't look that impressive, and Charlie knew from his review of the property file that even after sacrificing the tennis court for a new annex building, the mission was still pressed for space. He was wondering whether his office would be on the ground or first floor when he heard the door behind him open and a young man appeared. With his tall, athletic frame clad in a polo shirt and khakis, the guy looked as ready for the front nine as a day at the office.

"You must be the new MCO. I'm Drew Landon. Welcome to Havana."

Standing to take the outstretched hand, Charlie saw the same benevolence in the young man's eyes as in his smile. "Charlie Hillier."

"Sorry about the wait. I wasn't expecting you until tomorrow."

As he tried to place Landon's age within the low twenties — he looked young enough to pass for a student — Charlie couldn't help wondering whether Winston Gardiner had realized that *two* rookies were going to be in charge of embassy administration when he had assigned Charlie to Havana.

"I decided to drop in for a quick look around. I don't want to put you out, but if you could just show me where my office is …"

"It's no trouble." Landon looked at his watch. "Why don't I give you the dime tour, then maybe we can grab a late lunch?"

Charlie nodded and followed Landon as he punched in a code on the terminal next to the forbidding glass-and-metal door separating the reception area from the rest of the building.

"The head of mission's in Port au Prince until tonight, but I'll show you his office anyway," he said, leading the way through the open door and up the nearby stairs. "Good man, by the way," he added, as he punched in his code again at the top of the stairs and they entered the zone that housed the ambassador and his assistant.

"Afternoon, Martine."

A formidable grey-haired woman peered at them over her glasses from the other side of her desk.

"This is Charlie Hillier, the new MCO. Charlie, meet the ambassador's executive assistant, Martine Monette."

Charlie's lips twitched with an involuntary smile at the sound of his new official title. He had always wanted an acronym of his own. This particular one, short for Management Consular Officer, actually blended two formerly separate positions, before budget cuts had trimmed the ranks of the Foreign Service. The new position was responsible for both consular cases and the myriad administrative matters at the embassy, from human resources, to property and housing, to finance.

"Welcome to Havana," she said, with a curt smile.

"I was just showing Charlie around …" Landon glanced toward the ambassador's open door.

"You can have a quick look." She waved at the door and returned her attention to her computer monitor.

Landon seemed surprised by the invitation and went straight for the door. Standing in the doorway of the office, Charlie was impressed with its size and decor, furnished as it was with mostly modern pieces, accented by a few antiques and some wonderful artwork.

"Very nice."

"You should see the residence," Landon said, before pointing out some framed photographs of the ambassador with various senior departmental officials, as well as the prime minister. Next, Landon led them back out into the main part of the embassy and introduced him around to the few people they met as they made their way from section to section. The numerous empty offices, Landon explained, were due to a conference being held in Old Havana. After a brief tour of the ground floor, Charlie was surprised to find himself back at the main reception area.

"So, where's my office?"

"Oh, we're next door."

Charlie assumed he meant the modern-looking annex building, so he was puzzled when, back outside, Landon led them in the opposite direction, past the lane where the embassy van still sat, and then up a flight of exterior stairs over what looked like the garage.

"The admin section's back here," Landon said, as they reached another locked door and he entered his access code. The door opened onto a long and narrow hallway with offices on either side. Landon stopped in front of the second door.

"This is you."

Charlie hesitated at the door and, as he poked his head inside, his heart sank. The office was small, its walls of the same shiny material as the ones in the corridor — like the inside of his grade four portable, except white instead of faux wood. The sole window was shuttered from the outside and the glass was crisscrossed with what looked like masking tape.

"Hurricane mitigation," Landon said, following Charlie's gaze to the taped windows.

"Hurricane mitigation," Charlie parroted, as he took in the rest of the office and its battered furniture. The desk and cabinets looked like they had been pulled out of the basement at headquarters and shipped here in an open boat, possibly through a hurricane. He thought of the spacious digs he had left behind in Ottawa and felt like turning around and going back to the airport. A couple of shrivelled plants sat on the desktop, and he noticed that the back of the rolling chair was listing sharply to the right. Whereas the main building had been pleasantly cool, Charlie could feel beads of sweat forming on his forehead after just a few seconds in the close air of the office.

"Like I said, I wasn't really expecting you until tomorrow." Landon paused, noticing Charlie's crestfallen look. "But don't worry. We'll get you settled away, maybe with some new furniture."

*Can you please take me back to that nice building next door?*

"Oh, this will be fine, I'm sure," Charlie said, waving away any concern.

"Have you seen your SQ yet?" Landon asked, using the departmental lingo for staff quarters.

"Uh, no."

"Why don't we grab some lunch and then I'll take you out to have a look. You're going to like it, I promise."

Charlie was still staring at the rickety chair and feeling the first hint of sacroiliac pain. "I'm sure I will," he said, his deflated tone suggesting the opposite.

"There's the OR," Landon said, as Carlos slowed the van so his two passengers could get a good look. Set apart from the other houses in the leafy neighbourhood to the west of Miramar, the sprawling white stucco villa that served as the Canadian ambassador's official residence was well back from the road, nestled on a lush green lawn. In fact, the only other structure in sight was a dilapidated brick tower across the road.

"Jaimanitas," Carlos said as he swung the van around, stopped at the edge of the curving driveway, and pointed toward the large house beyond.

"I heard there was some connection to Hemingway," Charlie said, as he surveyed the sprawling house.

"Everything in Habana has a connection to Papa," Carlos said, giving Charlie a broad grin.

"Grant Mason, of Pan Am, had it built in the thirties for him and his wife, Jane," Landon continued. "Hemingway had quite a thing for her, apparently. Anyway, we'll get you in to see it soon. It's beautiful on the inside."

"I'll bet," Charlie said, as the van moved back in the direction they had come.

"You're just around the corner."

"From here?" Having seen his office, Charlie had imagined his new house as a corrugated metal shack, but that would be decidedly out of place in this part of town, so there was still hope. A couple of minutes later, they stopped on a tree-lined street in front of a very attractive villa. It was much smaller than the official residence, but it was bigger than the house he had left behind in Ottawa.

"I told you you'd like it," Landon said, seeing Charlie's expression. "The head of political wanted it, but his wife wouldn't uproot the kids from their existing house."

As they walked up the gravel path that dissected the front lawn, Charlie couldn't believe his eyes. This had to be a four-bedroom house, at least. Surely this didn't fit within the government guidelines for housing single employees?

"Isn't it a bit … *big*?"

"It's the foreign service, Charlie, not the foreign legion," Landon cracked, as he searched for the key to the front door. "But seriously, we did sort of luck out with this one. It just came available a couple of weeks ago, and the Cubans offered it to us first, for a song. We've been looking for a single-family for a while — the last MCO had three kids and they were in an apartment that really wasn't suitable."

"And there aren't any families that … need it?"

"Right now, most members of our Canada-based staff are single or couples; the ones with families are content where they are. But you might be in trouble if we have another family posted next summer."

Charlie waited by the front door as Landon fumbled with a ring of keys before finding the right one and fitting it into the lock. The door came open with a satisfying click.

"*Su casa*," Landon said, swinging the door open and letting Charlie go first. Stepping inside, all he could think to do was offer a silent prayer that no one with a family would be assigned to Havana for the duration of his posting. Despite the intense heat outside, the interior of the house was cool, likely because of the high ceilings and tile floors, which combined to give it an airy feel.

Landon led the way through the furnished dining room, family room, and study, before heading upstairs to show him the four spacious bedrooms. Arriving in the master, Charlie glanced at the massive wrought-iron bed before noticing that a little balcony lay beyond the floor-to-ceiling French doors on the other side of the room. Opening the doors and stepping outside, he gasped at the sight of the shimmering azure rectangle of water below.

"It has a *pool*?"

"I told you it was nice."

"When do I move in, again?"

Landon laughed and looked to Carlos. "When's the electrician coming?"

"He say tomorrow."

"He's been saying that for a week." Landon grimaced.

"*Mañana,*" Carlos repeated, with a nod of assurance. "For sure."

"What's wrong with the wiring, anyway?" Charlie asked.

"Nothing major, just some of the lights are on the fritz in the basement," Landon replied. "We'll have you in by the weekend; Monday at the latest."

They returned downstairs to complete their tour of the house, with Charlie marvelling at the spacious kitchen and the lush greenery surrounding the pool in the garden. It was with great reluctance that he accepted Landon's apologies for having to bring the tour to an end, due to some unfinished business back at the office.

"We'll probably get you in to see the ambassador tomorrow morning, around ten," Landon said, as Carlos pulled the van away from the curb.

"Hmm?" Charlie had barely heard him, focused as he was on watching the villa — *his villa* — disappear in the rear-view mirror. "Sure. That sounds good."

"There are some decent restaurants in that little mall next to the hotel. I'd offer to take you into town, but I've got some stuff to do tonight. Maybe I can show you around Old Havana on the weekend?"

"I'd like that." Charlie felt re-energized by the brief visit to his new house. It was almost enough to make him forget the sight of his office. "If you want tickets to a show, you tell me," Carlos was quick to offer. "Or maybe cigars?"

Charlie found himself wearing one of Carlos's infectious grins. "Thanks, Carlos, I might just take you up on that."

Charlie sat at one end of a long, polished boardroom table. Sharon and her divorce lawyer James Leitch, nicknamed (aptly, in Charlie's opinion) Jimmy the Leech, were seated in the distance at the opposite end. They were smiling and whispering together, while Charlie sat alone. Every few seconds, the lawyer would shout a new demand across the space between them and Charlie would nod in agreement, unable to respond in any other manner.

"We want your share of the house," he demanded with a sneer. Charlie nodded slowly. "And all the furniture," Leitch continued, clearly relishing each new demand and the automatic nod from the other end of the table that it produced.

"We want your pension too, Charlie — all of it." He was laughing now, and Charlie could see that Sharon was enjoying herself, too, but he remained powerless to resist.

"Okay, but where's *my* lawyer? Um, shouldn't he be here?"

"I killed him," Leitch replied, as he and Sharon burst into manic laughter. "We want your car, your salary, and all of your underwear," he continued, dabbing away tears, as Charlie nodded again. "Oh, and Charlie," he added, the smile disappearing from his face as he looked at Sharon and pulled what looked like a machete out from under the table. "There's one more thing she wants."

Charlie sat bolt upright in his bed, his body bathed in sweat, his heart pounding in his ears and his hands clasped around his crotch. It was several seconds before he recognized his surroundings and began to breathe again. He got out of bed and padded to the mini-bar, squinting at the interior light as he fumbled for a bottle of water. He gulped at the cold liquid in the dark until the bottle was empty, his nerves still jangling from the nightmare.

Stepping out onto the balcony, Charlie took in a lungful of the musty, salty air and leaned on the railing. Though he could see nothing but inky blackness past the lights of the pool below, he could hear the waves crashing along the ragged shoreline beyond the grounds of the hotel. A few stray notes of Spanish guitar rose above the sound of the swell, though it seemed too late for the hotel bar to be open. He peered over the rail at the still waters of the enormous pool, with its lagoons and swim-up bar, and thought of the happy couple on the plane. Perhaps they were somewhere in this very hotel, resting naked in each other's arms, their only concern whether to tour the old city or hit the beach in the morning.

Charlie tried to put them out of his mind as he stared out into the starless night and listened to the waves, until the ghost of a chill on the onshore breeze sent him back inside.

# CHAPTER 3

Charlie sipped his lukewarm coffee and tried to find a comfortable seated position. The newish chair he had found behind his desk when he came in was a definite upgrade over the relic from the day before. In fact, the whole office had undergone a transformation, with the windows, floor, and furniture having been scrubbed clean and the dead plants removed. After getting his pass and access code from the security officer, Charlie had been visited by the resident IT expert, who set up his computer account and got him ready for his first real day of work. He was reading an email summary of his first consular case — a tourist from Moose Jaw who had lost his passport on what appeared to be a drunken junket into Old Havana from Varadero — when Landon appeared at his doorway.

"Ready?"

Charlie hopped out of his chair and searched his desk for a pad of paper. Michael Stewart was a career diplomat on his fourth posting, his second as head of mission, and he was unanimously described as decent and down to earth. Still, there was something unnerving about having an ambassador as your boss. Finding a pad and donning his jacket, Charlie followed Landon over to the main building, through the secure entrance and up the stairs to the ambassador's reception area.

"You can go right in, gentlemen," Martine said, barely looking up from her computer.

The ambassador was seated at his massive desk, poring over a report of some kind when they entered. He looked up and took off his glasses. "Come on in," he said, coming out from behind the desk and shaking Charlie's hand first. "I guess you're our new MCO?"

"Yes, sir. Charlie Hillier."

"Call me Michael, please. Welcome to Havana," he said, as they arranged themselves on facing sofas. Charlie knew from reading his bio that Stewart was in his late fifties, but there was something about the man, perhaps an aura of confidence, that defied age. While Charlie straightened his tie and sat ramrod straight, Stewart crossed his long legs and assumed a leisurely pose, his tan linen suit a second skin. "What kind of housing have we got lined up for Charlie?" Stewart was looking at Landon and his top leg began to swing gently up and down, showing off a highly polished brown Oxford.

"We're putting him into the new one. It should be ready this weekend." Landon looked at Charlie and added. "We hope."

"The one around the corner from the residence? Oh, well. You'll be very comfortable there," Stewart said. "I wish I could credit that one to your diligent efforts, Drew," he added, grinning at Landon, "but I think it had more to do with that aid package we announced last month."

"And here I thought someone at ImCub must really like me," Landon joked. "ImCub's the arm of the Cuban government responsible for leasing property to diplomatic tenants," he added, turning to Charlie.

"Well, let's hope we have as much luck with a new embassy site," Stewart said, clapping his hands together.

Charlie had been briefed on the situation before leaving Ottawa. The current embassy was too small, and in need of a major retrofit. The Cubans had floated the possibility of selling land to Canada for a new building, something they generally didn't do but seemed willing to consider for some of their diplomatic tenants. Charlie had heard that Stewart was keen on the idea, and on making it happen within the two years left on his own posting.

"I've been reviewing the property file," Charlie said, wanting to appear just as keen.

"Then you know we need a new building." Stewart became more serious. "We're bursting at the seams here, and if the changes people are talking about come to fruition," he said, stroking his fingers over an imaginary beard — a gesture that Charlie knew was the universal reference to Castro, "well, you can imagine. I've invited the president of ImCub to this weekend's reception. You can meet him yourself." Landon had already told Charlie about the reception to be held on Saturday night at the official residence. "I understand you spent some time in property management in Ottawa?"

"Yes," Charlie replied, momentarily distracted by a five-by-seven portrait of a Labrador retriever in a gilt-edged frame on the side table. He hadn't noticed it when he had scanned the office from the doorway the day before, and it seemed out of place in the otherwise formal setting. "I was mostly on the finance side," he said, looking away from the picture and concentrating on embellishing his property credentials. "But I was involved in some major greenfield projects." He hoped Stewart wouldn't ask for much in the way of details. Charlie had authorized a lot of payments to contractors, but he hadn't exactly been close to, let alone in charge of, the actual projects. A critical path to him could just as easily mean a well-worn trail to the building site's porta-potty as a key project management term.

"Well, that's excellent news," Stewart said, leaning forward on the sofa and gesturing with a manicured hand, "because I intend to make this a reality, and I'll need your help to keep Ottawa on side."

"Of course."

Stewart spent ten minutes on other priorities, none of which seemed even remotely as significant to him as securing a new embassy site, before returning to the property file. Charlie kept his reservations about having the whole thing built in two years to himself, and the meeting concluded with a personal invitation to attend the weekend reception at the official residence.

"He seems like a decent guy," Charlie said, as he and Landon made their way back to the administration building after the meeting.

"I told you."

"What's with the picture of the dog?"

"That's Teddy." Landon laughed, but only briefly. "The ambassador's a serious animal lover — so is Mrs. Stewart. The last gardener got the boot because they didn't like the way he talked to the dog."

"I'll keep that in mind for Saturday night."

As they reached the secure door and Charlie punched in his code, he turned to Landon. "You said you *hoped* I'd be in my house by the weekend. I thought you tracked down that electrician."

"I did." Landon sighed as they went into Charlie's office and sat down. "And he swore he'd be there on Saturday morning, but you just never know when it comes to local labour."

"Is it a safety issue?" Charlie asked. "Because I can probably live without basement lights for a while."

Landon shrugged his shoulders. "I don't think so, but I can double-check the inspection report the guy from Ottawa did up a couple of weeks ago, if you like."

"Would you mind?"

What little furniture and personal effects Charlie had shipped from Ottawa had arrived ahead of him and were sitting in the garage downstairs, and he was eager to get settled. His new place was fully furnished and Sharon had grabbed most of the furniture in the settlement anyway, but there were a couple of items that she and Jimmy the Leech had let him keep, including an antique desk and chair that he especially liked. He saw no reason to delay his moving into what would be his new home on account of a little electrical problem.

Charlie stood in the expansive backyard of the official residence, a glass of champagne in his hand, listening at the edge of a cluster of guests for the punchline to the Australian political officer's joke about his first week in Havana. The blue water of the pool shimmered behind him, and the sound of crickets filled the night air, cooled to a comfortable temperature by the gentle breeze that stirred the tops of the trees. It was such a perfect evening, or would be, if Charlie weren't so preoccupied with wondering what he was doing there. He jumped as the crowd burst into laughter, and took a sip of the champagne. He was already halfway through his second glass and he would have to watch it, in case he had to make small talk with the ambassador, or worse, some Cuban official. He scanned the crowd again for Drew Landon, or any other familiar faces from the embassy. Seeing none, he briefly considered a stroll to the other side of the patio, but the thought of trying to incorporate himself into yet another group of strangers was more than he could bear at the moment. So he stayed where he was, pretending to be relaxed.

Social situations had always been difficult for Charlie, for reasons he could never fully understand. Whether it was some innate flaw in his physiological makeup, or an acquired tic, he always seemed just a little ... *off*, as though he were operating in a parallel world just slightly out of synch with everyone else. He had struggled with it through university and law school, thinking the awkwardness would eventually fade, but it still plagued him twenty years later. Standing there in silent agony, he could only marvel at the irony of his current situation. A lawyer who hated to argue, Charlie had successfully abandoned his legal training years ago and settled in to a perfectly bland bureaucratic career. How fitting that his role as faithful husband to an unfaithful wife would eventually force him to transform himself into a diplomat who couldn't schmooze. Was it any wonder he was so screwed up? He tipped back his glass and was looking for a waiter when he felt a hand on his shoulder.

"Charlie Hillier," Landon said, gesturing to the woman at his side. "I'd like to introduce you to Martina Blanco, Argentine special envoy for trade."

"Nice to meet you," Charlie said, shaking her hand and feeling a combination of relief at Landon's arrival and pleasure at Blanco's warm smile.

"Martina's specialty is agriculture."

Charlie guessed she was in her early twenties, and was about to ask whether this was her first posting when they were joined by another woman, who pecked Blanco, then Landon, on both cheeks as Charlie looked on. While Blanco was attractive, her acquaintance was stunning. Charlie found himself so absorbed by her smouldering brown eyes that he barely registered that Blanco was speaking.

"This is Amirjit Saini," she said. "She's with the Indian embassy. Amirjit, meet Charlie Hillier."

"Pleasure," Charlie said, shaking her hand.

"Charlie's our new MCO," Landon said, patting him on the shoulder.

"Oh, really?" Saini tilted her head to one side. "I'm a consular officer as well. You must be really new."

"I just arrived this week."

"Then you're here at an exciting time," Blanco said, referring to the recent historic meeting between the U.S. president and Raúl Castro. Opinions were mixed on whether this would amount to a significant change in the short term, but there was no question it was a milestone in Cuban history.

"Yes, interesting times."

"Where were you, before Havana?" Saini asked.

"Actually, this is my first posting," Charlie said, recognizing a slight widening of the eyes in the two twenty-something women. "I've been with Foreign Affairs for a long time, but I've been at headquarters until now," he felt the need to explain.

"A refreshing change, I hope?" Blanco offered.

"It's hard to argue otherwise in this environment." He gestured to their surroundings with his empty champagne flute and both women smiled, though Charlie recognized something in Saini's eyes that was at odds with the white flash of her teeth.

"Havana's my first posting, too," she said. "Martina's the veteran among us."

"Where were you before Havana?" Charlie asked, trying not to show his surprise at Blanco's experience.

"I have been in Brussels and New York, at the UN in both cases. But Havana seems like home to me. I studied here for three years. I am very happy to be back."

"The work here is challenging," Saini added, "but the people and the place are charming, as I'm sure you'll discover." Charlie was about to respond when a tall Cuban man appeared at the edge of their little group. Landon's reaction on seeing him made the man's importance clear.

"Señor Ruiz, what a pleasure." Landon shook his hand, then turned to the others, starting with Blanco. "Gustavo Ruiz, director general of Inmuebles Cubana, this is …"

"We've met," Blanco said, as Ruiz stepped forward to embrace her on both cheeks. "But I don't believe you've met Charlie Hillier, the new Canadian MCO, and Amirjit Saini, consul with the Indian embassy."

Ruiz gave Charlie's outstretched hand a perfunctory shake on his way to a two-cheek peck with Saini, which took considerably longer. He remained planted next to her as the conversation continued, and Charlie was so busy trying to think of an appropriate segue into possible building sites in the diplomatic area of Miramar that he barely noticed when Saini wrapped her arm in his and leaned against him. His furtive, sidelong glance at her when he realized they were standing arm-in-arm was met with such an easy smile that all he could do was respond with a dopey grin.

"You were going to show me the inside?" Saini pointed toward the residence.

He stared at the house for an awkward moment before recognizing the part he was being asked to play. "Of course."

"If you'll excuse us," Saini said, leading the way toward the house, tugging Charlie past Ruiz. "So nice to see you again, Señor Ruiz."

They strolled across the patio and inside the drawing room of the rambling villa, where pockets of guests stood around chatting. They stopped in front of a large painting.

"I'm sorry about that," Saini whispered, withdrawing her arm from Charlie's. "It was terribly rude of me, but I'm afraid Mr. Ruiz's reputation precedes him."

"My pleasure," was all Charlie could think of saying. He didn't really know what Saini's remark meant, and he didn't much care, but he was missing the sensuous feeling of her soft, warm skin on his. She was even more beautiful in the muted light of the drawing room.

"I suppose you haven't had a chance to do much in the way of consular work yet?" she asked, apparently keen to gloss over the reasons for her improvised escape.

"No, not really. I've been focused on getting my bearings, so far. I'm sure you have a wealth of experience, though. How long have you been here?"

"Almost three years. I meant what I said earlier, about the work. It really has been worthwhile."

"You must be nearing the end of your posting, then?" A waiter passed by and they exchanged their empty champagne glasses for full ones. "Will you go back to India?"

"I haven't really decided. I was considering something in South America," she said, trailing off. "What about you, Charlie? What brought you to Havana?"

"Mmm," Charlie mumbled, swallowing a mouthful of champagne while considering his answer. He knew the truth was out of the question, and decided to keep things vague. "I was looking for a change, really. I know it sounds a bit corny."

"I don't think it's corny at all," Saini said, with a genuine smile. Charlie was still considering pinching himself as he stood next to this exquisite woman in the opulence of the ambassador's drawing room, sipping champagne and chatting, when a familiar voice brought his dreaming to an abrupt end.

"Charlie. Good to see you. Having an enjoyable evening, I hope?"

"Oh, hello, Ambass— Michael. Yes, thank you."

"I'd like you to meet my wife, Katherine," Stewart said, as Charlie came face to face with the tall, graceful woman with an intelligent sparkle in her eyes at Stewart's side. "Charlie's our new MCO," Stewart added, pausing as he glanced at Saini.

"Oh, this is Amirjit Saini," Charlie said, hoping he got it right — he had never been good with names. "Meet Ambassador Michael Stewart and Katherine Stewart. Amirjit's with the Indian embassy."

"So, you've just joined us, then?" Katherine Stewart asked him, after exchanging greetings with Saini.

"Just got here on Monday, yes."

"Well, I hope you're enjoying yourself and not letting him work you too hard," she said, laying a slender, jewel-encrusted wrist on her husband's arm.

"I'm doing my best."

"Charlie was good enough to show me around the inside a little," Saini said, looking around the room. "It really is a beautiful house, but I must be getting back outside. It was a pleasure to meet you."

"Charlie's got the place around the corner," Stewart said to his wife, as they watched Saini leave. "So we're practically neighbours."

"It's a very nice neighbourhood," Charlie remarked, wondering if being so close to the official residence might be a liability. Then again, it wasn't as if the houses were in sight of each other.

"You've got your family with you, then?" Katherine Stewart sipped her champagne.

"Charlie's flying solo," Stewart said, as Charlie noticed a slight change in his wife's expression.

"I'm divorced," he felt the strange need to say.

"In that case …" Her smile returned. "Havana's just the place for you. Just watch out for the staff," she added, a frown appearing at edges of her pert mouth. "The locals will be falling over themselves when they find out there's an unattached man in town."

"Really, Katherine," Stewart scoffed, as Charlie tried to work out whether she was joking or not. He smiled anyway.

"I'll bear that in mind."

"Isn't that…?" Stewart began, before his wife followed his line of sight and finished his sentence for him.

"Hector Garcia. Yes. And he's looking bored. I'd better get over there. It was so nice to meet you, Charlie. Enjoy yourself."

"A pleasure to meet you, too," he said, as Katherine Stewart flitted gracefully across the drawing room toward the patio.

"He's in charge of Havana's protected buildings," Stewart said, as they watched his wife greet the Cuban official with an elegant embrace. "Katherine's been after him for weeks to let her hold a reception for one of her clubs in a heritage building near the Cathedral." He took a sip of champagne before adding: "And she has a habit of getting her way."

"She's certainly very charming," Charlie said.

"Relentless, actually," Stewart replied. "Poor Hector doesn't know when to throw in the— Oh, look who it is. Come with me."

Charlie was halfway across the room, following Stewart's long strides, when he realized they were headed toward Gustavo Ruiz, who was standing alone by the pool munching on a canapé.

"*Buenas tardes, Gustavo.*"

Ruiz's smile at meeting the ambassador seemed to fade when he noticed Charlie standing next to him.

"I'd like to introduce you to Charlie Hillier."

"Yes," Ruiz said, shaking his hand. "We have met already this evening."

"Well then," Stewart continued. "The first of many meetings, I'm sure, on the way to securing a site for our new embassy."

"I'm looking forward to working with you on that very important file, Mr. Ruiz," Charlie said, though Ruiz's thin smile was less than encouraging.

"There is much work to do, Señor Hillier," he finally said, after an awkward silence.

"Well, we're certainly keen to get started." Stewart plucked a caviar-laden cracker from a passing tray. "These are quite good. You should try one."

Ruiz nodded, taking a bite. "Almost as good as what the Russians once served."

"Times certainly have changed," Stewart said, waving off the tray. Charlie had driven by the Russians' massive and largely deserted diplomatic site out in Miramar and imagined they must have had quite a presence in Havana in their day. He wasn't sure whether Ruiz was dissing the caviar or just making conversation. If it was meant as a dig, Stewart was unfazed, and continued to chat easily with Ruiz, while Charlie decided to watch in awe as Stewart gradually eroded Ruiz's gruff façade with a subtle combination of charm and humour. He was caught off guard when the ambassador suddenly patted him on the shoulder.

"Listen to me, going on. Charlie here is keen to fill you in on our property requirements, Gustavo, and I see Katherine is looking for me."

Charlie struggled to think of something insightful to say, as Stewart slipped away and Ruiz sipped his wine for a moment, before breaking the silence himself.

"How long have you been in Havana?"

"Just a week."

Ruiz nodded, as though he understood. His dark eyes were making Charlie increasingly uncomfortable, and as a nervous reaction, he began rattling on about his flight from Canada, the weather there, and similar nuggets of information that were obviously of no interest to Ruiz. While he babbled, his mind was imagining Ruiz's position in the diplomatic property program as a front for his real role in Castro's secret police, tasked to add to an already thick file they had been gathering on a certain Charlie Hillier.

"So, you are in charge of property matters for the embassy?"

"Hmm?" Charlie was absorbed by the image his mind had conjured of Ruiz standing over him in some dingy basement interrogation cell, waving glossy pictures of his ex-wife wrapped around Lars the Swede. Then he remembered Ruiz had asked him a question.

"Yes … I'm in charge of property."

"You don't like your current location?"

"Oh, it's a wonderful location," Charlie said, quickly. "It's just that we're at capacity. Beyond it, really." Ruiz nodded. "And your …" He paused to think of the right word, though his English was excellent. "… *personal needs* have been met, I hope?"

It took Charlie a second to realize he was referring to his new house. "Oh, yes. Yes, it's very nice. Near here, actually."

Ruiz seemed impressed. "I know it well, then. You are very fortunate."

"So everyone keeps telling me. I haven't actually moved in yet, though."

Ruiz set his glass on the tray of a passing waiter. "I have another engagement this evening, Señor Hillier, so I must leave now. We shall meet soon to discuss your embassy's needs, yes?"

Does that mean there *is* a site? Charlie wanted to ask, but he decided not to push his luck, and fumbled instead for his business card. "I look forward to hearing from you," he said, before Ruiz set off toward the living room. He was about to head over to the buffet table when Landon appeared out of nowhere.

"How did that go?"

"Okay, I guess," Charlie replied, though he wasn't sure he had made any actual progress. He decided to concentrate on the positive. "He wants to have a meeting."

"Did he mention a site? Something on Fifth Avenue, maybe?"

"Sorry." Charlie shook his head. "Guess we'll have to wait and see. What was all that about, with Saini?"

"I was going to ask you the same thing." Landon was grinning.

"She ditched me in the drawing room, as soon as Stewart and his wife showed up. Does she have some history with Ruiz?"

"I don't know. Ruiz has a reputation as a bit of a player. That much I do know. They must have crossed paths before. Maybe he made a move on her."

"He seemed to know all about my SQ," Charlie added.

Landon shrugged. "That's his job."

"I just thought it was a bit … odd."

"Havana's a small place, Charlie. And the diplomatic community's even smaller. Everyone knows everyone. But it's nothing to be concerned about," he added, patting him on the shoulder. "Speaking of your place," Landon continued, "I talked to the electrician this afternoon."

"You mean the guy who was supposed to be there this morning?"

Landon shrugged. "He had some excuse or other, but the bottom line is, I don't know if we can count on him to get it done any time soon."

"Maybe I should do it myself," Charlie said, omitting to mention that his previous experience in electrical home repair was limited to installing a very standard furnace thermostat — a job he had botched so badly that he had almost burned the house down. It had quickly become

Sharon's favourite dinner party anecdote, and Charlie had always laughed along. It didn't seem as funny now, somehow.

"Or you could just leave it," Landon said, oblivious to the dark cloud that had just parked itself over Charlie's head. "I could put it on the to-do list for the next time one of our maintenance guys comes down from Ottawa. As long as you don't mind not having any lights in the basement."

"No problem," Charlie muttered, taking a slug of champagne and enjoying the growing buzz it was giving him. He had no idea when the next scheduled maintenance visit was, and he really didn't give a shit. He didn't plan on spending any time in the basement, anyway.

"I figured you'd want to get in there ASAP," Landon said. "So I arranged for Carlos to help us with getting your crates over there from the embassy tomorrow. It shouldn't take us long, if you're up for it."

Charlie's cloud dispersed at the news. "You don't have to do that, on Sunday no less."

"I've got no other plans," Landon said, shrugging his shoulders. "Come on, let's get something to eat."

Charlie set down his end of a crate and mopped his forehead with the back of his arm. "That's it."

Carlos gently deposited the other end of the crate on the dining room floor and smiled. "You need a *cerveza*, Charlie."

"Now you're talking," Landon said as he arrived behind them and set a cardboard box down on top of one of the crates.

"I wish I had some, but—"

"I got you a little housewarming present," Landon said, pulling a six-pack of Cristal out of the top of the box.

"You think of everything," Charlie said, as they made their way out to the backyard. He and Landon leaned over the side of the pool and splashed cool water over their faces, while Carlos sat in the sun, a little grin teasing the corners of his mouth.

Arranging their chairs poolside, the three opened their beers and Carlos raised his in a toast.

"To your new *casa*."

"Thanks for helping me move in, guys," Charlie said, taking a sip of the beer. It was like liquid gold in the midday sun.

"So, did you enjoy yourself last night?" Landon asked.

"Yeah, it was nice to meet some people," Charlie replied. "Martina seems very nice," he added. He had noticed she and Landon were both gone by the time he had left for the hotel, and he was still trying to figure out whether they had left together.

"I dated her for a while, a few months back," Landon said, sipping his beer. "We're still friends, but that's it. So if you're interested …"

"Oh, I didn't mean it that way, but she sure is attractive," Charlie said. "And her friend, from the Indian embassy …"

"Amirjit. Isn't she something?"

"She is beautiful." Carlos was nodding.

Landon looked surprised. "I didn't know you knew her, Carlos."

"I make it my business to know all of the beautiful women in Habana." He grinned as he savoured a mouthful of beer. "I give her a ride back to her embassy from that conference last week."

"I think she's got a boyfriend," Landon said.

Carlos frowned. "No boyfriend."

"How do you know?"

Carlos gave Landon a broad smile. "Maybe she tell you yes, because she knows you are a wolf."

"You're messing with me, aren't you, Carlos? I can always tell."

Carlos's face was an inscrutable mask as he turned to Charlie.

"Maybe she likes her men a little more … how you say?"

"You mean *older*?" Charlie was grinning.

"Invite her to your new *casa*," Carlos waved his bottle toward the house, "and find out."

"Now there's a plan," Landon agreed. "A little housewarming party."

They lounged in the sun and chatted for a while before Landon drained his beer, got up, and stretched. "Well, Charlie, can you handle the rest on your own?"

"You bet. Thanks again, guys, really."

"*No es problema*." Carlos patted him on the back.

Seeing them out, Charlie returned to the living room and the assortment of crates and boxes scattered over the hardwood floor. He would unpack for a while, then go for a swim. There was no reason to push himself. He had all the time in the world.

Charlie sat alone by the pool puffing on a cigar, its aromatic smoke dancing in the night air as he dangled his feet in the cool water. The sound of Latin music wafted out from a neighbouring yard, interspersed with peals of high-pitched laughter. He watched the smoke waft up into the night sky, and marvelled at the bright canopy of stars overhead as he contemplated his first week in Havana.

Landon and the rest of his embassy colleagues seemed nice, as did Ambassador Stewart. As for the details of his new job, Charlie considered himself a quick study. What he lacked in experience he would make up for easily enough with a little hard work. Even the previous evening's reception had been all right, once he'd gotten over his initial discomfort. He imagined himself a year from now, jumping easily from one conversation to another and allowed himself to think briefly of Sharon, if only to assure himself that wherever she was sleeping, it wouldn't be anywhere half as nice as his new villa in Jaimanitas.

With the first week under his belt, Charlie was beginning to feel better about the decision to come to Cuba. He would have to call Winston Gardiner and thank him again for the opportunity. He took a long pull on the cigar and focused on the unfamiliar sights and sounds brought to him on the warm Caribbean breeze. Ottawa, and the unpleasant memories it evoked, seemed distant indeed, and for the first time in months things were finally looking up.

He should have known better.

# CHAPTER 4

Charlie stood over the coffee maker, waiting for the last of the water to run through. It had been after midnight before he had sprinkled his things among the existing furniture at the house, but his excitement at getting into his new place, combined with this morning's invigorating dip in the pool, had overcome any fatigue. Even his office was looking better today, with the sun streaming through the opened shutters and falling on the two potted plants his assistant had presented him with that morning. Charlie didn't usually go for office foliage, but he had to admit they brightened up his neatly arranged credenza, and it was a nice gesture from his assistant, Alena.

Returning to his office with a fresh cup of coffee, Charlie scanned his email, then turned his attention to the file on his desk. His second consular case involved another Canadian tourist who'd had a little too much fun in Havana. The auto-parts salesman from Edmonton had spent the night in custody after what the police report described as an "altercation" with a prostitute. Not surprisingly, his story was different, but regardless of what had actually happened, the passport had been misplaced somewhere along the way. Charlie was trying to guess which parts of which version of the story were closest to the truth when his phone rang.

"Señor Hillier."

He sat upright as he recognized the voice. "Señor Ruiz?"

"I hope I am not interrupting something important."

"No, not at all. I was just catching up on my email."

"I was thinking about our discussion the other night, about your embassy's needs," Ruiz said. "I may have a site that is suitable for you."

Charlie was leaning forward in his chair now. "Well, I'd certainly be interested in hearing more."

"I propose that we meet as soon as possible. Are you available this week?"

"Of course," Charlie replied, unaware of his schedule, but certain that it could be rearranged to accommodate any meeting to discuss a new embassy site.

"I'll have my assistant contact you with the details of the meeting."

Before he had a chance to get any more information, Charlie found himself listening to a dial tone. Just as he set the phone down, it rang again, but instead of Ruiz's assistant calling with a firm meeting time, he recognized the voice of the ambassador's executive assistant, reminding him about a staffing report that Stewart needed before the end of the day.

"He'll have it," Charlie said, hanging up with a sigh. He had hoped Stewart's absence next week to attend a conference would have gotten him a reprieve from what looked like a time-consuming, not to mention boring, exercise. Still, his day was relatively free, and perhaps by the time he finished, he would have news about the meeting with Ruiz. Fortifying himself with a sip of the potent coffee, Charlie pulled out the staffing folder and set to work.

"Is that you, Charlie?" Stewart's words boomed from the recesses of his spacious office. Charlie stiffened at the voice. With no sign of the ambassador's assistant by four o'clock, he'd had no choice but to deliver the staffing report himself. He didn't relish the prospect of a cross-examination on the contents of his work.

"Yes, sir. It's me," he replied, poking his head around the door. Stewart was seated at his desk, a broad smile on his face.

"Come in, have a seat."

"Thanks."

"Any word on the meeting?" Stewart put down his fountain pen and leaned back as Charlie settled in one of the two chairs facing the ambassador's expansive desk. He had mentioned the call from Ruiz at an early afternoon briefing, and had instantly regretted doing so before a meeting was confirmed.

"I'm sure they'll call tomorrow."

"Excellent. We have to get them, and keep them, engaged. We don't want to lose this one, Charlie."

"Absolutely." He noticed the collective *we*, though he had a hard time imagining Stewart would be doing much from his week-long Americas Summit in Panama City. "I'll make sure you're copied on any important correspondence while you're away."

"That reminds me," Stewart said, snapping his fingers. "Katherine's decided to join me for the week, and I really hate leaving Teddy with the housekeeper." Stewart was silent for a moment as Charlie sat there wondering whether he was expected to say something. "I don't suppose you'd be willing to look after him for a few days? It would mean so much … to Katherine."

"Um, sure," Charlie heard himself saying.

"It's just that yours is the only other house with a big yard, and it's in the neighbourhood, so it would be just like home for Teddy. He can be such a big baby." Stewart grinned. "We're going to meet some friends in Costa Rica after the conference. Just for a few days."

"I, uh, don't know much about dogs," Charlie said, realizing that the term of his dog-sitting assignment had just been subtly extended.

"Oh, not to worry." Stewart waved a hand. "He's a piece of cake."

"Should I pick him up in the morning?" Charlie asked. At least he would enjoy one more night of peace before being stuck with the official mutt.

"Best you come by tonight. Around seven would be good." Stewart shuffled some papers into a file folder. "I'd have him dropped off, but it will be so much less upsetting for him to have you appear on his turf, so to speak."

"Right."

"My goodness, is that the time?" Stewart looked at his watch. "I'm never going to get everything done at this rate."

Charlie realized he had been dismissed, and started for the door.

"So, seven sharp then?" Stewart looked up from his papers and smiled. "We've got to be at a reception by eight, you'll understand."

"See you at seven."

"Thanks again, Charlie."

"My pleasure, sir."

"It's Michael."

Charlie pulled into the driveway of the official residence and gave a friendly wave to the security guard, remembering that a little hut would soon be installed outside his own place, and that from then on, he, too, would officially be under diplomatic guard. It would feel strange, he thought, to have his very own guard. The guy outside the ambassador's residence emerged from his hut looking decidedly drowsy, and Charlie wondered whether his arrival had interrupted an early-evening nap.

"He's here for the dog," came a woman's voice from the direction of the house. Charlie turned to see Katherine Stewart standing by the open door as the guard gave a lethargic wave and returned to his post.

"This is so good of you, Charlie," she said, as he arrived at the door. She tilted her head to the side and narrowed her eyes before adding: "I certainly hope Michael didn't pressure you to do this, because that just wouldn't be ..."

"Of course not," Charlie lied. "I love dogs."

As if on cue, Stewart stepped aside and Charlie heard the sound of barking and claws skittering across tile. He stood there frozen in place, with a grin pasted to his face and his guts clenched in fear as the big lab careened toward him.

"There's my big baby!" Stewart said, grabbing the dog by the collar at the last second, intercepting its lunge at the doorstep.

"Hi, Teddy," Charlie said, trying very hard to keep the wobble out of his voice as he removed his hands from over his crotch, where they had instinctively wandered, and extended one toward the dog, as though over a vat of bubbling nuclear waste. "Good boy."

Letting the dog go, Stewart looked on with a smile as Teddy lurched forward, sniffing Charlie and wagging his tail furiously as he emitted a series of grunts and barks.

"Look, he adores you," she said, just as the dog's sniffing zeroed in on Charlie's groin.

"Ah, there you are." Michael Stewart arrived at the door just as Teddy was completing his inspection of Charlie's privates. "José's bringing his things around," he added, looking at his watch.

"So, Charlie," Mrs. Stewart said, "I take it Michael's told you everything?"

Charlie looked to the ambassador, who was ready to jump in.

"Yeah, so he gets one of the big scoops a day of the dry food, and a half can of the other stuff, and he goes through a couple of bowls of water a day."

"And whatever you do," Mrs. Stewart added as the gardener appeared with a wheelbarrow laden with an enormous bag, a case of dog food, some bowls, and a blue rubber bone, "don't let him outside."

Charlie nodded, then realized the implications of this information. "You mean if I take him for a walk?"

"I mean, at all," Mrs. Stewart said, the smile gone from her delicate features. "There's a long lead that you can stake down in your backyard for when he does his business, but other than that, he'll be inside."

*I have to keep this thing inside my house for the next two weeks?*

"Don't worry," the ambassador added quickly. "He's house-trained."

Charlie stepped out into the driveway to open the trunk of his car and, while the gardener loaded the food and paraphernalia, Stewart clipped the leash onto the dog's collar.

"Thanks again, Charlie. We'd really better hurry, Katherine."

"No problem," Charlie mumbled, opening the back door and watching the dog leap in. It occurred to him that the tan fabric inside his recently arrived car might not be the best choice for chauffeuring animals.

"And don't forget to take him out at least three times a day," Katherine Stewart said, standing by the car as Charlie got in.

"But he's house-trained, right?"

"Oh, yes. It's just … better that way."

*Is the fucking dog house-trained or not?*

"Bye, Teddy," she said with a wave, as Charlie pulled away. The dog had jumped into the front seat before he had left the driveway.

"Down, boy," Charlie said, looking around the mass of fur for oncoming traffic and trying to ignore the smell of putrefying meat coming from Teddy's panting mouth.

# CHAPTER 5

Charlie lay in bed staring at the slow rotation of the ceiling fan blades, the only sound a low, rhythmic murmur from the large mound of golden fur curled up on the floor by the side of the bed. After an uneventful ride home, he had introduced the dog to his temporary home, and it had seemed content to sniff around. It was only when Charlie decided to go for a swim and tied the dog's leash to the railing by the back door that all hell broke loose. Teddy had barked non-stop for fifteen minutes, destroying the peaceful dip that Charlie had in mind, and forcing him to retreat inside before the neighbours sent out a hit squad. He wondered what other traits, apart from maniacal barking, the Stewarts had neglected to mention.

Charlie sighed as he caught sight of the time on his clock radio: it was past one in the morning and he was wide awake. He switched on the reading lamp and reached for the home repair book he had picked up at a second-hand bookstore in Ottawa, just after moving into his apartment. Charlie had never been particularly handy, and hadn't bothered to acquire any do-it-yourself skills in his years with Sharon. It had never really mattered to him before, and even Sharon's occasional teasing hadn't fazed him. But her ditching him for a younger man had made him consider his un-handiness in another light, perhaps as a sign of a more fundamental deficiency in his manhood. He scanned the index and flipped to the section on electrical fixtures, and he was intrigued by the instructions for basic wiring, and the importance of the grounding wire. No wonder he had almost burned down the house in Ottawa, he thought. He looked at the diagrams and wondered whether he should take a shot at fixing the light in the basement. It looked pretty easy in the pictures, and he knew where the main switch was. There would be enough light down there during the day to work. What the hell, he thought. He had nothing planned for the morning.

He skimmed through a few more sections of the book before setting it back on the night table and switching off the light. He found himself comforted by Teddy's deep, rhythmic breathing, and decided that maybe having a dog around for a couple of weeks wouldn't be so bad. After all, apart from a collegial friendship with Landon, who was more than twenty years his junior, Teddy was all he had. Lying there in the dark, it occurred to him how alone in the world he really was. He could literally slide off the face of the planet and who would care? Not Sharon, that was for sure. He wondered whether she would have even the slightest twinge of remorse on reading his obituary broadcast over the departmental email system. *Colleagues will be saddened to learn of the passing of Charlie Hillier, a ...* He couldn't even imagine the text that would follow. On paper — and in all honesty, in reality — his career over the past twenty years sounded dismal, and he could only hope the communications people who wrote those things were pretty creative. He considered his legacy beyond work and felt even worse. *Charlie leaves behind ex-wife Sharon ...* No, they didn't usually mention ex-spouses, especially ones whose extramarital closet-humping had been so spectacularly discovered. And with no kids to mention, who was left?

*Charlie leaves behind Teddy, a Labrador retriever he babysat for a couple of weeks before he weighted himself down and wandered into Havana Bay….*

Charlie rolled over and cringed at the grating squeak from the bed frame as his weight shifted. It was annoying at the best of times, more so in the midst of a sleepless night. Even the dog had stirred, but as it put its head back down and resumed snoring, Charlie's thoughts turned to Sharon. As much as he hated her for what she had done, he couldn't help missing her, and wondering if everything would have continued as normal if it hadn't been for that stupid Christmas party. Maybe he just needed to get laid, to give himself a little perspective. Since the split, Charlie had had precisely two sexual encounters, neither of which had been particularly satisfying for anyone involved. He rolled over again in frustration, eliciting the same metallic screech. This time it travelled from his ears down the length of his spine.

Bolting out of bed, Charlie dragged the metal bed frame sideways a couple of feet, creating another grating noise that could only be bad news for the hardwood floor, but he was beyond caring. He fell back on the bed and rolled around heavily before satisfying himself that the squeak was gone. On his back again, he closed his eyes to the big fan blades, but it was hopeless. He got up and walked over toward the bathroom, but didn't get more than a foot before stubbing his toe on something hard and sharp. A stream of expletives emerged from his mouth, as he looked down and spotted the protruding edge of a floorboard. Charlie clutched his bleeding toe and hopped the rest of the way to the bathroom, wincing in pain.

It took him a while to staunch the bleeding and apply a bandage, and when the pain had subsided to a dull throbbing, he came back out to investigate the floorboard. He realized that it had been covered by the bed, but now lay on the direct path to the bathroom. Charlie stood there and sighed, considering whether he might be better off just putting the bed back to its original position. But the board was obviously the source of the squeaking.

*Eeny, meeny, miny, mo …*

With his toe still throbbing, Charlie made his choice and was about to start dragging the bed back when a thought occurred to him. He set off in search of his toolbox and returned a few minutes later to find the dog awake and looking at him with an air of puzzlement.

"Sorry, Teddy. This won't take long."

He opened his home repair book to the section on flooring, but was disappointed to find no quick fix. Rather, the only proper solution for a warped board seemed to be replacement, and in order to do that, he would have to pull up two other rows of planks, back to the wall, and he didn't have a replacement board anyway. It occurred to him that he might be able to switch boards, relocating the warped one closer to the wall and out of harm's way, but it all seemed like a lot of work. He sat staring at the floor for a while, then at his home repair book and, finally, at the clock.

"Maybe this wasn't such a great idea," he said, as the dog wagged its tail, but he decided to see how easily he could pry up the moulding and was surprised when it came free on the first try. Within minutes, he had pulled up the first row of planks and, as he made his way back to the area of the warped floorboard, he noticed something odd. Instead of the white plastic underlay that he found everywhere else, there appeared to be a dark spot as he approached the warped board. He had to remove the third row to be sure, but he soon found himself staring at a hole about a foot across. Instinctively, he reached in and retrieved a plastic bag wrapped around something heavy and rectangular, about the size of a large brick.

"What have we got here, Teddy?"

Charlie carefully removed the plastic cover, to reveal another layer of clear plastic, around something off-white in colour. He used his screwdriver to puncture the plastic lining, and froze when a puff of powder emerged from the hole in the tight wrap. After a few seconds of staring at the package, Charlie wet his index finger, dabbed it in the powder, and placed it in his mouth. He felt suddenly dizzy.

*What the fuck are you doing?*

He rushed to the bathroom and rinsed his mouth with bottled water, then swallowed a couple of mouthfuls to try to dilute whatever he had ingested. As he stood over the sink, he looked into the mirror and saw the terror in his own eyes. Cuba was no place to be caught with a couple of pounds of narcotics in your possession. He returned to the bed and stared at the plastic-wrapped brick. Despite the fact that he wouldn't know cocaine from baking soda — his big screen–inspired taste test being of no help — he knew this had to be coke, or possibly heroin. And this was no recreational-use baggie, either. He picked up the brick and guessed its weight at a couple of kilos before setting it back on the pillow as though it were infected with the Ebola virus. His first thought was to call the embassy's head of security, or the police, or both, right away. That was what you were supposed to do, right? Then again, it was almost two in the morning. It could probably wait until first thing tomorrow. As he sat there staring, he realized that his hands were shaking.

Charlie headed toward the bedroom door; then, fearing Teddy might try to eat it, he returned for the brick and took it with him. He made his way down to the kitchen and pulled a bottle of Scotch from one of the cabinets and poured himself a double. As he sipped, he told himself to relax, that he would place a call first thing in the morning and let the embassy security officer take care of everything. He was beginning to calm down when a thought occurred to him. What if the house was under surveillance and the cops showed up the following morning, only to find him curled up with a couple of pounds of coke and half his bedroom floor missing? They might think he had no intention of disclosing his stash, or that he was moving it from one hiding place to another. Images from *Midnight Express* flooded his mind and he decided that he might be better off making the call right away.

He looked at the empty base for his cordless phone and remembered he had left the handset out by the pool. With the brick still tightly in his grip, he slid the patio door open and walked out by the pool, deciding not to turn on the floodlights. As he reached the table and spotted the handset in the moonlight, he realized the dog had followed him outside and was turning to shoo him back inside as he reached for the phone.

"Back inside Teddy," he whispered, as the dog stopped and looked at him.

Charlie felt the handset first, followed by a fuzzy sensation on the back of his hand that was as unfamiliar as it was unsettling. As he turned from Teddy to the table, and his eyes adjusted to the dim light, Charlie could make out a shape on his hand. But it took a couple of ticks for his brain to register the distinct outline, on the back of his hand, of an enormous tarantula.

In the same fluid motion, Charlie's hand shot back toward his body, shedding the frightened spider back onto the table, while his whole body turned and recoiled in an evasive manoeuvre that would have been quite effective, had he not been standing a foot from the pool's edge. Before he knew what was happening, Charlie was in the water, but not before his other hand, the one holding the drugs, had jarred painfully off the edge of the pool deck, slamming the brick onto the tiled edge and splitting the plastic covering. As Charlie's head came up out of the water, he could see the two halves of the brick teetering on the edge of the pool deck, and he managed to gurgle an instinctive "No!" as he watched Teddy bounding toward him. The last thing he saw, before the seventy-five pound Lab landed on his head, was both halves of the brick being kicked into the water by the dog's hind legs as it dove in after him.

Charlie came up for the second time just as the dog popped to the surface and yelped.

"Get out of the goddamn way!" he shouted, as the dog's kicking pushed the ever-shrinking brick out of his reach. He was trying to shove Teddy aside when he realized the dog was labouring, and likely ingesting mouthfuls of the now drug-laced waters of the pool. Luckily, they were within a few feet of the shallow end, and as soon as he was able to move them into this depth, Charlie got his arms around the dog's belly and pushed him up onto the pool deck. Charlie waded, then swam out to where the brick had gone in, but by the time he reached it, only the plastic wrap remained, next to some sodden, off-white clumps still floating on the surface. He grabbed the plastic and swam to the side, just in time to see Teddy jump up and start racing around the pool.

"*What the…?*"

The dog was on its third frenzied lap when Charlie realized it was probably high. Hopping out of the pool, he grabbed the dog by the collar midway through its next fevered circuit and barely managed to get the straining animal inside before it tore off up the stairs. A few seconds later, Teddy was back, only to set a new course through the living room, the kitchen, and then back upstairs again. Standing there dripping onto the kitchen floor, Charlie stared at the plastic wrap. The dope was gone — all of it. Whatever wasn't coursing through Teddy's system had dissolved into the pool. Would anyone believe Charlie had been that clumsy? What if someone tested his pool water?

*What have you done?*

As his mind swam with the possibilities, Charlie made his way upstairs for some dry clothes, barely aware of the dog racing in and out of the upstairs rooms. Pulling a dry T-shirt over his head, he walked over to the hole in the floor and knelt down, trying to peer into the dark recess. Still shaken by his encounter with the tarantula, Charlie used a screwdriver to poke around in the hole, hoping to scare away any lurking critters in the process. He dug around and finally found a flashlight in the bottom of the toolbox. He flicked it on and shone it into the hole, but he could see there was nothing in there.

He was still staring at the hole as Teddy trotted past him into the ensuite and began lapping at the water in the toilet bowl. Dragging the dog away by the collar, Charlie brought him downstairs, but when they got to the kitchen, the dog ignored his water and went straight for his food, wolfing down what was left in the bowl in a matter of seconds.

"I guess the munchies are kicking in," Charlie said, getting another scoop of dog food from the cupboard and topping up the dish. As Teddy ate, Charlie sat at the kitchen table and looked out at the pool again. There was no drug trade in Havana, or so he had been told. He had no idea what the penalty for drug trafficking was here, but death didn't seem implausible. Yet Charlie had stumbled on a lot more than a personal stash, and whoever owned it must have been prepared to sell it to someone who was also willing to take the risk.

Someone crazy.

Someone who wouldn't be happy to find out that Charlie had accidently dumped the precious commodity into his pool.

Not happy at all.

# CHAPTER 6

Charlie tried to concentrate on the consular file in front of him, but it was no use. He pushed aside his third coffee of the morning, the first two having done little more than increase his anxiety since bumping into the embassy's head of security. Gord Connors was a big man, but his even manner had a very calming effect, most of the time. The sight of him at the front gate this morning though, had sent Charlie into such a panic that he had barely been able to respond to Connors's friendly greeting, let alone look him in the eye. Charlie could only think one thing: *Maybe he knows.*

Charlie toyed with the idea of spilling the beans, but decided against it after an internal debate that lasted as long as it took him to walk from the front gate to his office door. At best, Charlie would look like an imbecile, and at worst, a liar. He was also concerned about Teddy, who had finally crashed out at about 3:00 a.m., and was still sleeping soundly when Charlie left for work. He had checked the dog's breathing before he left and he seemed fine, but he wasn't exactly a veterinarian. What if Teddy had permanent damage from ingesting God only knew how much cocaine, heroin, or whatever it was that Charlie had stumbled onto? He'd had two phone calls so far from the housekeeper, complaining about Teddy's apparent inability to control his bladder or bowels. And this was her first day. Worse yet, what would the ambassador do if he found out? Or Mrs. Stewart?

"We still on for that consular visit this afternoon?"

Charlie looked up to see Landon standing there, looking fresh. "Yeah, I thought we'd leave around eleven," he said, with an enthusiasm he didn't feel for the two-hour drive to the prison in Pinar del Rio.

"You feeling okay?"

"Sure," Charlie replied, realizing he must look as exhausted as he felt and searching Landon's eyes for confirmation. "Just a little tired, that's all." He looked at his watch. Despite the file being open in front of him for the past two hours, he hadn't really digested any of the information. He had to stop worrying about things he couldn't control.

"Say, Drew. What do you know about the guy who used to live in my house?"

Landon scratched his top lip with a finger. "Nothing much. Why?"

It was a perfectly reasonable counter-inquiry, for which Charlie was unprepared. "Just curious," he began, wishing he hadn't asked. "I found some … personal items."

"Anything interesting?" Landon was grinning.

"Not really. Just wondering how to get in touch with him, or her."

"I can find out."

"Don't bother," Charlie said quickly as his assistant appeared at the door and Landon withdrew. "See you out front at eleven."

Charlie sat in the interview room sweating, trying to ignore the shouts from down the hall and the stench of body odour that permeated the stifling air. The idea of being detained in a place like this was troubling enough, but Charlie found it even more unsettling on the heels of his late-night discovery under his bedroom floor and he was trying not to let his mind wander over the possible ramifications as he sat in these inhospitable surroundings. Even Landon, who had no such worries and who had chatted throughout the drive west from Havana out to the prison, seemed subdued by the environment as they waited in silence. Prison Santa Ana was a minimum security facility, but from what Charlie had seen of the place so far, he hoped he never had to set foot inside a maximum security institution in this country.

Both men jumped as the heavy metal door squeaked open. A middle-aged man was led to the other side of the table by a burly guard. After directing his prisoner into the chair, the guard secured the handcuffs to a thick iron ring welded onto the tabletop. The guard muttered something in Spanish and left the room.

"Mr. Martin?" Charlie said, comparing the man across the table with the information from the file in front of him. He looked a decade older than his actual age, and as a successful hotelier, Charlie had pictured Tate Martin in a suit — or a nice polo and crisp chinos, at least — not the sweat-stained, light blue prison garb he was wearing.

"You're from the embassy?"

"Charlie Hillier. And this is Drew Landon." He slid his card across the table as Landon did the same.

"Thank God," Martin said with a sigh as he scanned the cards. "You've got to get me out of this hellhole."

Charlie saw the desperation in the man's eyes and wanted to help.

"Are you being mistreated?"

Martin shrugged. "Isn't everyone here? Look around."

"Why don't we start with how you got here," Charlie said, taking Martin's answer as a qualified no. "We've read your file, but maybe you could expand a bit."

Martin gave a snort. "I'm here because I played by the rules ... or didn't, depending on your perspective." Seeing the puzzled looks across the table, Martin continued. "Look, I've been in the hotel business in Cuba for ten years, and I know how things work here. At least I thought I did." He paused to wipe a droplet of sweat from over his eye "You need a permit for everything under the sun here, right? So, when I paid for my annual liquor licence, I added the usual 'fee' and figured everything was cool. Next thing I know, I'm being shaken down for more, and not a few of pesos either. I'm talking thousands ... of *dollars*."

"You're saying you were asked to pay a bribe?" Charlie said.

"I'm saying the usual bribe wasn't enough," Martin replied. "So when they came back for more, I balked, just to knock it down a bit, that's all. I knew I would have to pay; it was just a question of how much. But before we even had a chance to negotiate, I get a visit from the cops. Next thing I know, I'm in here."

"Charged with bribery," Charlie added, looking down at the file.

"For them to charge *me* with bribery is a joke. That's how everything gets done here. Don't you get it?"

"I hear what you're saying, Mr. Martin, but you understand the problem — bribing a public official is a criminal offence in Cuba, and, well, you're not really denying it." As he spoke the words, Charlie realized how naïve they sounded.

"What the hell am I supposed to do? If I refuse to pay, I get my hotel shut down. Ten years I've gone through the same routine with no problems. Why now?"

Charlie had to admit the guy had a point, and he seemed pretty credible.

"I'll tell you why," Martin continued, lowering his voice. "It's that new hotel going up on José Martí Square, across from the Inglaterra. Nobody seems to know who's funding it, but whoever it is, they've got big-time connections."

"You think you were set up by your competition?" Charlie was mindful of one of the few nuggets he had learned from his brief articling rotation in criminal law: that everyone in jail was innocent, put there by some conspiracy or another. And with all that time in a cell to think, people could come up with some pretty creative theories. Still, Martin seemed genuine, and Charlie knew that there was a lot of corruption in Cuba, Havana especially.

"It's obvious, isn't it?" Martin said, more as a plea than a question.

"Have you had access to a lawyer, Mr. Martin?" Landon asked.

"Yeah, sure," he said, with a sigh. "But I don't have a lot of faith in the Cuban legal system."

"Is there anyone you'd like us to contact in Canada?" Charlie asked. He hadn't seen any mention of a wife or family in the file.

Martin shook his head. "Havana's home. I just never thought I'd end up like this," he added. "Is there anything you guys can do?" he asked, the defeat evident in his voice as well as his posture.

"We'll file a consular report, and do what we can to make sure your rights are respected, but we have to let the legal process run its course."

Again, hearing his own words, Charlie couldn't help thinking how impotent they sounded. Martin was obviously thinking the same, slumping farther into his chair, as though someone had loosened a valve somewhere and let out all of his hope.

"In that case, I may never get out of here."

# CHAPTER 7

"There's the U.S. interests building!" Landon yelled into the windswept back seat of the taxi as the driver of the pink convertible 1957 Chevy fought the massive steering wheel all the way along the seaside road running from Miramar into Old Havana. With the embassy's drivers all in service, Landon and Charlie had hailed the cab for the trip into the city for the two o'clock meeting at the municipal architect's office, deciding to take the opportunity to have lunch in town for a change of scenery.

Charlie had been looking out at the blue waters of the Caribbean and watching the waves crash into the breakers just the other side of the seawall, the spray coming up over the side and soaking parts of the road. He followed Landon's outstretched arm and saw the ultramodern American building, more intrigued by the sea of enormous black flags waving in the breeze immediately next door.

"What's with the flags?" he yelled back, as the wind swept a mist of seawater through the back of the car.

"I guess Castro didn't like some of the news," Landon replied, as Charlie noticed a digital news banner on the other side of the building, its rolling red text largely obscured by the flags. As they passed the building, a series of giant billboards with unflattering slogans and caricatures of the current American president came into view.

As they carried on toward the old town, Charlie was struck by the beauty of the buildings fronting onto this particular stretch of the Malecón, but also by the extent of damage to some of their once-grand facades. The paint had long ago flaked off, and was being followed by the mortar in many cases. A few were so badly eroded that they were propped up by wooden supports, presumably to keep them from falling down altogether.

Landon took advantage of a lull in the wind to provide some commentary as Charlie stared at the passing buildings.

"Hurricanes have done a lot of damage in the past few years," he said, as they passed a particularly dilapidated property.

"Do people live in them?" Charlie noticed clotheslines strung across several of the balconies.

"A lot of them, yeah. But more and more are becoming unsafe. I hate to think what this strip will look like in ten years." Landon swung around and pointed across the bay, to the old Spanish fortress at the tip of the northern peninsula. "There's El Morro." He patted the cab driver on the shoulder and said something in Spanish that got a nod. The cab pulled over into a little square off the Malecón a few seconds later.

"We'll walk from here," Landon said, settling up with the cabbie and hopping out over the passenger door. They had discovered, on hailing the taxi, that the doors were welded shut. "The architect's office is a couple of blocks that way," he added, as Charlie clambered out of the back seat.

Landon led the way across a little square and through the winding, narrow streets as Charlie marvelled at the sights and sounds around him and listened to the description of the various points of interest. Much like out along the Malecón, many of the buildings were in various stages of decay. But here, in the narrow and filthy streets, Charlie found himself walking within inches of people's living quarters. He felt like a voyeur as each open window he passed offered a glimpse of Cuban domestic life. A couple sharing a coffee at their kitchen table; a man lying on his bed under a rusted, motionless ceiling fan; an old woman rocking in a chair, just inches from the street. What struck him about the people he saw was their apparent indifference to the intrusion into their lives of passersby. He was also shocked to see the living conditions of some, whose single-room quarters were so small that they had taken over a part of the street, either by setting up a table or chair by the front door, or by simply sitting there – torso in the doorway, legs spilling out onto the cobblestones.

But intrigued as he was by the bizarre sensation of walking down what seemed at once a crowded street and a part of someone's living space, Charlie was amazed by the architecture and the differing level of decay from one building to the next. They passed a dozen crumbling hovels, and then came across a gem with an internal tiled courtyard covered in greenery and centred by a water fountain under an Andalusian patio. Even in its state of general disrepair, and with the panes of glass long gone from the atrium roof, the building was still stunning. To imagine this area in the fifties was to conjure up a streetscape so rich that its current state was all the more heartbreaking.

They passed by four men playing cards in front of an open doorway, which disgorged a gaggle of laughing children, chasing one another in a spirited game of tag. Ten feet farther, there was a pile of rotting garbage so foul that they had to plug their noses as they passed.

"That's Cuba for you," Landon said, noticing Charlie's reaction. "The restaurant's over there," he added, pointing across the little square they had just entered.

They took a seat at one of the open tables on the restaurant's patio.

"So, what brought you to Havana, anyway?" Landon asked, as a waitress arrived with menus. "I understand you were in HR back in Ottawa."

"I started out in finance, actually," Charlie said, opening the menu, "then moved into HR. As for what brought me here," he said, gazing around the square. "I don't really know. Just looking for a change, I guess."

"Well, MCO in Havana'll sure be a change."

"I'm thinking of it as a challenge, too, I suppose," Charlie lied, preferring the statement to the truth — that he just wanted to get as far away from Ottawa, and Sharon, as any job could take him. As he looked across the square at the little trio playing a mixture of guitars, bongos, and some sort of wooden stick instrument Charlie had never seen before, he decided this place fit the bill. "I just went through a divorce, and ..." He paused to see if Landon's face betrayed any knowledge of Sharon's indiscretions before continuing. "I stayed out of the rotational stream for a long time because my wife ... my *ex*-wife wanted to stay in Ottawa. So I found myself suddenly free."

Landon nodded as if it made perfect sense. "Well, if you're looking to get over a divorce, you picked a pretty good place. There are plenty of beautiful women in Havana."

"How 'bout you? Why'd you choose Havana?"

"You mean apart from the beautiful *señoritas*?" Landon laughed. "Wasn't much of a choice, really. It was either here or Abuja."

"That's somewhere in Africa, right?"

"It's the capital of Nigeria."

Charlie understood perfectly, given his own limited options. "Hopefully, we both made the right choice."

They ordered their meals and chatted over drinks as the patio filled with the lunchtime crowd.

"So, what do you think Ruiz is going to offer us?" Landon said. "Maybe something's come up on Fifth Avenue?"

"I don't know, but I guess we'll find out tomorrow." His assistant had received confirmation of the meeting just before Charlie had left the embassy.

"Not bad progress, considering you've only been here a week. The ambassador will be thrilled that you got a meeting already."

Charlie felt a glow of pride, but it was soon dulled by the image of all that cocaine floating in his pool. He had tried to forget about what had happened by focusing on work, but it was always there at the back of his mind, and whenever it popped up, he had to struggle to reign in the ever more horrendous scenarios his freewheeling imagination produced.

"I'd like to see what they're offering before I start getting his hopes up," he said, returning his focus to the conversation.

"Well, whatever it is, I think it's a step in the right direction." Landon raised his glass. "And a good sign for your prospects here."

"Cheers," Charlie said, clinking his glass off Landon's. For all he knew, he would be returning from tomorrow's meeting with a solution to the ambassador's number one problem. In that sense, things *were* looking positive, even if was just dumb luck. He chose to push the lingering fears farther to the back of his brain, if only to allow himself to enjoy a brief moment of satisfaction.

# CHAPTER 8

Charlie sat in the leafy garden restaurant and sipped his bottled water as Ruiz told a story about a Spanish hotel developer in Varadero. *La Cocina* was one of the better private restaurants — *paladares*, as they are known in Havana — and Charlie certainly couldn't argue with the setting. The vine-covered pergolas kept the midday sun at bay, and the competing background sounds of Spanish guitar and the bubbling of a fountain at the centre of an artificial pond added a relaxed atmosphere, broken only by laughter as Ruiz delivered his punch line.

"So, Señor Hillier," he said, as the laughter subsided and the menus arrived. "What do you think of your site?"

"I'm very impressed," Charlie replied, genuinely. The morning meeting had turned into an impromptu visit to the site on the prestigious Quinta Avenida, where an aging administrative building was currently located. The size of the site, as well as its location, made it perfect for the new embassy, and the presence of an existing office building meant it was unlikely to be contaminated by any significant environmental liability. He would have to get advice from the engineering, planning, and security experts, but he was having a hard time thinking of any serious hurdle. Still, he had to be careful. "It's a wonderful location. Definitely worthy of further investigation."

"It is a shame your ambassador is not here to view the site for himself," Ruiz said, a little frown clouding his aquiline features.

"I'll send him a report this afternoon," Charlie assured him. "And I'm sure he'll be anxious to see it himself when he gets back next week."

Ruiz seemed satisfied, and as he perused his menu, the rest of the table followed his cue, and the conversation soon shifted to Cuban food. Charlie was treated to an explanation of some Cuban staples by Ruiz's second-in-command, seated directly opposite. The man was explaining a pulled beef dish he was considering for himself as Ruiz looked on.

"It's peasant food, Señor Hillier," Ruiz said, with a dismissive wave. "The swordfish is excellent though."

"I'm sure they're both good," Charlie said, noticing the other man's glum expression. Because the man had spent five minutes describing the dish for his benefit, he decided to try it when the waitress arrived.

The conversation soon shifted back to the embassy site, and the more he heard, the better Charlie felt. They hadn't talked price yet, but the timing worked, and the assurances from the Cubans about the permitting and planning process sounded genuine. It was all going so well.

The meals arrived, for all but the Cuban directly opposite Charlie. He insisted, as any good host would, that everyone start without him, and after some mutterings and glares in the direction of the kitchen from Ruiz, they all began. It was only when the last meal eventually arrived, and Charlie caught the expression of disgust across the table within seconds of the first bite being taken, that he knew something was wrong.

Charlie had spent the past five minutes eating rancid meat.

He supposed he couldn't be blamed for not noticing anything wrong with the dish, since he didn't know how it was supposed to taste. In any event, he assured his apologetic hosts he hadn't eaten that much and that he felt fine. In reality, he was seriously debating whether to run to the washroom and force his fingers down his throat as a preventive measure, but while Ruiz made a show of dressing down the waiter, and apologizing profusely, Charlie accepted a substituted plate of chicken and beans and the lunch continued. In fact, after his initial horror, he felt just fine. A close call, but nothing more.

"So, Charlie," Ruiz said, as they finished their meals and the waiters cleared away the plates. "What do you think of Havana so far?"

"I think it's charming," he said, glad that Ruiz had started calling him by his first name. "I haven't really had a chance to see much of Old Havana, but I look forward to exploring it."

Ruiz smiled. "You must visit the Museo de la Revolución," he said, referring to the former presidential palace that Landon had pointed out on their way to the municipal architect's office the day before.

"It's on my list," Charlie said. "And I'm told the Gran Teatro de la Habana is one of a kind."

"There's a Spanish company there for the next few months," Ruiz said. "I hear they are excellent."

They continued to chat over coffee and dessert, and by the time the two groups parted in front of the restaurant, Charlie was pretty sure they would have a deal before too long. He and Landon hopped in the embassy van, eager to get back to the office and start planning the next steps.

Charlie sat in one of the wing-back chairs in the ambassador's office, wishing he was at home paddling around in his pool. He and Landon had been on their way out for the day when they were summoned by the acting head of mission to give a debrief of the day's events. Charlie had been warned about Miles Johnston, and could only think the man was living up to his reputation. Whereas Stewart wielded his authority with a quiet confidence, the chargé d'affaires had a different approach — one that did little to inspire either confidence or loyalty, and belied an underlying insecurity.

"What do you mean you didn't talk price?" he snapped. Landon looked to Charlie, who took a deep breath before answering, feeling oddly short of breath.

"Well, we focused on the specifications of the site, and its suitability …"

"How the hell do we know it's suitable if we don't know how much they're asking?"

"We do have a follow-up meeting scheduled for tomorrow," Charlie continued. "We expect that's when …"

"Why the hell didn't you say you had another meeting set up? You don't have to tell me how things work in Cuba," Johnston fumed. "Just make sure they know we're not going to get taken to the cleaners."

"Yes, Mi… sir," Charlie said, with as much enthusiasm as he could muster. He was feeling suddenly clammy. Landon sensed something was wrong and picked up the slack, describing the strategy for the next meeting. Johnston seemed appeased, and Charlie had managed to utter a few words about bringing down a team from Ottawa to check out the site for themselves when his bowels began contracting so forcefully that he thought they would empty right there, on the very rug that Stewart had made a point of mentioning he had picked up at the Grand Bazaar in Istanbul. But he managed to quell his straining stomach and steer the meeting toward its conclusion, with Landon's help, and was actually feeling pretty good about his chances of surviving the debrief as it wrapped up. He was within a foot of the door, with Johnston looking on and grumbling about something when Charlie was overcome by a wave of nausea so intense that by the time he was done, a few short seconds later, his projectile streams had hosed down not only the prize rug, one of the chairs, and the coffee table, but Johnston himself, who stood frozen in place, his eyes wide as saucers.

Charlie closed his eyes and sighed as he lay on the bed, his mind replaying the awful scene. *Thank God for Landon,* was all he could think. He had gotten him out of there in a hurry, and within the hour, Charlie had been cleaned up, seen by the embassy doctor, and driven home with some pills and a promise that he could expect to suffer no more dire consequences than having to spend the best part of the evening in the bathroom, provided he kept himself hydrated and took the medicine.

As a new disturbance made its way through his system, Charlie tried to focus on the day's progress on the new embassy site, but it was no use. Barfing on the acting head of mission in your first week on the job was difficult to forget, no matter what else you accomplished. And things had been going so well….

Charlie was wondering how he could ever face Johnston again when he heard the distinctive clang of the doorbell, followed by a skittering of paws on the tile and Teddy's barking. He briefly considered staying put — he didn't feel much like moving from his current location for a number of excellent reasons — but after a few seconds the doorbell rang again, and Teddy was at the bedroom door now, his barking

growing louder and more insistent. Charlie sighed, got out
of bed, and slipped on a pair of shorts, the now-incessant
ringing grating his already frayed nerves.

He got to the bottom of the stairs and flicked on the outside light, casting the shadow of two figures across the frosted
glass by the front door. He paused for a moment, wondering whether he should open it, as Teddy weaved through his
legs and sniffed at the bottom of the door. Because Charlie
had moved into the house ahead of schedule, the diplomatic
guard that would normally be posted outside hadn't yet been
arranged with the Cuban Ministry of Foreign Affairs. He
decided a quick look through the peephole was in order, and
was surprised to see two young women standing there, one of
whom was pressing the doorbell with an annoyed expression
on her pretty face. Even in his feverish state, and through the
distorted little lens, he could see they were harmless enough.

As the door swung open, Charlie registered their obvious surprise and tried to interpret its meaning. True, he was
sweating, pale, and had just spent the past couple of hours trying to rid himself of a formidable bout of diarrhea, but still …

"*¿Uh, es la casa de Javier?*" said the one with her hand still
on the doorbell, breaking the silence as she glanced from
Charlie to Teddy, who was straining to sniff out the visitors.

"No." Charlie ran the back of his hand over his forehead
and wiped the sweat on the bottom of his T-shirt as he held
onto Teddy's collar with the other hand.

"Chu speak English?" said the other, perking up.

"Yes."

"Wanna party?"

Charlie looked at the two young women. They were
dressed in halter-tops and skirts so tight that parts of them
were spilling out in strategic locations. "Um, I'm really not
feeling that great."

"Come on baby, we make you feel *reeeaaal* good," the younger one said, running her finger down Charlie's arm. He felt his stomach clench and he shifted his weight slightly to try and alleviate the pain.

"You a friend of Javier?" asked the other.

"I'm sorry, I don't know any Javier," Charlie said, as his stomach resonated with the sound of another gurgle and he began to push the door shut.

"This your place, baby?" The older woman gave him an appraising eye.

"Um, hum," he managed to say, doubling over slightly as another cramp hit him, along with an urgent need to get back to the bathroom. "Sorry ... you've got the wrong address," he said, shutting the door against their protests, locking it, and racing to the downstairs bathroom.

Charlie lay there in the dark, praying that the worst had passed. It had been several hours since his last run to the bathroom, and the knots in his stomach seemed to be unravelling a little. He reached for the glass of water by his bed, but it was empty, so he slowly brought himself upright, swung his legs out over the side of the bed, and tiptoed out of the bedroom, careful not to disturb the snoring dog. After guzzling a bottle of cold water from the fridge in seconds flat, he stood in the dim light of the kitchen, catching his breath from the effort. Though he was relatively confident that he was out of the woods, he still felt awful, and the thought of going into work in a few short hours and facing everyone, Johnston especially, was not making him feel any better. He could imagine the chatter around the embassy after he had been driven home this afternoon.

*Did you hear? The new MCO yakked all over the charge d'affaires….*

And the ambassador's chair, his coffee table … and his rug.

It took a determined effort for him not to descend into further worst-case office scenarios, but as he looked at the clock over the stove, Charlie realized that his little barf-fest wasn't the worst of his problems. It had been only forty-eight hours since he had discovered the dope under his floor-boards and then dropped it into his pool.

*Jesus!*

Returning upstairs, Charlie popped another pill. After chasing it with a gulp of water, he made his way past Teddy over to the balcony. Outside, there was little sound, apart from the crickets, and he stood there for a moment just enjoy-ing the warm night air. Turning to the train wreck that had been his day, Charlie tried to be positive. Accidents happened, and people got sick, he told himself. On the positive side, the property file was advancing rapidly, and even Johnston had seemed grudgingly satisfied, if not impressed, with the new site. Well, before Charlie had thrown up on him, at least.

Glancing down at the pool below, Charlie wondered whether the water was safe. He was no scientist, but surely dissolving that much cocaine must have had some effect. Would it just evaporate? He had half expected to find an assortment of jacked up wildlife doing laps in his pool when he got up this morning. Fortunately, Teddy seemed fine, though the housekeeper had complained that he had peed on the floor a couple of times during the day. He had been so busy that he had barely thought about his discovery, or whether to share it with anyone, like Landon, or the embassy security officer. Maybe it had been under the floor for years, long forgotten by a previous occupant of the house. In any case, there wasn't much he could do about it now.

As he leaned on the balcony railing and looked out over the glimmering water of the pool, the only thing that came to his mind was Sharon.

How could she?

# CHAPTER 9

Charlie read through a draft of an email he was about to send to Ottawa, asking the property officer responsible for Cuba to assemble a team for a site visit in order to address the architectural, engineering, security, and legal issues arising from the proposed new embassy project. He had never met the regional property officer, but Landon seemed to think he was pretty keen, so Charlie felt that organizing the visit in the next couple of weeks was feasible. He stared at the screen for a few more seconds, then hit send, just as a burst of laughter erupted down the hall. It was nearing closing time, and most of the staff were heading down to the bi-monthly Friday afternoon social at the little poolside cantina in the embassy's courtyard. It was a scorcher outside, and the perfect occasion for an ice cold beer.

Charlie still felt a little self-conscious about his spew-fest in Stewart's office just forty-eight hours earlier, but he had forced himself to come in on the day after and go straight to Johnston with his apologies. The chargé had been gracious in assuring Charlie that no apology was required and that no harm had been done. Even the ambassador's prized rug had survived a thorough cleaning without sustaining any permanent damage.

Landon had attended the meeting with the Cubans to discuss price, and their opening number was within the expected range. Stewart had been briefed by email and seemed pumped about the Fifth Avenue site. As for actually signing the deal, Charlie had only a general sense of what needed to be done at this point, but he was confident he would know a lot more when he got a response to his email from Ottawa.

"Coming?"

Charlie looked up to see Landon standing at the door, looking at his watch.

He logged off his computer, shuffled some papers for Monday morning, and joined Landon in the hall.

"How quickly do you think the team from Ottawa can be here?" he asked, as they made their way outside into the hot afternoon sun.

"Depends on their availability," Landon replied as they passed in front of the main entrance to the embassy grounds and nodded at the guards. "But it'll take a couple of weeks for the visas."

"Shit, I forgot about that." Charlie frowned, realizing the visa delay would make the expectations he had just sent out on timing sound hopelessly naïve. He was mentally pushing back the project timeline by a couple of weeks as they rounded the corner of the main building and the pool area came into view. A few people were gathered under the awning outside the little bar, and a dozen more were sitting at tables on the pool deck.

The still blue water looked inviting, but Charlie couldn't imagine stripping down to a Speedo in front of his colleagues, and had a hard time imagining anyone else in this crowd doing the same.

"Does anyone ever use the pool?"

"Kids mostly, on the weekends."

As he made his way through the crowd, exchanging greetings and smiles with the Canada-based staff, and the few local employees who were there as well, Charlie began to self-consciously wonder whether the smiles were genuine, or whether everyone was grinning at the arrival of the infamous new MCO. Had they all been having a laugh at the expense of "Chucking Charlie," or maybe "Hurling Hillier," before he and Landon had arrived? He tried to repress these thoughts as he arrived at the bar and a young political officer he had met on his first day stood aside to give him a berth at the bar.

"Charlie, how are you doing?"

Charlie hesitated at the thought that the inquiry might be a reference to his recent illness, as opposed to mere conversation. He decided to interpret it as the latter and smiled in return.

"Doing well, thanks, Jeff. How 'bout you?"

"I was just telling Joanne here that Anne and I are off to Cienfuegos on the weekend. Have you met Joanne?"

"Um, no." Charlie had noticed the striking young woman next to Jeff Cook as soon as he had entered the little bar. She gave him a broad smile and extended a delicate hand. "Hello, Charlie. Welcome to Havana. I've heard you're making quite an impression."

Charlie felt himself flush.

"Locating a site so quickly, I mean," she added, with such an empathetic smile that his confidence was immediately restored.

"Great place, Cienfuegos," Landon chimed in, ordering a couple of Molsons.

"Joanne was telling me about her experiences there last year," Cook said.

As the conversation evolved into things to see and do in Cienfuegos, Charlie couldn't help wondering why Landon hadn't mentioned the existence of the lovely Joanne, and was making a mental note to inquire later when he got his answer.

"This is Joanne's husband, Bryan," Landon said, pointing to the young man passing the beers over the counter.

"Right. You're in political?" Charlie guessed.

"Yeah, but I always wanted to be a bartender," the young man said with a grin, reaching over the bar to shake Charlie's hand. "Bryan Kincaid. You all settled into your housing?"

"Yes, thanks, but I'm still trying to get used to the heat." Charlie dabbed at his forehead with the back of his hand as he sipped the cold beer.

"It beats the rainy season, I'll tell you," Kincaid said, as Landon nodded. "So where's your place, anyway?"

"Charlie's got the new one, out in Jaimanitas," Landon said.

Kincaid whistled. "So, you're the lucky dog. I hear it's pretty nice."

"Yeah, it's great." Charlie wondered if he should play it down, just in case. But if he was interested in bumping Charlie out of his new digs, Kincaid gave no indication.

"So what are you guys doing this weekend?"

"No big plans," Landon replied. "I thought I might show Charlie around Old Havana."

"You interested in tickets to the Tropicana? Joanne got a couple of comps from the Aussies but we can't go. Her parents are here for a visit this week. It's an outdoor cabaret," Kincaid explained, seeing Charlie's puzzlement. "If you've never been, it's worth going, and tickets aren't cheap. It'd be a shame for them to go to waste."

"It's fun," Landon agreed, as he sipped his beer.

"Done then," Kincaid said, going behind the bar to fish the tickets out of his jacket pocket and hand them over to Charlie. "Tell me all about it on Monday."

Charlie continued to chat as one beer turned into two, and the conversation moved on to the recent rapprochement between the Cuban and American leaders, and what it might mean for Cuba. The television at the far end of the room had a live CNN broadcast from Miami, where thousands of expatriate Cubans had gathered to protest the event, in stark contrast to the more positive reaction practically everywhere else. The reaction within Cuba itself had been muted. The consensus in the Canada Club seemed to be that Castro's younger brother, although reportedly more liberal, would not likely oversee any major change, especially with Fidel still in the wings. Charlie took it as a good omen that he was arriving at such a turning point in Cuba's history, and he was feeling positive as the crowd began to thin and the embassy driver announced the last run of the afternoon. Heading out toward the main gate, Charlie chatted with the Kincaids about good day trips from Havana, while Landon talked to one of the embassy drivers. As the van filled up, Landon waved Charlie over.

"Carlos'll pick you up first, around nine-thirty, then he'll get me on the way. The show's at ten."

Driving home, Charlie was feeling much better. His physical symptoms had pretty much gone within forty-eight hours, and with the work week at an end, a night out on the town was just what he needed.

The housekeeper would have left him a meal, after which he would have time for a dip in the pool. The sun was shining as he drove west, and life was good.

# CHAPTER 10

Charlie was sitting out back by the pool, puffing on a cigar and sipping the last of his after-dinner coffee when he heard the doorbell. He looked at his watch and sighed. It was only nine. Carlos was early, and Charlie was still in his swimming trunks. He set the cigar down in the ashtray and threw on a T-shirt as he headed inside and toward the front door. But instead of Carlos, Charlie was surprised to open the door to a young woman who seemed just as taken aback to see him. She looked ready to bolt, as they both stood there, staring at each other.

"Can I help you?" he said, trying not to stare at the woman's chest, which seemed to be straining the fabric of her top. He couldn't help wondering why for the second time in less than a week, a provocatively-dressed and uninvited woman had shown up on his doorstep.

"Javier not here?" she finally said.

*Who the hell is Javier?*

"No, there's no Javier here."

As she considered his answer, she caught Charlie looking at her and ran a finger down the chain hanging around her neck, fingering the little pendant that hung directly over the swell of her cleavage. She gave him a playful grin.

"You wanna have some fun?"

Charlie kept his eyes on hers as he stammered his reply. "I'm … I have to go out in a little bit."

"Won't take long, baby," she added, moving closer as Charlie held his ground at the door.

"Who is Javier, anyway?" he said.

Rather than answer, she seemed to sense that he wasn't going to be able to give her whatever she had come for. *"Buenas tardes,"* she said, with a quick smile as she turned to go back down the path.

Charlie shut the door and headed into the living room, peering out through the shuttered window as the woman reached the end of the path, then paused by the side of the road. Charlie wondered how long she was going to stand there when a car pulled up and she opened the passenger door. He could see the driver's face by the dome light as she got in the car, and even from fifty feet away, Charlie could tell this was one guy he didn't want to cross in a dark alley. His dark-complexioned, square features under close-cropped dark hair gave him a military air, and a large scar was clearly visible across his upper cheek, as the man turned to look toward the house. Charlie jumped back from the window and stayed hidden until the car revved up and moved off into the night. As he made his way upstairs, he tried to make sense of the two strange visits. One could be written off as a wrong address or another mix-up, but two? He was beginning to wonder whether this Javier had been running a brothel out of the house before Charlie moved in. Another thought crossed his mind, long enough to send an unsettling bubble of air through his chest, but he dismissed it as paranoia. Tonight, he was determined to have some fun for a change.

Charlie was leaning against the seawall along the Malecón, the woman's softer parts pressed into him as they kissed. Her mouth felt warm and wet against his, but … what was that smell? His smile turned to a frown, and as he opened his eyes, he recoiled in horror.

"Bad dog!"

Charlie wiped the slobber off his face as Teddy barked and swished his tail against the bed frame. Holding back the urge to vomit, Charlie rushed to the sink to douse his face with water. The brief wave of nausea gone, a throb from the core of his brain took over and had him riffling through the drawers of the vanity for Tylenol. Finding it, he popped a couple of pills in his mouth and chased them with a mouthful of bottled water. As he swallowed, he caught sight of his reflection in the mirror and was horrified. Apart from the severe bed head, his eyes were bloodshot and puffy, and his lips were parched. Not only did he look like shit, but he realized he was still wearing the same shirt he had come home in. He sighed and returned to the bed, deciding to collapse back into the tangle of bedding, rather than venture out into the bright light outside on the balcony. It was almost eleven in the morning, he noticed, as he tried to remember the last time he had slept this late — it had to be ten years or more. He heard the sound of the dog squirming expectantly by the foot of the bed and sighed.

"It's all right, Teddy. Just don't … Oh, forget it," he muttered, changing his shirt and slipping on a pair of shorts to head downstairs. He was still yawning as his bare foot sank into something warm and soft as he reached the bottom of the stairs. The overpowering stench hit his nostrils before his eyes identified the fresh pile of dog shit enveloping his right foot.

"House-trained, my ass," he grumbled, hopping to the back door with the dog following close behind. Once outside,

Charlie grabbed the leash and clipped one end to Teddy's collar and the other to the railing. "Bad dog," he repeated, wagging his finger and rubbing his foot on the dewy grass at the far end of the yard. After washing it under the outdoor tap, he returned inside to clean up the rest of the mess while Teddy whined outside. With his appetite for breakfast shot, Charlie decided he might as well fill Teddy's food and water bowls before bringing him back inside.

"You're going outside every hour, on the hour," he said as the dog lapped at his water and Charlie set up the coffee maker.

Sitting at the kitchen table, nursing his first cup of the potent Cubita, Charlie thought back to the night before, beginning with the rum-soaked show at the Tropicana, and the bar-hopping expedition Landon had led them on afterward. They had bumped into half a dozen of Landon's friends, mostly Australian and Dutch, and clearly closer to his age than Charlie's. But they had been very welcoming, and Charlie had done his best to keep up with the younger crowd as they downed round after round of Cuba Libres. He vaguely remembered dancing at one point, and being part of some sort of conga line, but there were significant gaps after that. As he sipped his coffee, patches of the ride home emerged in his mind's eye. Landon was at the curb outside the club, talking in drunken Spanglish to a wiry young Cuban man as Charlie and one of the Aussie girls looked on. Charlie remembered piling into the back of a Lada that looked ready to fall apart. But most of all, he remembered the overpowering stench of gasoline. He could see the astonished look on the girl's face as she squeezed into the back next to him and looked into the open trunk area behind the seat at the metal jerry can, and what looked like a fuel line running into it through an opening that left plenty of room for the fumes to escape. He remembered the smile on the young Cuban driver's face as he turned around to give them a reassuring wink as the engine sputtered to life and echoed through the bare metal interior of the car, a glowing cigar stub pinched between his lips.

"Holy shit," Charlie muttered aloud, as he sat at the kitchen table. How they hadn't been incinerated on the ride out to Miramar was a miracle. He wouldn't have set foot in that deathtrap in a million years if he'd been sober. But there had been enough Havana Club flowing through his veins at the time to make him completely oblivious to the risk of riding in the back of a moving Roman candle, and he couldn't help grinning at the thought of it — the traditionally cautious Charlie Hillier, bombing along the Malecón at four in the morning, laughing with the others as they made their way west in the imminently combustible Lada. He remembered seeing the beginning of a sunrise behind them, but the rest was fuzzy. He had made it home and into bed though, and was none the worse for wear, apart from a headache. Besides, he didn't have much on his agenda for the day. Deciding his stomach was ready for food, Charlie poured himself a bowl of cereal and glanced at the home repair book he had left on the table. Flipping through it as he chewed, he looked down at the dog.

"We've got nothing better to do today, Teddy. Think I can fix the basement light?" The dog looked up at him, cocked his head to one side, and gave an encouraging bark. Charlie smiled.

"Me too."

Charlie stood on a chair in the basement staring at the light fixture, then at the diagrams in his book, then back at the fixture. Somehow, the two didn't seem to relate. Maybe this wasn't such a good idea, he thought, as he looked at the nest of wires hanging out of the ceiling.

*There's only supposed to be three.*

Charlie sighed, looked at the dog, then returned his attention to the diagrams. It wasn't rocket science, for God's sake. What kind of a man was he, if he couldn't string up a god-damn light fixture? He took one of the wires and hooked it up to one of the contact points, then connected a second wire. He reasoned that the only uncovered wire had to be the ground, and hooked that up to the only part of the fixture that looked remotely like the grounding contact shown in the diagram.

That left two more wires.

The fixture had a built-in pull chain, but Charlie had noticed a switch on the wall near the bottom of the stairs — for some reason it had been placed around the corner, so that you had to know it was there to find it. Seeing no other light in the basement, or other worldly purpose for the wall switch, Charlie assumed it was for the overhead light and figured the odds were good that he could get either the chain or the switch working, but probably not both. Determined not to quit now, he did a little eeny, meeny, miny, mo and connected one of the wires to the only contact point left, then tied some electrical tape around the end of the last one and tucked it back up into the ceiling box. He took one last look at the diagram, then back at the fixture.

Close enough.

He screwed the fixture back into its bracket and inserted a bulb before heading over to the main panel in the corner of the basement.

"You ready, boy?" he said, before flicking the main power switch back on and closing his eyes. Instead of the shower of sparks that he half expected, Charlie opened his eyes to see the bulb burning brightly. The previously dingy basement took on a whole new look as well.

"Pretty good, huh, Teddy?"

The dog wagged his tail and followed him over to the bottom of the stairs, barking each time the light went out in response to Charlie's flicking of the wall switch.

"Knew I could do it," he said as the ring of the phone interrupted his moment of glory. He looked at his watch, pleased that the whole exercise had only taken him two hours, then flicked off the light and headed upstairs, the dog following close behind.

# CHAPTER II

Charlie was sitting at the end of the bar, nursing a mojito and wondering why he had bothered to come out at all. He would have preferred to stay in after his late Friday night, but Landon had been insistent that he shouldn't pass up a Saturday in La Habana Vieja.

They had been at the bar for half an hour already, with no sign of a free table, and God only knew what damage the official mutt was doing back at his house. To make matters worse, Charlie had quickly become an awkward fifth wheel to the foursome that had formed at the bar next to him: Landon and an attractive Cuban woman and a German acquaintance who was married to the woman's friend. Landon had whispered something about a sister who had been unable to make it, and had tried to keep Charlie involved in the conversation, but it was difficult when they were all sitting in a row at the bar. He sipped his drink and surveyed the room, trying to gauge when the next table for five might come open, and wasn't encouraged. He was half listening to the conversation next to him and considering an exit strategy when he spotted a stunning woman making her way through the crowd. He concentrated on his drink as she slipped into the opening next to him and waited for the bartender. She was tall and sultry, dressed in a tight-fitting black dress. Her perfume was light and fresh.

"*Hola*," she said, her white teeth shining in contrast with her smooth brown skin.

"*Hola*." Charlie noticed a mischievous sensuality in her eyes as she looked him over.

"American?"

"Canadian," he answered, after she had placed her order with the bartender.

"I'm Charlie, by the way," he added.

"Maria. What brings you to Havana, Charlie?" she asked, sliding onto the barstool next to his.

"I work at the Canadian embassy."

"How interesting."

"Your English is very good," Charlie said.

"Thank you. I have the chance to use it a lot in my own work," she said, as the bartender delivered her drink.

"*Salud*," Charlie said, as they each sipped their drinks. "And what line of work are you in?"

She stirred her drink as she seemed to ponder the question. "I work for the Ministry of Culture."

"Really?" Charlie fished a business card out of his wallet and handed it to her, trying to remember the name of a man he had met at the ambassador's reception that he was pretty sure worked for the Ministry of Culture. Or was it sport?

"I don't have a card," she said, looking at his and repeating his title. "Consul. That sounds very important."

"Not really." Charlie could see Landon had noticed their new neighbour, so he made the appropriate introductions.

"Maria's with the Ministry of Culture," he added.

"I just work in the office," she said, with a demure smile.

"I didn't get your last name," Landon said.

"Aguirre."

"Well, Maria Aguirre, I hope you'll join us for dinner."

"Thank you," she said, "but I can't. I have to meet some-one later."

Charlie tried not to show his disappointment, though by looking at her he shouldn't have been surprised. What were the odds such a beautiful woman would be alone on a Saturday night in Havana? They continued to chat, and when the bartender said it would be at least fifteen more minutes for a table, Charlie decided to order another drink.

Maria fanned her face with a napkin. "It's so hot."

"It is warm, isn't it?" There was a breeze blowing outside, but in the crowded bar, the ceiling fans did little to circulate the heavy air.

"It's a good night for swimming," she said, with a little laugh.

Charlie nodded, his mind conjuring up an image of this woman gliding through the blue waters of his pool. "I may just have a dip myself when I get home," he said, immediately wishing he hadn't. Not many Cubans had a pool in their backyard. But if she was offended, she certainly didn't show it. Instead, she inched closer to him as his drink arrived. She stirred the sugar in her own, put her chin in her hand, and spoke in a softer, almost intimate tone.

"So how do you like your work, Charlie? It must be fas-cinating."

He tried his best to make his day-to-day work sound fascinating, and he felt he was doing a pretty good job of it, judging by her reaction. She asked him about Canada, and how it differed from Cuba, and as she listed the things he must see during his time in Cuba, Charlie found himself transfixed by her sparkling eyes and glowing skin. He was so taken with her that he had almost forgotten about Landon and the rest of his dinner party behind him.

"It's really too bad you can't join us for dinner," he said, resigned to the fact that he would soon be deprived of her company. But she surprised him when she smiled and beckoned him closer with a crook of her delicate index finger.

"I'm not really meeting anyone," she whispered. "I just never eat here. It's too noisy for my liking. Good for drinks, though," she added with a smile.

"Would you like to eat somewhere else?"

"But you're here for a meal with your friends."

"To be honest," he said, lowering his own voice this time. "I only really know Drew," he said, pointing behind him with his thumb. "And I was sort of thinking the same thing about this place — and it's so hot," he said, wiping a trickle of sweat from his temple.

"I know a little place just a few streets over with wonderful seafood. Why don't you join me? Your friends too."

Charlie leaned back on his chair and looked at Landon and the rest of the group, as Maria pulled out a cigarette. He waited for the right moment to tap Landon discreetly on the shoulder. After a brief and whispered discussion that was lost in the background noise of the crowded bar, Charlie turned back to Maria.

"They're going to stay here," he said, as Landon glanced over to Maria and smiled. Charlie leaned in closer. "One of the girls really wanted to eat here, so he doesn't want to offend. Otherwise …"

"Of course," she replied. "But we should go soon, so we are sure to get a table."

"Right," Charlie said, reaching into his pocket for some money. Fate seemed to have put him in a position to share a meal alone with this lovely woman, and he was anxious to get going before the arrangement changed. With a hurried good-bye to Landon and the others, Charlie followed her to the front door. Once outside, Maria slipped her arm in his and led them off down the street. As they turned the corner onto a wide boulevard, a warm ocean breeze blew in and momentarily dispersed the sultry night air. Maria brushed her dark hair back from her face and sighed.

"It's so much nicer out here," Charlie said, as she led them into a dark side street that ran into a little plaza. The restaurant was on the far side, its patio outlined by twinkling white lights adorning an iron railing that enclosed a half-dozen tables.

After a brief exchange with a waiter, Maria looked to Charlie and smiled.

"We're in luck."

Moments later, Charlie found himself sitting across from her, with the bright Cuban stars overhead and the soft pulse of Latin music drifting from inside the restaurant. Charlie had to resist the temptation on several occasions to pinch himself, reluctant to believe his luck at stumbling into such an enchanting dinner companion. And whether it was the crisp white wine she had ordered for them, or the mojitos already in his system, Charlie found himself strangely at ease with Maria. She seemed genuinely interested in his work, and he was fascinated in turn by her description of her own life in Cuba. Food and wine came and went as they chatted easily, and before he knew it, Charlie noticed that two hours had passed and the waiter was serving their coffee. Fearing the end of the evening, he was waiting for the appropriate moment to suggest an after-dinner walk, or anything else that might extend it, when she finished her coffee and looked at him with that mischievous twinkle in her eyes.

"Did you say you something about going for a swim tonight?"

Charlie froze with the little coffee cup at his lips and looked at her. Was she pulling his leg?

"I was thinking it would be a nice evening for it, yes." He searched her face for a sign that she was toying with him, but sensing the time was now or never, he took the plunge. "You could join me if you like."

"I thought you'd never ask."

"What a beautiful home," Maria said, as Charlie fumbled with the front door key. She was holding on to his arm as they stood on the front porch, and the sensation of her voluptuous body pressed up against his was making the usually simple task of inserting and turning the key quite a challenge.

"Teddy?" he called out as the door opened. A few seconds later, the dog appeared, looking as though he had just awoken from a long nap. "I'll just give him some food," Charlie said, as Maria followed him to the kitchen. While he filled Teddy's bowls with food and water, Maria looked out over the backyard.

"It's a lovely pool."

"And it's a perfect night for a swi—" As he straightened and turned, he was surprised to find her standing so close behind him that he almost knocked her over. But rather than recoiling at their sudden proximity, Maria wrapped her arms around his waist and pulled him closer.

"Later," she said, as he stared into her dark brown eyes. "We'll swim later."

Charlie lay on his back with Maria by his side, her arm draped over his torso. He didn't want to move for fear of disrupting the glorious warmth that coursed through his entire body.

"You are a great lover, Charlie," she purred, lifting her head to look at him. He just stared at her, searching back through the archives of his mind, skipping entirely over Sharon, and the one other woman he had dated seriously in university. There was that cheerleader he'd had a drunken one-nighter with back in high school, but she didn't come close, either. Maria Aguirre was the hottest woman he had ever slept with, by a wide margin.

"But you have made me very thirsty," she added, running a finger down his arm.

"Let me get you a drink," he said, though he didn't move. He wasn't sure he could. His whole body felt like rubber.

"You stay here," she said, getting up. He continued to lay still, his eyes the only part of him that moved, in order to follow her progress from the bed to the door, in all of her naked splendour. Only a woman with a body like that could be so unconcerned by her lack of clothing. Just watching her cross the floor was enough to stir him again, and when she reappeared a few minutes later at the door, a half empty bottle of Cristal in her hand, there was a conspicuous lump in the sheets.

"You are a very bad boy," she said, jumping on the bed and brushing up against him as she brought the bottle to his lips and he raised himself up on his arms. "You're going to need this."

He took a long sip of the cold beer and watched as she kissed her way down his chest. When she got to his stomach, she looked up at him and smiled.

"Finish your beer, and lie back down."

Charlie took another long swig and set the bottle on the bedside table. As he lay back and watched Maria's dark tresses moving over him, he felt such a combination of joy and relaxation that it was as though he were drifting on a cloud toward another dimension. As the pleasure increased, Charlie felt his eyelids grow heavy and he let them close, unable to reopen them as a broad smile creased his lips.

# CHAPTER 12

It was the singing of the birds that he heard first, their excited chirping bringing him gently around. Next was the sound of laboured breathing, coming from the warm body lying next to him in the bed.

*Maria…. She was real!*

Charlie smiled and reached for her, content to leave his heavy eyelids closed and rely on his memory of the previous night. But rather than the soft, supple skin he was expecting, he found himself caressing a soft patch of … fur.

"Teddy!"

The dog jumped up in surprise and bounded off the bed, barking and wagging his tail furiously as he gauged whether it was safe to venture back toward his interim master.

"Sorry, buddy," Charlie said, rubbing a hand over his face. "I was sort of expecting someone else." The dog yawned and continued to wag its tail as Charlie sat up and looked around the room for a sign of Maria. Her clothes were gone.

He couldn't remember her leaving.

Come to think of it, he was having a hard time remembering much after she had returned with the beer. Well, apart from the first couple of minutes, which he had no trouble remembering in vivid detail. He looked under the sheets to confirm that he was naked, but as for actually closing the deal the second time, he was drawing a blank. He glanced at the bedside table and noticed that the beer bottle was gone.

Getting out of bed and throwing on his boxers and a T-shirt, he headed downstairs. Maria's shoes were gone. He looked out by the pool, but there was no sign of her there, either. He went to the front door and noticed immediately that it was unlocked. He stepped outside and glanced over toward the little guard hut, where the guard was preoccupied with a piece of loose caulking on the outside of the window. Charlie was debating whether to approach him when the guard waved.

"*Buenos días.*"

"*Buenos,*" Charlie replied, remembering that the guard had been on duty when Charlie and Maria had arrived back at the house the night before. He walked slowly over to the hut. "Uh, what time did my friend leave this morning?" he asked, catching his reflection in the window and realizing he was standing there in his underwear.

"She no leave this morning, *Señor,*" the guard said, with a grin. "Las' night."

"She left last night?" Charlie couldn't conceal his surprise. "What time?"

"Late."

"Like, midnight?"

"*Dos horas.*"

"Right," Charlie said, looking up at the sky to add, before he turned to leave: "Beautiful, huh?"

"*La Señora … si, mucho.*"

Charlie ignored the wolfish grin and returned to the house, hoping a hot cup of Cuban coffee would refresh his memory of the events of the previous evening. As he made his way to the kitchen, he noticed the basement door was ajar. He was pretty sure he had closed it, he thought, as he stared at the door. For most people, it was the type of thing that might be easily forgotten, but Charlie had a rather obsessive habit of closing doors, especially basement doors. Had the dog pried it open? He frowned and looked at Teddy, who was sniffing himself in the corner, and immediately decided the idea that he had reared up on his hind legs to manipulate the doorknob with his paws was ludicrous.

"Whatever," he muttered to himself, closing the door and shuffling off toward the kitchen and the coffee maker. With a fresh pot brewing, he filled the dog's bowls and got himself some breakfast.

As he chewed his cereal and sipped his coffee, Charlie replayed the evening in his mind, starting with their first roll in the sheets shortly after their arrival back from the restaurant. He had no trouble remembering that, and doing so left a smile on Charlie's face so broad that even the dog seemed to notice, as it cocked its head and watched him from the foot of his chair. Also burned into his memory was the vivid image of Maria's naked profile slipping gracefully across the bedroom floor on her way for refreshments, as were the contrasting sensations of the cold beer she had returned with and the growing warmth of his arousal....

But that was it.

Had he experienced such an earth-shattering orgasm that it had short-circuited his memory, even rendered him unconscious? Maria was smoking hot, to be sure, but it still seemed a bit of a stretch. Perhaps it was the cumulative effect of the alcohol he had consumed over the course of the evening. The more he thought of it, the more likely that scenario sounded. After all, he had combined mojitos, wine, and beer, albeit in what he felt at the time were relatively modest quantities. But booze had a habit of sneaking up on you, and Charlie had never been much of a rum drinker.

He sat there, sipping his coffee and revelling in the memory of what had been a most enjoyable evening, the sudden unconsciousness aside. More troubling than his unexplained power failure was the fact that she had left without giving him the opportunity to say goodbye, or to get her number. He knew her name, but the odds of finding someone by looking them up in the phone book weren't good. This was Havana, after all.

Charlie took his coffee out by the pool and sat in the shade, breathing in the fresh Sunday morning air. There wasn't a cloud in the sky and he could sense that it was going to be a hot one. Maybe he would take a drive out to one of the beaches on the other side of the city. As he sat there looking at the pool, his thoughts of travel plans for the day were soon eclipsed by visions of the lovely Maria Aguirre. To whatever force of fate had thrust her in his path last night, he was truly grateful.

# CHAPTER 13

Charlie was returning from a hurried lunch at the nearby sandwich bar when he saw the van pull up to the embassy gates and felt a wave of unease as he stood on the opposite corner, waiting to cross. His initial excitement at being able to arrange a very quick visit by the headquarters property team had gradually given way to anxiety as he realized that he was largely accountable for the visit's success, or failure. He had thought he would reserve a few hotel rooms, set up a couple of meetings, and that would be that. But as the number of meetings grew, so did the difficulty of coordinating everyone's schedule with those of the various Cuban authorities. Charlie's head was swimming with the times and locations of a dozen meetings to be held across town over the next four days, and while there had seemed to be plenty of time at first, he was now seriously wondering whether they would be able to fit everything in. Since confirming the dates with Ottawa the previous week, he had been inundated with emails from the project manager, architect, engineer, and lawyer, who were now disembarking from the van inside the embassy's gates. Now, he would have to respond to their questions first-hand, rather than through the comfortable filter of his office computer.

Arriving at the front gate, Charlie gave the guard a smile and headed straight to the driveway and the three men standing outside the van, squinting into the bright afternoon sun. They were looking around as though they had just been beamed onto the surface of Mars from the comfort of their air-conditioned workstations in Ottawa.

"Welcome to Havana," he said, approaching a heavy-set man in his fifties. "I'm Charlie Hillier."

"Oh. Hi, Charlie. Bruce Redden," he replied, identifying himself as the project manager. "This is Dan Hart and Antoine Lefebvre," he added, pointing to the two other men, whose names Charlie recognized as the architect and engineer, respectively. Charlie was about to ask them about their flight when he realized they were one short. How could he forget the lawyer, whose litany of pointed emails had kept him hopping over the last week? His own legal background aside, Charlie felt his spirits rise at the possibility that she hadn't made the trip, his general impression of his legal peers having been forever tainted by his economic disembowelment at the hands of Jimmy the Leech.

"And Jillian's in there somewhere," Redden said, gesturing to the back seat of the van, concealed from Charlie's view by its tinted windows.

"Just looking for my file," came the reply from the far recesses of the vehicle's interior. Charlie had developed a mental image of Jillian Gray, whether due to the sharp precision with which she crafted her emails, or to the general impression created by the title "government property lawyer." In any case, the image was distinct and tended toward anal, bookish, and dowdy. When Gray finally emerged a few seconds later and stood in the bright sunshine, Charlie was taken aback.

"God, for a moment there I thought I had left some documents on the plane," she said, standing up straight and smoothing the fabric of her pinstripe pantsuit. Gray had to be close to six feet tall, with glowing auburn locks framing freckled skin and piercing green eyes. Charlie was trying to reconcile his preconceptions when he realized reality was staring back at him.

"Charlie Hillier," he said, closing his mouth and trying a casual smile. "I hope your flight was okay?"

"Jillian Gray, Justice," she said, flicking a piece of her hair from her eyes and holding out her hand. "It was fine, but I'm not dressed for this weather."

"Come on inside, where it's cool," Charlie said, motioning to the stairs that led up to the side building. "We've got a couple of empty offices where you can set up for the week." He noticed Gray's glance at the back of the van and understood. "You can leave your luggage in the van. Carlos will drive you over to the hotel when you're done here."

"What time are we meeting with the head of mission?" Redden asked, as they made their way up the stairs.

"Three," Charlie said, checking his watch. "He just wants a quick briefing," he lied, knowing there was never anything quick about a visit to the ambassador's office. "First time in Cuba?" he asked the group, as they assembled outside the secure door and he entered his code.

"Antoine and I worked on the renovations on the main building a couple of years ago," Redden said.

"First for me," Hart said, as they all turned toward Gray.

"Me too, unless you count Varadero," she said with a grin as the door beeped and Charlie swung it open. As they entered, they were hit by a blast of air-conditioning.

"That's better," Gray said as the door closed behind them. Charlie led the way down to the large spare office at the end of the hall.

"Here you are." He paused by the door and looked at his watch. It was almost two-thirty. "Have you eaten? I could try to get some sandwiches brought in…."

"We had lunch on the plane," Redden said, settling behind one of the desks as Hart and Lefebvre jockeyed for the only other computer in the office.

"If you want to call it that," Gray said, looking up from her BlackBerry as the others chuckled. "Do you have another office? I don't need a computer, but a desk would be nice."

"Of course," Charlie said, resisting a powerful urge to offer her his own office and scrambling for an alternative. "There's a meeting room two doors down that you can have for the week," he said, with no idea whether it was available. He was also acutely aware, in the silence that followed, of the attention of the three men that he had just condemned to a cramped office designed for two for the same period of time.

"Thanks," Gray said, her focus back on her tiny screen as she followed him out into the hall.

"I'll come and get you when it's time to go over for the briefing," Charlie said to the group as he turned to head back to his own office.

"Oh, Charlie?" He turned and almost bumped into Gray, who was standing right next to him in the narrow hallway. "Where's the lady's room?"

"Last door on the right," he said, following her down the hall toward his own office. His attempt not to stare at her shapely backside in the narrow hallway was futile, and he barely heard her joke about the weather in Ottawa, but managed a laugh at the appropriate moment when he reached his office door and disappeared inside. As Gray's light fragrance hung in Charlie's nostrils, he realized that all the dread he had been feeling about the week ahead had vanished, replaced with a different feeling altogether.

"So," Ambassador Stewart said, with the introductions out of the way and everyone settling into the sitting area of his large office. "Welcome to Havana. I hope you have a very productive visit."

"Well, they certainly have a very busy schedule," Charlie said from his chair at Stewart's right.

"You're going to meet with the Cubans tomorrow?" Stewart leaned back in his chair and tapped a manicured finger on his chin.

"Yes, in the morning. Then we're talking to a couple of developers tomorrow afternoon — one Canadian, one French," Charlie continued, pulling out his agenda. "Uh, then it's the architects and a project manager on Wednesday, and the planning office on Thursday."

"What about the local lawyer?" Gray asked.

"Oh, I forgot. That's on Wednesday, too."

"You *are* going to be busy," Stewart remarked, looking at the Ottawa team and adding: "Did you drive by the site on the way here?" Charlie had given the driver strict instructions to point it out on the way in from the airport.

Redden nodded. "It looks good from the point of view of size, and I assume you like the location."

"The location is excellent," Stewart said.

"We couldn't get a security officer teed up in time for this trip," Redden said. "But they'll be sending someone in the next couple of weeks to check it out. We'll have a better idea after this week what the plans will look like, but as I said, the size should accommodate whatever security features they'll want to see."

Stewart looked on thoughtfully as Redden spent twenty minutes going over the general expectations for the configuration of a new building, taking everyone through the boxes the Ottawa team would be looking to tick during the week ahead. Hart and Lefebvre weighed in on their specific areas of expertise along the way.

"And who are these developers?" Stewart asked when they had finished.

"The Canadian one did the renovation on that hotel near Parque Central," Charlie said.

Stewart snapped his fingers. "The Capital, of course. That was a good job."

"And the French one has done several hotels out at Varadero, and recently did the Venezuelan embassy."

"We'll have to tender the construction, of course," Gray jumped in, "and the architectural work, as well, so these are just preliminary discussions."

Stewart's features clouded for the first time in the meeting. "How long will that take?"

"Depends on the value," she replied. "But I would think a couple of months for the architectural work. The construction will be done later, once we have a design."

"Hmm," Stewart was frowning now.

"And we'll have to make sure the site is free of legal claims," Gray continued casually, oblivious to the ambassador's darkening features.

"I don't want to lose this site over legal niceties," he said.

"Neither do I." Gray smiled. "But we don't want someone from Miami showing up at our door with title documents a few years down the road, after we've invested millions." Stewart looked at Gray as a pall of silence fell over the room, causing the others to fidget. She seemed unperturbed, eventually breaking the silence without the slightest appearance of unease. "But I've already seen a preliminary title search and sent the particulars to Washington, so we should know more by the end of the week."

"Washington?" Charlie didn't see the connection, and the others looked just as puzzled.

"That's where the foreign claims were registered in the sixties," Gray replied easily.

"Oh." Charlie coloured slightly. This woman was sharp. And cool as a cucumber, as well.

"You're using Sam Sanchez?" Stewart asked Charlie, referring to the local lawyer, a Canadian ex-pat who had come to Havana from Toronto ten years ago.

Charlie nodded.

"Well he's a bright guy, and he knows how things work here," Stewart added, glancing at Gray for a fleeting moment before turning back to Charlie. "Do you have a dinner planned for the Cubans?"

"Yes, at that new *paladar* you suggested, tomorrow night."

"Excellent. Well then, I wish you the best of luck. Let me know if there's anything I can do to help."

"Of course," Charlie said, as they all stood and shook hands again. The group filed back outside. Standing in front of the main building, waiting for Redden to emerge from a pit stop at the men's room, Charlie took the opportunity to sound out Gray's impression of the meeting.

"The ambassador's all right," he began. "He's just keen on getting the project going."

Gray tucked a piece of hair behind her ear and smiled. "They all are. Believe me; I've seen enough of these projects to know the dynamics. But don't worry," she added quickly, seeming to sense his discomfort. "It's not usually a legal issue that sends these things sideways. Right guys?"

"Yeah, right," Hart said, as he and Lefebvre exchanged looks.

"So, can we check into the hotel now?" Gray said, as Redden appeared.

"I'll get the driver to run you over there right away," Charlie said. "Pickup will be at eight-thirty tomorrow morning."

"Sounds good," Redden said, as they moved toward the main gate.

"I didn't arrange anything for dinner tonight," Charlie added, before heading off in search of the driver. "But the hotel has a couple of restaurants, and there's that plaza nearby."

"Yeah, we're fine," Hart said.

"I'm looking forward to a dip in the pool," Gray said, as she slipped a pair of designer sunglasses over her eyes. "It's stifling."

"Well, have a good rest, and we'll see you in the morning."

# CHAPTER 14

It was two-thirty in the afternoon on the first full day of their visit, and Charlie was feeling as though the team had been there for a week already. The morning meeting with the Cubans had stretched a good two hours over the allotted time and had led to a hurried lunch before the ride downtown to the developer's office, where they had just been led into a large conference room. As they arranged themselves around the table, waiting for their hosts to arrive, Gray took a seat next to Charlie, set out a yellow legal pad, and pulled a shiny black pen out of her jacket pocket.

"So how did we end up talking to these guys, anyway?" she asked.

"Word of mouth, basically," Charlie said, pleased that she had chosen not only to sit next to him, but to also deem him worthy of her inquiries. He hoped to God the mysterious bean side dish that had accompanied his chicken lunch wouldn't wreak havoc on his breath. "They've done a lot of construction in Havana, as well as the stuff out in Varadero that Stewart mentioned. They were going to try to arrange for us to have a walk-through of the Venezuelan embassy."

"Oh, good," she replied, as a woman appeared behind them with a tray of coffee. Hart and the others were looking out the open window, commenting on some architectural feature of the adjacent building, as the woman set down little cups of espresso. Charlie felt the need to make conversation with Gray.

"So how's the hotel?" he asked, before remembering that had been his first question upon greeting Gray at the embassy this morning. If she noticed the gaffe, she gave no indication.

"It's very nice," she said. "Big rooms."

"First time in Havana?" he said, scrambling to recover from his blunder.

*You asked her that yesterday. What the fuck's wrong with you?*

The appearance of several men at the meeting room door saved him from further embarrassment. The two groups exchanged greetings and business cards before sitting down to begin the meeting.

"Well, we're so glad you were able to meet with us today," said the man at the head of the table. Charlie glanced at his card — Société Immobilière, Daniel Leblanc, President. Leblanc was dressed in an elegant linen suit over a sky blue shirt, and his watch was probably worth more than Charlie's car, though that wasn't really saying much. Leblanc carried on with a welcoming speech, then introduced the other three men as a VP, engineer, and project manager, respectively. After that, Leblanc launched into a company bio, accompanied by a glossy brochure of the major projects SI had completed in Cuba. Charlie was impressed by the presentation, and he noticed Gray and the others scribbling notes from time to time.

When Leblanc had finished, the Canadian side took turns asking questions about the company's various projects. Gray seemed particularly interested in their experience in getting permits from the Cuban authorities, and how the requirement to hire Cuban labour had been dealt with in their other projects. Lulled by mid-afternoon fatigue and the subtle scent of Gray's perfume, Charlie's mind began to wander. He wondered if Gray was married, and glanced at her left hand. No ring. She was probably dating some rich class-action litigator and happy to avoid marriage altogether.

He frowned as he thought of how his own fifteen-year experiment with the institution had turned out, and felt the now-familiar sense of … what was it, anyway? Shame, he supposed. How could have he have missed the signs?

At first, he had taken refuge in the almost bearable notion that Sharon's infidelity was limited to a one-off fling with the Swedish Meatball. But the more he thought about it, the more his mind brought up uncomfortable memories from his past. Like the time about five years ago when he had arrived home early from a business trip to Toronto. His meeting had wrapped up ahead of schedule and he had managed to get an earlier flight back. He had called out upon entering the house, with no reply, and was surprised when, a few seconds later, he went downstairs to get something out of the basement freezer and found Sharon standing there next to a burly tradesman, looking awkward. At the time, he thought nothing of her hurried explanation of the electrician's presence — she had called him to fix the dryer plug. He remembered the man seeming very preoccupied with the panel in the rear corner of the laundry room, but then again, wasn't that what electricians were supposed to do? He didn't recall feeling any suspicion at the time, only annoyance that she had called an electrician in the first place, as though Charlie were incapable of even taking a look at it first. And though this sensitivity may have obscured his objectivity at the time, it was odd how his memory presented the scene so differently now. Her skirt had seemed rumpled, and her blouse was untucked at the back — both rare occurrences for someone as fastidious about her appearance as his ex-wife.

And had she seemed flushed? Or was that his memory supplementing the facts in light of more recent events?

Charlie's mood darkened even further as he thought of the dismantling of their decade-and-a-half union — a process that had begun with Charlie's decision to leave the house after their mid-January heart-to-heart. His divorce lawyer would quickly tell him that by doing so, Charlie had essentially evicted himself forever from the matrimonial home by voluntarily leaving, and it soon became apparent to him that being an innocent cuckold didn't get you much sympathy in a divorce settlement these days. After the dust had eventually settled, Charlie was left with no wife, no house, and not a lot of money to show for the past fifteen years. Just thinking about it now made him want to …

Charlie snapped out of his brooding when he realized Leblanc was wrapping up the presentation and proposing a tour of the Venezuelan embassy. At least it was better than having to attend to that staffing report waiting for him back at the office.

"You okay?" Gray asked in the shuffle of papers that preceded their departure. "You seem kind of … preoccupied."

"What?" Charlie said, wondering if the hammering of his pulse that made his ears throb was audible to her. "No, I'm fine. I'm looking forward to the tour," he added, trying to convey a relaxation he didn't feel as they all headed to the door of the conference room.

# CHAPTER 15

Charlie stood over his kitchen sink, sweating as he removed the last of the shells from the lobster tails.

"You sure you don't want a hand?" Landon was leaning against the counter, sipping on a cold Cristal. "Why didn't you just get Marta to make dinner?"

"She made the salad, and the dessert." The housekeeper came in every couple of days, and usually left pre-made dinners in the fridge for him. "I figured I could handle the barbeque, and I wasn't really thinking about having to shell all of this shrimp and lobster. Anyway, it's done now," he said, reaching into the fridge for one of the distinctive green bottles. "Let's go out by the pool; it's too damn hot in here."

Heading into the backyard, Charlie and Landon sat in a couple of loungers by the edge of the pool. The sun had almost set, but the heat of the day still lingered in the air.

"When are they coming, anyway?" Landon asked, as Charlie leaned down to splash some of the pool water on his face.

"They called just before you got here to say they'd be a little late."

Landon nodded and sipped his beer. "So how'd it go this afternoon?" he asked. Though he had attended the morning meeting with the Cubans, Landon had skipped the afternoon session with Société Immobilière at Charlie's request, in order to make sure their famously unreliable Cuban carpenter actually showed up for a repair job at the head of the political section's house. The work was already weeks overdue and Charlie had enough on his plate already without Miles Johnston harassing him.

"It went well," Charlie said. "They were very professional, and from what we could see, they do pretty good work."

"What was the Venezuelan embassy like?"

"Looked pretty nice to me. Although Redden didn't seem overly impressed with some of the finishing work."

"That's the problem with Cuban labour." Landon shrugged and took a sip of beer. "How's your wiring, by the way? I could try to get that electrician over here again."

"Fixed it myself," Charlie said, with considerable pride. "But I've hardly been down in the basement. Speaking of repairs, did the carpenter finally show up and fix the goddamn door?"

"He was an hour late, and he took his time once he got there, but it seems like he did a good job."

"Thank God. One more snot-o-gram from Johnston and I'd have snapped," Charlie said with a laugh. The priority of the property team's visit didn't stop his usual workload from accumulating, and, even with both him and Landon going full tilt, he wasn't sure how he was going to deal with it all. There were maintenance problems at the embassy compound and at the various residences scattered around Miramar that required his attention, not to mention two separate HR complaints by locally engaged staff to investigate. To top it all off, Charlie had picked up a couple of new consular cases, both involving Canadian tourists. The report on Tate Martin was still his priority case, but it remained in draft form. Charlie knew he had to sign it off as soon as possible, even though the incarcerated hotelier's prospects looked bleak.

All in all, Charlie's current situation was far from the Caribbean picnic he had envisioned just a few months ago when he had planned his escape from Ottawa. He comforted himself with the knowledge that this was a particularly busy week, and that things would likely settle down when the property team returned to Ottawa.

"I thought we'd trade off meetings tomorrow," Charlie said, setting his beer on the ground and sitting at the edge of the pool as he dipped his legs in the water. "You can take the architects, and I'll take the lawyer."

"Sure."

Charlie noticed Landon's grin. "What?"

"Nothing. I've just noticed your sudden interest in, um, the law, that's all."

Charlie tried another tack. "Well, you've already met the local lawyer, and I haven't."

"Yeah, that makes sense."

"What's he like anyway?" Charlie continued, subtly shifting the focus of their conversation.

"Sam? He's very practical. We've used him on all of our leases, and he's done some other stuff for us since I've been here. He knows the head of mission pretty well, too."

"Sounds good."

"And Gray seems very ... knowledgeable," Landon said.

"Mm-hmm," Charlie took a sip of his beer and swung his legs out of the pool. "I'd better get changed," he said, shaking off the excess water. "Help yourself to another beer. I'll just be a minute."

Charlie climbed the stairs to his bedroom two at a time and soon found himself in his closet, staring at his clothes. Normally, his selection would have taken about ten seconds, but tonight, for some reason, he was undecided. Would the light blue button-down make him seem boring and frumpy? There was always that stripy shirt; the one Sharon had paid a fortune for in Toronto that he never wore. She had called it "edgy" or something like that at the time, but Charlie had always thought it a little too much. It occurred to him that he didn't really remember packing it, but there it was. He took it off the hanger and slipped it on now, taking a look in the mirror. It certainly wasn't frumpy, but it wasn't really him either. Then again, maybe he wasn't the same person he was a year ago.

After fumbling with the buttons, Charlie straightened his hair and returned to the closet for a pair of pants, stopping off at the dresser for a light squirt of cologne — another of Sharon's selections. He was fastening his belt when he heard the van pulling up out front. He ran into the bathroom for a last check in the mirror and was pleasantly surprised. He had acquired a little colour in the few weeks he had spent under the Cuban sun, and he looked quite dapper in his outfit. For some reason, that was important to him tonight.

"That was really good," Redden said, putting down his spoon. The others all echoed Redden's sentiment, and Charlie put up his hand.

"Wish I could take credit for the chocolate mousse, but it was the housekeeper."

They were all seated around the dining room table, the ceiling fan keeping the air moving and the temperature just right. It had been an enjoyable dinner, with the majority of the conversation focused on the property deal that was gradually taking shape as the week progressed. There hadn't been much in the way of personal information exchanged, though Charlie had learned that Lefebvre had worked with Redden on several other projects. It was also clear that Gray and Redden didn't much care for each other.

"Coffee?" Charlie offered, and got several positive responses from around the table. "Why don't we have it out back? It won't take a minute; you can go on out," he said, getting up from the table and heading to the kitchen as the others made their way outside. He emerged ten minutes later with a tray of coffees.

"Oh, I almost forgot," he said, returning to the kitchen after setting down the tray on the patio table. He was back a moment later with a box of cigars.

"You've got to try one of these," he said, setting it down on the table.

Hart, Landon, and Redden waved them off, but Lefebvre eyed the box with interest.

"Are they real Cohibas?" he asked, opening the cover and peering inside.

"Yes," Charlie said proudly. "They're Esplendidos. I'm no connoisseur, but I'm told they're a pretty good smoke. They'd run you fifty bucks a pop in Ottawa."

"And here?" Lefebvre asked.

"I think it was fifty bucks for the whole box. Go ahead, help yourself."

"Thanks." Lefebvre took one and accepted the cigar cutter from Charlie, who looked over at Gray. She hadn't said anything and he was wondering whether she was annoyed at the prospect of having to sit in a cloud of tobacco smoke. She surprised him, and the others as well, when she leaned over and took one out of the box and ran it under her delicate nose.

"I think I'll have one, too."

Charlie watched in amazement as she took the cutter

from Lefebvre, expertly clipped off the tip, and puffed the big cigar to life with the help of Charlie's lighter.

"I didn't know you were a stogie kind of girl," Redden said, as Charlie clipped the end of his own cigar.

"I'm sure there's a lot you don't know, Bruce," she replied, blowing out a cloud of blue smoke in Redden's direction. "About me, that is."

"These are great, Charlie," Lefebvre remarked as Charlie got his own going.

They all sat in silence for a few moments, the three smokers enjoying their cigars, Hart sipping his coffee, and Redden stewing over Gray's jab. The crickets were chirping in the background, and the smoke rose straight up in the warm night air, undisturbed by even the slightest breeze.

"I could get used to this," Lefebvre said with a grin as he took another puff. Charlie was watching Gray out of the corner of his eye. She really seemed to be enjoying the Cohiba.

"So how'd you end up in Havana anyway, Charlie?" Hart asked.

"Yeah, where were you posted before?" Redden chimed in.

"Well," Charlie began, tapping the ash off his cigar into the ashtray. "This is my first posting. I was in finance and HR back at Pearson."

"That's an interesting move," Redden said, with what Charlie felt was a challenging undertone.

"I got tired of Ottawa." Charlie picked up his cigar and started puffing on it. "And I thought this would be different."

"Well, it's different all right. I'll give you that," Redden added.

Charlie felt strangely self-conscious about his mid-life change of career, and his nervous puffing was generating quite a cloud of cigar smoke as he considered the possibility that Redden knew the real reason Charlie had hightailed it out of Ottawa at the first possible opportunity. Maybe he had heard the whole sordid tale of Sharon and the Swedish Meatball at some water cooler back in Ottawa. Was it even possible that Redden and Sharon might have…?

"I think it's great."

Charlie stopped puffing at the sound of Gray's voice. He turned to see her, leaning back in her deck chair, lazily blowing out a stream of smoke, punctuated every few inches by a perfectly-formed smoke ring that she created with a methodical crack of her jaw. They were all staring as she continued to talk.

"It takes a certain streak of independence to pull up stakes and just go, you know?" she said, to no one in particular. Then she turned toward Redden and added: "A lot of people haven't got the balls."

Everyone sat there in silence, waiting to see if Redden would respond, but he didn't, choosing to fiddle with his coffee cup instead. What Charlie felt, as he marvelled at the sassy, cigar-smoking woman sitting in the chair next to him, was a mix of gratitude and desire.

"So, what's on tap for tomorrow?" Lefebvre said, changing the subject.

"We've got the local lawyer coming to the embassy at nine." Charlie looked at Gray, then at the rest of the group. "I imagine you guys don't need to attend that one. "Then Sam, Jillian, and I will take the planning meeting while you guys talk to potential on-site project managers."

Redden stretched his arms over his head and let out a loud sigh. "I don't know about everyone else, but I'm beat. We should probably think about heading back to the hotel."

"I'll call the driver," Landon said, pulling out his BlackBerry. "It shouldn't take him more than a couple of minutes to get here."

"It's too bad I didn't bring my swimsuit," Gray said, looking at the pool. "It looks so inviting."

"Yeah, the water's great," Charlie said.

"Well, if this week continues the way it's been going so far," Lefebvre said with a smile, "we might be back in a few more to actually sign something. You can bring it then."

"You'll have us back for dinner?" Gray gave Charlie a mischievous look.

"Of course."

After chatting briefly about the agenda for the following day, and accepting their thanks for the meal, Charlie was seeing the group off at the front door. Returning inside, he decided to throw on a pair of trunks and have a quick swim. After paddling around in the warm water, he emerged by the table and lit the rest of his cigar. He enjoyed the sweet aroma of the Cohiba, and the warm night air on his wet skin, as he sat there listening to the crickets and thinking of Jillian Gray.

# CHAPTER 16

Charlie sat at the large meeting table, trying to look interested in what the municipal planning official was saying. It was late in the day and he was tired. He had given up trying to understand the man's machine-gun Spanish, preferring to rely on the local lawyer's interpreting skills. Sam Sanchez had moved to Cuba from Canada ten years prior and spoke both languages fluently. He, Charlie, and Gray had been there for more than two hours, and as vaguely interesting as the municipal permitting and approval process might have sounded when the meeting had started at three, it was definitely wearing thin now. And to make matters worse, despite the open windows and a fan in the corner that looked like something out of a museum, the air in the room was stifling.

Located in a side street off the Plaza de San Francisco, the building was like nothing Charlie had ever seen. Built in the Spanish colonial style, it featured an interior courtyard with an overgrown fountain in the middle, four floors rising up around the centre, and an Andalusian patio on the second level. In its day, its intricate arches and high ceilings must have been magnificent, but after years of neglect — like so many buildings in Old Havana — it seemed on the verge of collapse, with the plaster long gone from the ceilings and parts of the walls and support beams scattered here and there in an attempt to delay its eventual collapse.

A familiar buzz on his hip jolted Charlie from his daydream and he discreetly checked the incoming message as the city official answered one of Gray's questions on the procedural requirements for getting an architectural design approved for construction. Charlie wasn't surprised to see the message from Bruce Redden, to the effect that the meeting he, Hart, and Lefebvre were having with a potential project manager back at the embassy was running late, and that they would not be able to join the planning meeting after all.

*No problem*, Charlie thumbed back under the table, adding: *Meeting here going late too*, before slipping the BlackBerry back onto his hip and smiling apologetically at the two Cubans on the other side of the table.

It was after six when the planning meeting finally wrapped up, and the sky had darkened with rain clouds by the time they stepped out into the early evening air.

"Well, that was productive," Gray said as they stood in front of the old building.

Sanchez nodded. "As you can see, there will be no shortage of red tape, but a lot of it can be minimized by a good project manager."

"You mean someone who knows which palms to grease?" Gray remarked, giving Sanchez a sideways glance.

"I'm afraid it's just the way business is done down here."

"Problem is, there's no line item for payoffs in a government project budget, you know what I mean?"

Sanchez chuckled. "You needn't worry. On a project like this, it's all built into the developer's cost — overhead, if you will. You'd never get a real breakdown even if you wanted it."

"I get the feeling we probably don't," Charlie said.

Gray looked at her watch. "I don't know about you guys, but I could use a drink."

"The Floridita's just around the corner." Sanchez pointed toward the old town. "It's where Hemingway drank his daiquiris."

"If it's good enough for Hemingway, it's good enough for me," Gray said, as they set off across the Plaza de San Francisco.

"So your visit has been a success, then?" Sanchez asked as they made their way through the narrow streets, careful to stay out of the puddles and to avoid the scooters, Ladas, and ancient Chevys as they rolled by, belching out clouds of black exhaust.

"I think so," Gray said, adroitly sidestepping a massive pile of dog crap on the sidewalk. She had been admiring an ornate balcony a couple of flights above on the other side of the street. "God, I was just trying to imagine what this place must have looked like in the fifties. It must have been incredible."

"I'm sure it was," Sanchez agreed. "Maybe one day it will be restored to its former glory."

"But you're right about this week, it's been very positive. Wouldn't you say, Charlie?"

"Absolutely," he replied, with genuine enthusiasm. For him, the week had been a crash course in real estate development, and much of the detail was over his head. But if there was one thing he had taken away, it was that there was no obvious engineering, architectural, or legal obstacle that put the proposed project at risk. So far, so good.

"Look at that," Gray said quietly as they walked by an open doorway. The ceiling over the entry had collapsed, but through a small doorway in the back they could see a tattered couch and a daybed on which an old woman was sitting, listening to salsa music playing from a little transistor radio. "I can't believe these are people's homes."

They were within sight of José Martí Square when the rain clouds erupted, spilling a warm torrent on the unsuspecting pedestrians below.

"Come on, we're almost there," Sanchez yelled over the shrieks of the children taking shelter in doorways left and right.

They sprinted through the rain and arrived at the Floridita, where the smiling valet spun the revolving door for them. Inside, the air was cool and smoky, with the majority of the tables in the front occupied. Sanchez made a beeline for the bar and commandeered three stools in the corner, near the Hemingway statue, before yelling an order over the din to the red-vested bartender.

"This is nice," Gray said, brushing her wet hair back from her face and flicking the excess water off her suit jacket. Charlie had kept most of his head dry with the leather folder he had been carrying around all week, but his pants were soaked. He was looking down at them when he heard Gray laughing.

"A little damp?"

"You could say that," he replied, watching her settle herself on the bar stool next to him. If he had to endure a long day of boring meetings for the opportunity to have a drink with her now, then so be it. The daiquiris arrived with a plate of fried plantain chips.

"To a successful week in Havana," Sanchez said, raising his glass.

Cold and sweet, the slush hit the back of Charlie's dry throat like a salve, and tingled all the way down to his stomach.

"Oh, these are good," Gray said, looking over at the life-size statue of Hemingway in the corner, leaning over the bar. "I can see why he came here often. And it wouldn't take too many of these to get roaring drunk."

"I think his record is eleven," Sanchez said. "Or maybe it's fourteen."

"I'd be on the floor after about four." Gray took another sip. "But it would be fun trying."

They chatted for a while, mostly about Sanchez's experiences in Havana and how much things had changed since he had arrived. They had almost finished their second round when Sanchez waved the waiter over and ordered a third.

"Then I've got to be on my way," he said.

"You can't join us for dinner?" Charlie asked.

"I promised a friend I would help her move some furniture into her new apartment. It's actually my girlfriend's sister; otherwise, I would have gladly joined you. Are you still here tomorrow night?"

"No, we fly back tomorrow afternoon," Gray said. "At least, I do."

"But you'll be back soon, I hope?"

"It's a distinct possibility."

"Oh, I have a feeling you'll be back before you know it," Charlie said.

"My turn," Gray said, as the waiter arrived with their daiquiris. She handed him some bills over the protests of her two bar-mates.

"You're going to get soaked," Gray said to Sanchez, looking out at the rain cascading down the windows.

Sanchez waved his hand. "My apartment is just around the corner."

"Know any good places to eat near here?" Gray asked. She looked at Charlie. "Unless you want to head back out to Miramar and meet up with the others."

"I think they were going to do their own thing," Charlie said, finessing the truth. He hadn't actually heard from them since the brief message to the effect that they were behind schedule, and he wasn't about to check his BlackBerry now.

"There's a pretty good restaurant right here, if you don't want to get wet," Sanchez said, pointing to the rear of the room. Charlie hadn't realized there was a dining room, in addition to the bar. "It's a bit pricey for Havana. But in Canadian terms, it's still pretty reasonable."

"Sounds good to me," Charlie said, taking a sip of his daiquiri.

# CHAPTER 17

"Are you going to have dessert?" Gray asked, as the waiter removed their dinner plates.

Charlie was feeling pretty full after a feast of grilled dorado. "I don't know. You?"

"Let's see the dessert menu," she said, looking up at the waiter, who nodded and disappeared. The dining room was almost full, the crisp white linen in stark contrast to the red-brown carpet and velvet-covered chairs and the waiters' crimson vests.

"That fish was fantastic," Gray remarked. "How was yours?"

"Great. I'll have to add this place to my A-list."

"Do you eat out a lot here?"

"A couple of times a week, but not like this." Charlie gestured at their surroundings. "There's an Italian place near me that has good pizza and pasta. My housekeeper's a pretty good cook, too, thankfully."

She smiled. "That place we went to with the Cubans was nice, but the food wasn't as good as here."

"No, the *paladares* are really hit and miss. La Guarida is supposed to be really nice."

"One of the guys mentioned it the other day."

"It's in a really cool old building, and they say the food's excellent. Maybe we can go next time you're here," Charlie added, suddenly feeling awkward and thinking it had come out sounding a lot like he was proposing a date.

When the waiter arrived with the dessert menu, it didn't take Charlie long to zero in on the cheesecake, while Gray liked the sound of the apple torte.

"So," Charlie said, after the waiter had taken their orders, "how long do you think before Ottawa gives us the green light?"

"Depends on how quickly we can get all the paperwork in order," Gray said, curling a strand of auburn hair around her finger. "The environmental report should take a week or so, and Sam's report on title will take about the same. After that, it's just a question of Redden's boss making the call."

"And then you'd be back to negotiate the final terms with the Cubans?"

She nodded.

"So, realistically, late August to early September?"

"Probably. Hey," she added suddenly, "isn't that hurricane season?"

"We're in hurricane season now, technically."

She looked out toward the bar and the windows beyond. "Speaking of weather, it looks like the rain's stopped."

"Good," Charlie said, as the waiter returned with two large desserts and a pair of coffees. "We might have to walk some of this off."

By the time they stepped out of the Floridita, the rain clouds had dispersed, revealing a canopy of stars in the inky sky above them. The warm night air had an intoxicating freshness, and Charlie filled his lungs.

"What a beautiful evening," Gray remarked.

"Do you want to walk down the Prado to the water and get a cab from there?"

"Lead on."

After crossing the square, they strolled along the marbled walkway in the centre of Havana's main boulevard, the Paseo del Prado.

"It's such a strange place," Gray remarked, looking up at the mess of laundry lines strung across the balconies of what had once been the most exclusive apartments in all of Havana.

Charlie followed her gaze. "I know what you mean."

"You really are lucky," she said, "to have the chance to live in a place like this. And especially now. I mean, who knows how the country will change in the next few years."

"Yeah, it's certainly got its charms, if you can get over the things it lacks."

They continued to stroll, taking in the unique scenery. "So, you'll be here for, what, two years?" she asked.

"Maybe three. We'll see."

"And you're not married?" She said it casually, her eyes still on the buildings lining the Prado. He hesitated a moment before answering.

"Divorced."

"Oh, sorry to hear that. A long time ago?"

They were coming up to a group of teenagers milling around a marble bench built into the central walkway. The boys were showing off their dancing skills for the girls, to the music crackling from a battered portable radio.

"Actually, that's one of the reasons I took this posting. To get away from Ottawa."

"I didn't mean to pry."

"It's all right," he said, unsure what had prompted his uncharacteristic candour. He had made every effort not to utter Sharon's name in the past six months, let alone acknowledge any element of the pain she had caused. "My marriage just sort of fell apart one day, you know? And we both worked at Pearson, so …"

"Must have been awkward."

"You could say that, yeah."

"So, Havana's a new start for you, then?"

"That's the plan," he said, as they neared the end of the Prado. "Do you want to walk along the Malecón for a bit, or get a cab here?"

"Let's walk for a bit. I like the smell of the sea."

They crossed the street and stood at a light, waiting to cross to the promenade by the seawall. A pretty young girl in a miniskirt tottered on stilettos by the waiting cars, smoking a cigarette.

"I think she's looking to transact a little business," Gray remarked as the light changed and they started to cross. One of the cars had pulled over to the curb and the girl was leaning in the window.

"How about you?" Charlie said, after they had begun walking along by the wall. "Are you married?"

"No. Came close once, but I never took the plunge."

They passed a couple sitting on the wall, kissing playfully and sharing sips from a little bottle of rum. Ten feet further along, another couple had moved beyond simple kissing.

"Boy, they're really going at it," Gray whispered after they had passed. She had leaned closer to Charlie in the process, and he had felt something like an electrical current as they briefly touched. She looked out at a light off in the distance and gently tugged on his arm as she came to a stop. "That looks a long way out. I wonder where it's coming from."

"Who knows," Charlie said. "A Venezuelan tanker maybe?" They both looked out over the calm waters of the bay, the soft sloshing of water on the breakers below mingling with the competing sounds of a couple of passing motorbikes.

"Well, Charlie," Gray said, leaning on the wall and turning to face him. "You seem to have made the right choice. I can't think of a better place to escape to than Havana."

She was close enough for him to smell her perfume and the fresh scent from her hair. He stood there watching her for a moment, and to his surprise, she leaned in and kissed him. She stopped after a few seconds and pulled back, a smile on her face. This time, he moved into her and their mouths locked in a long embrace.

"I don't usually do this," she said, after they had come up for air a second time.

"Do what, kiss?"

"I mean mix work and pleasure," she said, with a laugh.

"Oh, right. Well, that makes two of us."

"I guess we should get a cab…. It's getting late."

"Sure," Charlie said, wondering what he should do next. Was she saying they should get a cab to his place? Or was she thinking she had made a horrible mistake and looking for an exit? He had no idea as he waved at a passing yellow cab.

"I should probably go back to the hotel," she said, as they got in the back seat, putting an end to his internal debate.

"*Meliá Habana, por favor,*" he instructed the driver. It was only after they were underway and an awkward silence had descended that it occurred to him that she might have been waiting for him to suggest an alternative, like a nightcap at his place. As the cab followed the seawall out to the tunnel, then along Fifth Avenue into Miramar, Charlie had almost forgotten Gray was sitting next to him in the back seat, he was so angry with himself over fumbling his one chance.

"I had a great time tonight Charlie," she said suddenly, breaking the silence. "Thank you." She put her hand on his and gave it a light squeeze.

"My pleasure," he said, as the cab took the ramp up to the hotel and pulled up to the front entrance.

"So, debrief with the ambassador at nine?" she said, as she opened the door to get out.

"Hector will be by at eight-thirty. Sleep well."

"You too."

As the cab pulled away and headed out toward Jaimanitas, Charlie reclined and closed his eyes. He could still smell her hair and feel her body pressed up against his. *First Maria Aguirre, now this,* he thought, as he opened his eyes and felt the warm breeze on his face. But whereas Maria was a question of animal attraction, pure and simple, there was something different about Gray. She was certainly beautiful, but she had stirred something that Charlie hadn't felt in a very long time. The only problem was, she was getting on a plane tomorrow afternoon.

As they drove west along the darkened streets, Charlie pulled out his BlackBerry and switched it on. He had turned it off for the evening but couldn't resist its siren call now, after several hours of neglect. He scrolled through a couple of messages and saw one from the head of security at the embassy, marked IMPORTANT. As he clicked it open and read the glowing text in the darkness of the car's interior, he felt his chest tighten.

A few hours earlier, while Charlie and Gray were having dinner, Amirjit Saini — the Indian consular officer he had met at the official residence in his first week — had been abducted from her Miramar home.

# CHAPTER 18

Charlie sat in the ambassador's office, half-listening as Stewart went on about the importance of maintaining the momentum that had been gained over the course of the week. Charlie was there in body, but since giving his initial summary of the week's events to open the meeting, his mind had been wandering between two different topics.

The first had been on everyone's mind since the general briefing at eight-thirty this morning to discuss what was known about the abduction of Amirjit Saini. The police had released few details, other than to confirm that she had been taken from her home, which had been ransacked.

Kidnappings were generally rare in Cuba, but they were unheard of in the diplomatic community. The news had cast a pall over the usually noisy cantina, where the entire embassy staff had gathered to hear the ambassador deliver the bad news. The dark rain clouds outside seemed to add to the gloom.

But it was the warning issued by the embassy's head of security that had sent a real chill through the assembled group. Security at the embassy itself was to be heightened, and in addition to being reminded of the personal security measures that had always been in effect, members of staff were also being asked to exercise increased caution when going out, until more details of the Saini incident became known. The diplomatic guards were to be doubled until further notice.

The other subject vying for Charlie's attention was sitting across the room. He had only to look at Gray as she sat there listening to Stewart and he was right back on the Malecón, the warm onshore breeze whipping her fragrant hair in his face as he held her in his arms. Though he had done nothing wrong, Charlie had nonetheless been avoiding direct engagement with Gray all morning. And though it seemed silly, he had the distinct impression, on the few occasions where they had shared a quick glance, that she was doing the same.

Charlie tried again to focus on the picture of Teddy on the side table as the ambassador rambled on, but it was useless. One minute he and Gray had been hot and heavy and the next it was goodnight and goodbye. Half drunk and horny was not the best way to cap off an evening, in Charlie's experience, and, with the news of Saini's abduction, it had taken him hours to get to sleep. And there would be little, if any, opportunity to talk to Gray alone after this meeting, since the whole team would be leaving for the airport together. It had occurred to him that she might be pissed off, or worse. Perhaps her noncommittal smile this morning had been designed to conceal the fact that she had spent the entire night in her hotel room framing the mother of all harassment claims — she was a lawyer, after all.

*Jesus, what were you thinking?*

Charlie felt clammy as he thought of the possible consequences. Had he forced himself on her? Had the daiquiris and the red wine obscured his ability to read the negative vibes that would have prevented a sober Charlie from even considering smooching a member of the Department of

Justice? He was mentally resigning his post and packing his bags when he realized someone was actually talking to him. He looked up, and the entire room, including Gray, was staring at him.

"Sorry?"

"Are you all right, Charlie?" Stewart said, his brow knitted with concern. "You look a little ... *off.*"

"Oh, I'm fine. I was just thinking ..." He looked away from Stewart as he tried to think of something, and locked eyes with Gray, "... about the legal report on title, and when we might get it from Sam." He looked back at Stewart and smiled, pleased that he had found something to say. Stewart was eyeing him suspiciously, and Charlie noticed that he had moved back into his chair a little, shifting subtly into a defensive pose. At least he wasn't rolling up the rug.

"That's a good point," Gray said, coming to his rescue. "I'll ask Sam to confirm his estimate, but I think he mentioned he would try to get us a draft report in about a week."

"Good," Stewart said with a nod, and looked at his watch. "Well, I think we've covered everything, haven't we Charlie?"

"I think so," Charlie lied. He had no idea what had been said in the last ten minutes, but he knew what the next steps were, so he wasn't too worried.

"Have we arranged a ride to the airport for these good people?"

"Eleven-thirty," Charlie replied. That much, he knew.

"Well then. Thank you for your excellent work this week, and I look forward to seeing you all again very soon to wrap this up."

They all shook hands, and then filed out of the ambassador's office, down the stairs, and out into the mid-morning heat.

"Well, I'm going to check my email and log off," Redden said, looking at his watch. "We've got twenty minutes, right?"

Lefebvre nodded. "I'm going to have an espresso. Anyone care to join me?"

"Sure," Hart said, as Redden headed off toward the administration building.

"Order me one," Gray said. "I just have to ask Charlie something about the legal report."

Hart and Lefebvre headed off toward the cantina as Charlie and Gray stood in silence.

"Listen, about last night," Gray began quietly. "I just want you to know, I don't usually act like that. It's not very professional."

Charlie stood there, wondering whether this was a trap — part of her harassment claim strategy, perhaps. He was about to formulate a strategic apology of his own, but then he stopped himself.

*Fuck it!*

"Well, I thought it was great. Actually, I was thinking it would be nice to check out La Guarida when you come back."

She looked at him, her face registering mild surprise. Charlie spent an anxious moment as he waited for more, but she only laughed softly.

"That could be arranged."

"Good. Now, let's go get that coffee."

With Gray and the rest of the Ottawa team gone, Charlie had come in to Old Havana in the hope that the charms of the city would cheer him up. He had stopped at Plaza Vieja for a bite to eat and had been disappointed with the food, and the walk back to the waterfront hadn't done much to lift his spirits either. On the contrary, the dimly lit streets that a couple of weeks ago had seemed so intimate and quaint now just seemed squalid and seedy. Even the Malecón had changed character, the hopeful anglers and suitors on the seawall replaced by drunks and pickpockets. There was also something ominous about the sea spray coming over the wall and soaking parts of the sidewalk, as though a rogue wave might come over at any moment and sweep Charlie into the inky blackness of Havana Bay. The last straw was an encounter with a cigar peddler who had become more and more insistent when he found out Charlie was Canadian, giving up only after following him for several minutes and rambling on about his sister in Toronto.

Charlie decided to cut short his planned walk down to the Prado, and doubled back toward his car instead. As he crossed the Malecón, he noticed a commotion near the market square, where a couple of police cars were stopped and people were milling around. As he skirted the crowd, he caught sight of the same cigar salesman he had encountered on his way west, just as one of the cops shoved him into the back of a patrol car. A woman was crying as the car pulled away, the man's face pressed to the glass of the rear window, an unmistakable look of terror in his wide eyes.

Unnerved by the scene, Charlie hurried to his car, and had almost reached it when his phone went off.

"Charlie?"

"Yeah, Drew. What's up?"

"Have you heard?"

"Heard what?"

"It's Amirjit. They found … her body, earlier this evening."

Charlie froze, his hand on the door handle of the car. "Holy shit! Where?"

"Washed up by the San Pedro docks."

"Jesus. Do they know what happened?"

"I just talked to Connors. He says there aren't any details, or they're not releasing them, anyway. I'm sure they'll update us in the morning, I just thought I should let you know." Charlie was barely listening, his mind taking him back to his only encounter with Saini at the official residence. He could still feel her warm arm on his as she led him away from Gustavo Ruiz. He had a vivid image of her beautiful face, with its bright smile and sad eyes. "You there, Charlie?"

"What? Yeah. I just can't believe it. It's so … horrible. Such a waste," he added, as the siren of a passing police car wailed.

"I know. It's awful. Where are you, anyway?"

"Down by the market. I'm just getting in the car to go home."

"All right. I'll see you in the morning. Be safe."

"Thanks, Drew."

Driving home, Charlie felt a longing for the safety of Ottawa, where nothing like this would ever happen. Until now, he had essentially thought the same of Havana — that its dark side was something foreigners never had to experience unless they went looking for trouble. As if to reinforce this new feeling of malevolence, a gust of wind sent a fine mist of water onshore, over the seawall and onto Charlie's windshield, to remind him that, on top of everything else, the heart of hurricane season was just around the corner.

Passing under the tunnel and heading along Fifth, the intricate spindles of the ficus trees took on an eerie quality in the dark, and Charlie couldn't help wishing the avenue could lead him not to his darkened house in Jaimanitas, but all the way back to Ottawa and his familiar house in the Glebe, where he might find Sharon on the other side of the door, welcoming him back from his foolish little adventure with a drink and a hug.

# CHAPTER 19

Charlie frowned at the cloud of black smoke coming out of the tailpipe of the Lada in front of him, thinking of the seventy bucks he had been forced to spend on emission-testing his two-year-old car back in Ottawa. One day, e-testing might find its way to Cuba, and when it did, he hoped he was in the garage business. He didn't bother to put up his window, preferring the acrid smell of exhaust and burning oil to the lingering smell of stale dog piss that permeated the interior of his previously pristine vehicle.

The smell aside, though, Charlie found himself actually missing the official mutt. He hadn't seen much of the ambassador since his return from Panama, and given the property visit and Saini's abduction and murder, there had been little time to discuss Teddy's welfare. The dog had seemed healthy enough when he had brought him back to Katherine Stewart, and he was pretty sure Teddy hadn't suffered any permanent effects from ingesting the narcotic-infused waters of his pool. Puking on the acting ambassador was one thing, but harming the official dog might just get Charlie posted to Tajikistan.

It occurred to Charlie that his discovery under the bedroom floor had become almost irrelevant in light of all that had happened since. Everyone was still reeling from the news just a week ago that Saini's lifeless body had been pulled out of Havana Bay, days after she was taken from her home. Though the police had said little, other than to confirm that the body they had found was, in fact, Saini's, the rumours had already begun to circulate through the diplomatic community. Saini had been beaten to death and then drowned ... she had been stabbed first, then drowned, or maybe shot.... Even the tight-lipped Cuban police couldn't deny that her death had been the result of foul play of some kind.

As for the drugs Charlie had stumbled upon, there was every indication that they had been long-forgotten by their owner.

He parked the car in the lot across the street and made his way up to the office, where he was just settling in with his morning coffee when Landon appeared at the door.

"Nothing new on the Saini case?"

Charlie shook his head as Landon took a seat. They traded theories about what might really have happened to her for a while, before moving on to work, and some survey documents that had come in from the Cubans on the new embassy site. Landon was on his way back to his office when he paused at the door. "I never asked you how dinner went," he said, returning to his seat.

"What dinner?" Charlie replied. He didn't think Landon knew he had eaten with Gray the night before she left, and was considering his answer when Landon continued.

"You know ... *Maria*. We were so caught up in the property visit, I completely forgot. She was somethin' else."

"Oh," Charlie said with a little smile. "Yeah, she was something, all right."

"Where'd you go?"

"Little restaurant in the plaza nearby, I don't recall the name. Had a really nice meal, though."

"And?"

Charlie could tell Landon wasn't going to be placated by vague recollections, so he gave a brief outline of the events of the evening, careful to avoid any mention of his apparent loss of consciousness.

"Man, I can't believe — I mean, I knew from the way she was acting at the bar that she was really into you," he added quickly, "but, wow, what a *hottie!*"

"She was beautiful," Charlie agreed.

"Have you seen her since?"

"Well, I didn't get her number."

Landon was aghast. "How could you not get her number?"

"I … it was complicated."

"Wait a minute." Landon hopped up out of his chair. "She said she worked at the Ministry of Culture, right?"

Charlie nodded as Landon bolted out the door, returning a few seconds later with a little book.

"What's that?"

"The government directory. We'll just look her up." He began flipping through the pages. "What was her last name again?"

"Aguirre."

"Right. Here we are, Culture. Aguirre, Aguirre. There's a Carlos Aguirre, but no Maria."

"She said she was just a clerk. Maybe she's not listed."

"Hmm, maybe not. Hey, wait a minute; I'll call my contact at protocol…."

"I don't know," Charlie said. "I don't want to get her in trouble."

"Nah," Landon said with a shake of his head. "This guy's not gonna give her any trouble. Unless you don't want me to…."

"Give it a couple of days." Charlie gave a friendly wave of his hand. "If I haven't bumped into her again, maybe you could call."

"Sure," Landon said. "You let me know."

Charlie wasn't sure why, but he wasn't surprised to find that Maria's name was not in the directory. In fact, the more he thought about it, the more perturbed he felt. What were the odds of an encounter like that happening out of the blue? Still, if she had been out to roll him, she hadn't done a very good job. He had done a quick inventory around the house the morning after, but apart from finding the basement door ajar, nothing seemed out of place. And there had been nothing missing. He had found his wallet, which was full of cash, sitting on the dresser in plain view. No, he was being paranoid, he decided. Maybe she wasn't a one-night stand kind of girl and had felt embarrassed by their evening together. Anyway, Charlie wasn't really interested in following up.

"Yo, Charlie!"

"Hmm?" he said, realizing that Landon was speaking, but oblivious to the topic his young colleague had moved on to.

"I was just saying it looks like the property team'll be back in three weeks."

"Oh yeah? I haven't checked my emails yet this morning."

"Redden sent a trip report. Must've done it on the plane. Says he expects to get approval this week to proceed with negotiations to buy the site, and they're going to pre-screen a shortlist of developers at the same time," Landon said, getting up. "I'll let you read it. He's asking for us to follow up on those details the Cubans were supposed to give us about the site."

"Oh, I meant to ask you," Charlie said, as Landon paused again at the door, "Are you going to this thing at the Venezuelan embassy tonight?" He pointed to the invitation he had received the previous Friday from Société Immobilière. It was no surprise that Daniel Leblanc had made sure they were on the guest list, and Charlie fully expected to be harassed all night long for details on Canada's construction plans.

"Yeah, I wouldn't miss it," Landon said. "Hey, maybe Maria will be there."

Charlie shrugged. He doubted a clerk from the Ministry of Culture would be invited to the grand opening of the new Venezuelan embassy. "I've got my car if you want a ride."

Charlie was in a rotten mood as he drove home along Fifth. The reception had been the predictable schmooze-fest and, as expected, Daniel Leblanc had been all over him for details about when they might be going to tender on the new embassy project. The fact that they hadn't even bought the site yet didn't seem to matter to Leblanc, who was acting as though he already had the construction contract in hand; transparency and best value in government contracting apparently being foreign concepts.

And though Charlie knew it was unrealistic to expect to have seen her there, he had caught himself glancing around the room on several occasions looking for Maria Aguirre. But with no sign of her, and after suffering through some bad canapés and downing a couple of Cristals, Charlie had been anxious to leave. Landon had met up with his Aussie friend and was planning to hit a bar or two after the reception — Charlie wondered where he got his energy — so he had made a solo exit.

All the way back along the Malecón, Charlie's mind was whirring. There was still no news about who might have abducted and killed Amirjit Saini, which in itself was unsettling, but ever since Landon's impromptu search through the Cuban government directory, Charlie found himself increasingly preoccupied with his strange encounter with

Maria Aguirre. Was there any reasonable explanation for his suddenly passing out after a couple of sips of a beer? If she didn't work for the Ministry of Culture, who did she work for? And why had she given him a false name? The possibility that she had slipped something in the beer had been playing on his mind all day, and he was pretty sure he didn't see her take a drink from the bottle after she had appeared in the bedroom. He had admittedly been focused on other matters at the time, which, it occurred to him now, only reinforced his suspicions.

Reaching Jaimanitas, he turned off Fifth onto a side street, then onto another as he made his way home. As he drove along the dimly lit street, darkened even further by the tall hedges, he noticed the lights of a car behind him and was surprised when a red light flashed in his rear-view a few seconds later. As he pulled over, his first instinct was to wonder whether he had been driving erratically, and the second was to count how many drinks he had consumed at the reception: precisely two. Satisfied that he had done nothing seriously wrong, Charlie rolled down his window and watched in his side mirror as a Cuban in uniform approached the car. "*Buenas tardes,*" he said in his best Spanish.

"Good evening," the young man answered. Whether it was because of Charlie's pronunciation, his skin colour, or the diplomatic licence plates, the officer seemed well aware that he was dealing with an English speaker.

"Is there a problem?"

"Your light is out." The man looked past Charlie into the interior of the car.

"My brake light?"

The cop shook his head. "No, the …" he seemed to be searching for the right word.

"Tail light?" Charlie offered helpfully.

"Yes. You need to get a bulb."

Charlie noticed that the young cop seemed very interested in the back seat, which was empty, and he was beginning to wonder whether the guy was planning on writing him a ticket or just standing there staring all night when he spoke again. "You from Canada?"

"Yes, I'm the MCO at the Canadian embassy."

"I have a cousin in Montreal."

"Great city," Charlie said, thinking some friendly banter might get him on his way again sooner. But the young cop's smile evaporated as quickly as it had appeared.

"Your name?"

"Charlie Hillier."

"You wait," the cop said, suddenly turning and heading back toward his car. Charlie noticed the flashing light had been removed from its roof, and he could see the outline of another person in the passenger seat. It occurred to him that he hadn't even been asked for his driver's licence.

"Um … what am I waiting for?" Charlie asked, leaning out the window.

The cop returned and gave him a thin smile. "You stay in the car, Señor. I check the plates," he said, as if that settled everything. Charlie was about to inquire further when he thought better of it. He was entitled to certain immunities as a result of his diplomatic status, but if the guy was just going to run his name against his plate number, he supposed he could wait.

He had been sitting there a good ten minutes, tapping his fingers impatiently on the steering wheel, before the cop finally got out of his car and returned to Charlie's driver's door.

"You should get the light fixed. Is dangerous in the dark," he said with a nod, and then he was gone.

"Right," Charlie said, turning the key in his ignition and pulling back onto the road as the other car did a U-turn and headed off in the opposite direction. He realized, as he pulled up to the gate outside his house a few minutes later and the guard emerged from the little hut to open up, that he hadn't bothered to check the light himself the whole time he had been sitting there on the side of the road. Parking the car in the driveway, Charlie left the engine running and the lights on and hopped out. A quick inspection of the tail lights revealed that they both seemed in perfect working order. Having closed the gate behind him, the guard was looking at Charlie as he stood there, behind the running car. Charlie waved him over and asked him to put his foot on the brake, then activate the turn signals. Everything worked fine.

"*Gracias*," Charlie said as the guard got out of the car, looking even more puzzled than before.

"*De nada, Señor,*" he said, before heading back to the hut, shaking his head.

Charlie shut off the car and made his way to the front door, his mind working through the possible explanations, starting with a loose connection. That was reasonable, he thought, as he opened the front door and stepped inside. He didn't get a chance to consider any other options.

Charlie was frozen in place as he caught sight of the living-room couch cushions on the floor, their stuffing spewing out of the torn covers. His first instinct was that Teddy had blown a gasket. But he had taken the dog back more than a week ago. As he looked more closely at the straight slash across each of the cushion covers, he recognized the work of a very sharp knife. He felt a shiver run down the back of his spine as he looked around the rest of the room and saw the cabinet doors open, books removed from shelves, and the few knick-knacks with which he had decorated the room tipped over. Someone had torn the place apart as though they were looking for something....

Charlie turned and ran out to the guard hut, located a good fifty feet from the house, near the fenceline. The guard seemed put out by Charlie's request to follow him, no doubt expecting to be asked to operate the gringo's car lights again for some unknown reason, but his shocked expression upon setting foot in the front hall said it all.

"*¡Madre del amor!*" he said, reaching for the pistol in his holster before advancing toward the kitchen, where the cupboards and drawers were all open, half of their contents lying in untidy piles on the floor. Charlie pointed to the patio door, still ajar, and it was immediately clear how they had gotten in.

After the guard had switched on the floodlights over the backyard and taken a quick look around, they went upstairs. Whoever had broken in had done a fairly thorough job of scouring every drawer, closet, and piece of furniture. The pictures were askew on the walls and Charlie's clothes were scattered all over the floor.

"Jesus!" Charlie muttered.

"*Policia,*" the guard countered, indicating his intention to return to the hut and call for reinforcements.

"*Si,*" Charlie said, pulling out his BlackBerry and punching in the number for the head of security for the embassy. As he sat on the bed, waiting for the phone to be answered and staring at the disarray all around him, he glanced at the floor beneath the bed and was overcome by a feeling of dread.

Charlie sat at his kitchen table while the embassy's head of security saw the last of the Cuban police officers out. It was almost midnight, and Charlie's mind was still reeling at the events of the evening.

"You okay?" Connors asked, returning to the kitchen.

"I need a drink." Charlie got up to retrieve a bottle of Scotch. "You want one?"

"Why not."

Charlie poured a couple of fingers into each glass and returned to the table. "Cheers," he said, taking a sip. "So, what do they think?"

Connors shook his head. "I think their main concern is explaining to their bosses how your place was ransacked while one of their guys was sitting out front with his thumb up his ass."

Charlie nodded. "He does watch a lot of TV."

"TV or not, he's still fifty feet from the house, so unless they were smashing plates in here, it's not really surprising that he didn't hear anything, and it's obvious they came in the back."

"What did they say about the cops who pulled me over?"

"They weren't cops," Connors said, sipping his Scotch. "They checked and there's no record of any of their guys pulling over a car with dip plates in Jaimanitas this evening."

"I knew it," Charlie muttered, feeling like a fool. "I never even checked to see if the tail light was out."

"Most people wouldn't. You said the car had a cherry on the roof?"

"Yeah. One of those removable ones, you know? I least I think so…. It wasn't there when I drove off."

"Well, they were definitely in on it. The way they had you wait around while they pretended to check your plates. They must have been in contact with whoever was in the house, and were giving them the chance to clear out before you got back." Connors rubbed his chin. "Who knew your schedule for this evening?"

"I don't know," he said, shrugging his shoulders. "Drew and Alena, and a few others at the embassy, I guess. I don't think I told the housekeeper. She leaves at five anyway."

"Who'd you talk to at the Venezuelan embassy?"

"I met their MCO, a new guy, just got here. There was a Dutch consular officer and his wife. Apart from that, I was mostly with Landon and his Aussie pals."

The two sat in silence, taking turns at their drinks.

"And you say nothing's missing?"

"Not that I can see."

"Well that's good," Connors said, as Charlie sat in silence, considering whether to voice the thought that had been pre-occupying his rattled mind for the past several hours.

He took a healthy sip of his drink before asking.

"Do you think this is related to Amirjit Saini?"

Connors paused, then shook his head. "I don't see how. They didn't seem interested in you, otherwise they would have either grabbed you when they pulled you over, or waited for you to come home and snuck you out the back door the same way they came in."

"But what were they looking for?"

"I don't know. Do you have anything especially valuable that you keep around here?"

"I don't have anything especially valuable, period," Charlie said with a bitter laugh. "My ex-wife and her lawyer saw to that."

Connors smiled. "Well, the Cubans have posted another guard out front, and one for the back, so you can rest easy tonight. We'll do up a full incident report tomorrow. Are you going to be okay? You could go stay in a hotel if you'd feel better."

"No, no. I'll be fine. Listen, thanks a lot for coming over. Sorry to wreck your night."

"No problem," Connors said, as he got up to leave. "And don't worry. We'll get to the bottom of this, one way or another."

"Thanks," Charlie said as he escorted Connors to the front door, noticing the guard in the booth had been replaced. After he had seen Connors out, Charlie went out back by the pool and sat on one of the loungers, trying to make some sense of the whole mess. He was trying to convince himself that his house had been the random target of thieves, albeit extremely well-organized ones, when he heard a rustling in the bushes at the far end of the yard and froze. He jumped out of his chair, his frayed nerves on full alert as a silhouette emerged from the bushes and waved. It was the second guard they had posted to watch his house.

"*Disculpas,*" he said, seeing Charlie's obvious alarm.

Returning inside, Charlie slid the patio door shut, braced it with a broom handle, and double-checked the lock on the front door before heading upstairs.

Stepping over the clothes strewn all over his bedroom floor, he decided to leave it all where it lay for now. It was late, and he didn't have the energy to begin the daunting cleanup. He flopped on his bed and stared at the ceiling for a while, comforting himself with Connors's opinion that that the break-in had nothing to do with Amirjit Saini. That worked for a couple of minutes, but he soon had to acknowledge another, far more worrying, possibility.

# CHAPTER 20

"I just heard," Landon said, arriving at Charlie's office door. "Geez, you look like shit," he added. "You okay?"

"I've been better. I didn't really sleep that well." In fact, he had barely slept at all. After spending most of the early morning hours going over ever-worsening scenarios in his head, he had decided to make a start at cleaning up the mess. After an hour's sleep, he had showered and waited for the housekeeper to show up so he could explain what had happened.

Landon nodded. "I heard someone posing as a Cuban cop pulled you over?"

"It was obviously well-organized," Charlie said, sipping his second coffee of the day and giving Landon an abridged version of the night's events.

"What are you even doing here? You should go … well, somewhere other than here."

"I've got to meet with Gord and fill out an incident report. You know the drill. Plus, he's supposed to be talking to the cops this morning, to see if they know anything more."

"Well, let me know if you're still around for lunch."

"Chicken place?"

"Sure."

Charlie sat at his computer, waiting for it to load up for the day, thinking about the mess he was in. He decided his only hope was to play dumb for Connors and the local cops, and hope to God he never had to convince the owner of the dope that he knew nothing about its whereabouts, much less tell them that he had dissolved it in his pool. When his computer beeped its readiness and brought him back to the real world, Charlie realized beads of sweat had formed at his hairline despite the air-conditioned chill of his office.

Focusing on his email and scanning the list of messages in his inbox, he zeroed in immediately on one message and clicked it open. It was from Jillian Gray.

> *Hi Charlie*
> *You must have some serious clout down there, because Redden and I got our visas already. Hope you can arrange meetings with the Cubans and the shortlist of developers for next week. I look forward to seeing you again and moving our transaction forward.*
> *JG.*

Charlie sat staring at the screen, his mind conjuring up his own personal highlight reel of Jillian Gray, starting with the image of her standing in his arms by the Malecón's seawall, the soft ends of her windswept hair caressing his cheek just before they kissed.

He sipped his coffee and reread the message, dismissing the opening flattery. Gray knew full well that it had been the ambassador's call that had expedited the visa process, rather than anything to do with him. He briefly considered whether she was mocking him, but quickly moved on to the last bit, about "progressing our transaction," which he thought was an interestingly ambiguous choice of words. He had read enough of Gray's emails to know that her language was usually very precise. So what was she really saying? Whatever its true intent, Gray's message lifted his spirits. In fact, he might have completely forgotten about the break-in if Gord Connors hadn't appeared at his door.

"Hey, Charlie. Glad to see you smiling again."

He clicked the message shut and waved Connors in. "You want to do the statement? Come on in."

"Actually, I thought we'd go over to the meeting room and do the statement there. The Cubans want to give us an update, too."

Charlie tried not to look nervous. He would just as soon avoid the update by the Cuban cops. But that might appear odd, and any appearance of odd behaviour on his part could be extremely dangerous at this particular point.

"Great," he said, getting out of his chair and reaching for his coffee mug. "I'll need a refill first, though. I really didn't sleep much last night."

After stopping by the break room for a top-up, they walked over to the neighbouring building and settled themselves at the large table in the second-floor board-room, Connors arranging some forms in front of them, Charlie gripping his coffee mug so hard his knuckles were turning white.

"So," Connors began, filling in the top of one of the forms. "We'll start with the incident report. I'm just going to fill in the standard information and ask you to take me through what happened from the time you left the reception at the Venezuelan embassy to when you called me." He looked up from the form and added: "You know how this works."

"Actually, this is a first for me."

"Well, just tell me everything you said last night. Then we'll have it typed up and you can sign it."

Charlie nodded and began the narrative, punctuated by sips of coffee as Connors scribbled. When Charlie got to the part where he was pulled over, Connors interrupted.

"You say you heard someone telling you to pull over. Did you hear a siren?"

"No, there was a flashing red light on the roof of the car."

"And how long would you say you were stopped by the side of the road?"

"All told, maybe ten or fifteen minutes."

"All right, carry on."

Charlie continued with the description of his drive home and arrival at the house, and his discovery of the break-in upon entering.

"You said you didn't think anything was taken."

"No. Nothing that I noticed."

"Okay, I need you to double-check today, if possible. And make sure you go through your shipping inventory. Make a note of anything missing … for insurance purposes."

Connors was still scribbling when the phone in the centre of the table rang. He hit the speaker button and the voice of the receptionist filled the room.

"Gord, there are two police officers here to see you. Shall I have someone escort them up?"

"I'll come get them," he said, hanging up. "Have a stretch, Charlie. I'll be right back."

Charlie decided to heed the advice and got out of his chair as Connors left the room, walking over to the window and looking out at the street below. A young man was polishing the fender of a rust-covered Chevy. He yawned and stretched and was about to return to his seat when he saw Connors's notes from the previous evening out on the table. Charlie leafed through them — an accurate summary of their discussion the night before, from what he could remember. He noticed another sheet of paper with the previous day's date in the left-hand margin, under the heading "Cuban Police," and was drawn to an underlined word: _suspicious_. He tried to read the rest of the text, but it was barely legible. Did it say "CH's story" was suspicious? It wasn't clear, but the mere possibility sent Charlie into a panic. There were other notes immediately below, but as he started to read them, he heard approaching footsteps and had to return to the other side of the table before they reached the door. Just as the men entered the room, Charlie shot a glance over the table to make sure he had not disturbed the papers.

"Charlie, this is Sergeant Gutierrez and Detective Viernes. They're both attached to the Ministry of Foreign Affairs."

"_Hola,_" Charlie said, shaking their hands in turn as everyone took a seat.

"We are very sorry for what happened," Gutierrez began, after coffee and water had been offered and refused.

"Thank you, I appreciate that," Charlie said, as Gutierrez smiled and his younger partner just looked at him. Something about Detective Viernes made Charlie nervous.

"And we want to assure you that we will take every measure to find these guilty parties. I have had a full report from my officers who were on the scene last night, and we have some further informations for you."

Charlie and Connors nodded, wondering what the new information was.

"We have confirmed that the persons who stopped your car on the street near your house were not, in fact, members of the Cuban police. We have reason to believe that they were part of an organized gang that targeted your house for the robbery," Gutierrez continued.

"Have there been other robberies of this nature?" Charlie asked, noticing that Viernes was still staring at him.

*What the fuck's he staring at?*

As if to answer, it was Viernes who spoke next.

"No. This is why we are very interested in this case, Señor Hillier. May I ask, was anything taken?"

"We don't think so," Connors interjected. "But I've asked Charlie to make a thorough search of the house today to identify anything that might be missing. We'll make sure you get a copy of Charlie's statement, as well, for your file," he added, pointing to the papers on the table in front of him.

"Thank you," Viernes said as a thin smile creased his lips. It was gone by the time he turned to address Charlie again.

"Do you keep valuables at your house? A safe perhaps?"

"No to both," Charlie said. He considered mentioning Jimmy the Leech's role in his relative poverty, to add some levity to the conversation, but decided against it. This Viernes character didn't seem like the kind to appreciate humour, even of the self-effacing variety. "I really don't have much of value," he continued, comfortable that this much at least was true. Almost depressingly so, he had thought, when he had done a quick inventory this morning. He had a crappy little TV/DVD combo, an even crappier stereo — he was pretty low-tech, even by Cuban standards — some ratty furniture, and some clothes. The only thing he considered remotely valuable was his antique desk, but its true value was mostly sentimental. "And there's no safe."

"Have you noticed anything strange since you moved into the house, Mr. Hillier?" Gutierrez asked as Viernes opened his notebook.

"No," Charlie said, shrugging his shoulders. "You mean like …?"

"Strange visitors, for example," Viernes said, jumping in. He looked up from his notes and fixed Charlie with a stone-cold stare.

"No," Charlie answered quickly. His decision not to mention the two visits by the scantily clad young women had seemed like a sound one when he had made it at about three in the morning. It was only now, under Viernes's stare, that Charlie was reconsidering his wisdom. He shifted in his seat and felt himself getting warmer as he considered the possibility that his house had been under surveillance all along. It also occurred to him that he had mentioned the visits to Landon. What if he had told Connors?

"I'm a single guy," Charlie said, deciding talking was better than sitting there squirming in silence. "New in town, you know? I haven't had a lot of visitors."

"Of course," Gutierrez said as Viernes scribbled some notes.

"Can I ask you a question?" Charlie said, looking at Viernes this time. "Do you think this is related to what happened to Amirjit Saini?"

"The Indian woman? Why would we think that?" Viernes replied.

"I don't know. One diplomat gets murdered and another gets his house robbed a week later. You don't think that's a strange coincidence?"

"We don't know what the motives were for the Saini woman's death," Gutierrez said, "but if they had wanted to kill you last night, Señor Hillier—"

"We wouldn't be meeting here this morning." Charlie finished the thought, applying the same logic Connors had the night before.

Gutierrez nodded his agreement.

"Is very strange, *non*," Viernes said, "that someone would go to such lengths to rob you when you have nothing worth stealing?" A pall seemed to descend over the room following Viernes's statement, and Charlie decided to keep his mouth shut this time.

"But we will find these thieves, that is for certain," Gutierrez said, jumping in with an enthusiasm that fit well with his good-cop role.

Charlie answered the rest of their questions, trying not to let Viernes unsettle him, and fifteen minutes later the meeting was coming to a close.

"We will maintain the extra guards at your house until this matter is resolved," Gutierrez said, "And you have our assurance that we will not stop until we have caught these men."

"Thank you," Charlie said, as they all got up and Connors escorted the two cops out of the meeting room.

"Was it just me, or was that Viernes guy acting strange?" Charlie said as they sat outside the canteen. Connors was sipping an espresso, while Charlie had opted for water.

"I've met him before. He's always like that. Don't let him bother you."

"He wasn't bothering me," Charlie lied. "I just thought he was, I don't know, *weird*." He wondered whether Connors had any idea he was holding out on him as well as the Cubans, and what he would say if he knew. "Maybe I'm just tired," he added, concealing his discomfort with a sip of water.

"Why don't you go home," Connors suggested. "Get some shut-eye and check your inventory."

"Yeah," Charlie said, "I've got to set up some meetings for the property team visit first, but I think I'll head out after that. I really do need some sleep."

"They're coming back already?"

"Next week."

"That was quick." Connors seemed surprised.

"I guess the powers that be are on board to get this deal done as soon as possible."

"Well," Connors said, finishing his coffee and getting up, "I'll have this typed up for your review, and you can sign it before you go, or take it home with you if you like."

"Thanks, Gord. And thanks again for last night. I don't know what I would have done without you."

"No problem."

Charlie watched him leave and considered his situation. He felt bad about keeping information from Connors, but he was too afraid to come clean just yet. More unsettling was that shifty Detective Viernes. Did he know something? Could he know about the girls showing up at Charlie's door? There was nothing incriminating about strangers ringing your door-bell, but when you start lying to the cops…. He realized that he was actively interfering with an official investigation, and wondered what the penalty for that was in Cuba.

"Hey, there you are."

Charlie's thoughts of being tossed into Havana Bay with concrete shoes from the heights of El Morro vanished at the sight of Landon approaching.

"I called over to set up that meeting for next week. It turns out Gustavo Ruiz is leaving for a two-week visit to Chile on Monday."

"Shit!" Charlie could see the week falling apart. "Stewart's not going to like that."

"They said we could meet on Thursday and Friday to hammer out the main commercial and legal terms, and the rest he could leave to his juniors the following week."

"But that's … the day after tomorrow. There's no way the property team can make it down that fast, not without—"

Charlie stopped, remembering Jillian Gray's message that they had already received their visas. He looked at his watch. It was quarter to twelve.

"Come on," he said, as he got up and started off toward the admin building. "Let's see if we can reach Redden."

Despite Charlie's best efforts at an early exit, Gustavo Ruiz's last-minute scheduling change had required some frantic planning between Havana and Ottawa, with the result being that Redden and Gray were to fly in the next afternoon, in time for meetings on Thursday and Friday. The rest of the team would follow on Sunday. It would be a hectic ten-day visit, but as he sat at his desk and shut down his computer for the day, Charlie was glad to have something to distract him. Since his and Landon's call to Ottawa at noon, he hadn't had an opportunity to think about the break-in, its possible connection to his discovery of the illicit stash under his bedroom floor, or even the unsettling interview with the Cuban cops that morning. And with Redden and Gray's imminent arrival, his plan to sleep in tomorrow was out as well. He realized that he had promised Connors that he would inventory his things, and he wondered where he would find the energy.

Still, even with the added workload and the stress that the visit would bring, it would move the file forward. As he sat there, gathering up the energy to leave, it occurred to him that in spite of all of the current turmoil in his life, he was smiling. He tried to convince himself that it was due to the possibility of closing the embassy deal and not the imminent return of Jillian Gray.

# CHAPTER 21

Charlie sat in the interview room, stewing in the infernal heat and dabbing at a trickle of sweat running down the side of his face, despite having mopped his forehead with a handkerchief thirty seconds before. It was a hot day outside, but nothing could have prepared him for the wall of heat that had assailed him on entering this place twenty minutes ago. It had been like walking into a blast furnace, the steaming air rank with the stench of sweat. He had decided to pay Tate Martin a visit just to check in, and been surprised to find that he had been moved from the Santa Ana minimum security facility in Pinar del Rio where he and Landon had first met the hotelier to the Villa Marista prison just outside Havana.

In preparation for the visit, he had made some inquiries as to the reason for the move and was still waiting for a response. But in the process, he had learned that while Santa Ana was pretty laid back, as Cuban prisons go, Villa Marista was quite the opposite, and was nicknamed the Cuban Lubyanka for its inhospitable conditions. From his grim surroundings, and the shouts and screams he had heard on the way to the interview room, Charlie was beginning to think the name was well-earned.

He was checking his watch and wondering how long they were going to keep him stewing here when the door opened with an earsplitting creak and Martin appeared, followed by two guards who hustled him over, sat him down roughly, and chained his hands to the table before disappearing through the door without a word, slamming it behind them.

"Tell me you're here to get me out of this place," Martin said before the echo of the door slamming faded completely. Charlie was shaken by the change in the hotelier's appearance since he had last seen him. Martin's features were gaunt and his filthy clothes little better than rags. Seeing the desperation in his eyes, Charlie wished he had better news.

"I'm afraid I'm just checking in," he said, unable to maintain eye contact. "I wasn't told that you'd been transferred here, otherwise I would have come sooner."

Martin gave a grim laugh. "I guess they figured Santa Ana was too much like Varadero for a gringo like me. They decided to give me some hard time instead."

Charlie considered asking whether he was being treated appropriately, then stopped himself. He was talking to a man, quite possibly an innocent man, who spent every day shoulder to shoulder with some of the most dangerous criminals in Cuba. He tried another tack. "I've been trying to find out why you've been transferred to a maximum security facility. And whatever the answer," he added, trying to sound encouraging, "I'll be making a formal request to get you transferred back to Santa Ana."

Martin snorted. "Don't waste your time."

"What do you mean?"

"I mean, they put me in this shithole for a reason, and I don't think I'm ever getting out."

"Why do you say that?"

Martin sighed. "I told you, man. They want me and my hotel out of the way."

Charlie nodded, remembering Martin's claim that all of his troubles were a result of him being in competition with a new hotel being built across the square from his.

"I don't even give a shit about the hotel anymore," Martin said, with a plaintive expression on his stubbly face as he wiped sweat from his eye. "They can have it. I just want to get the hell out of here … forever. You tell them that, Charlie," he added, leaning forward over the table. "You tell 'em they can have my hotel — all the blood, sweat, and tears I put into that place over the years — they can have it all if they just put me on a plane. I swear I'll never come back."

Charlie watched as Martin's expression became more desperate before his eyes. It was clear that his perspective had changed since the first visit, and while it might have something to do with his new surroundings, Charlie had a hunch there was more to it than that. He leaned forward himself, meeting him halfway across the metal table.

"Have you been threatened since you got here?" he asked, keeping his voice low.

Martin shook his head. "It's worse than that."

Charlie waited for an explanation, but Martin offered nothing more, other than to hang his head.

"I don't understand, Tate, and I can't help you if you don't tell me what's going on."

"I told you about the hotel across the square from mine, right?"

Charlie nodded. "In José Martí Square. Yes. What about it?"

"I found out who the main investors are." Martin paused, the only sound in the room a faint mechanical whirring in the ceiling and the splatter of a droplet of sweat falling from Charlie's eyebrow onto the table.

"Who are they?"

"Colombians," he whispered, his voice barely audible.

Charlie was surprised at first. Though he knew there were strong historical connections between Cuba and South America, he had thought it was mostly between Cuba and Venezuela. When he thought about it, though, he supposed it made sense, given that Colombia was right next door. "I'm still not sure I—"

"You don't fuck with the Colombians," Martin said, shaking his head.

"You think they're behind you being detained in the first place, or being transferred here?" Charlie asked, wondering if Martin's imagination wasn't working overtime in this oppressive heat. The days of Pablo Escobar were long gone.

"You have no idea. Just forget it." Martin threw up his hands and slouched back in his chair.

"Let me—"

"Don't do anything," Martin said, shaking his head again. "You'll only make it worse, believe me."

"Listen, I'm not saying I don't believe you," Charlie said. "There's definitely something odd going on here. But let me start with the request to have you transferred first. They can't possibly justify keeping you in here," he added, looking to Martin for confirmation. The other man shook his head wearily, then shrugged.

"Okay, whatever. You put in your request, but don't be surprised if it goes nowhere."

# CHAPTER 22

Charlie sat in the spacious lobby of the Meliá Habana Hotel, watching the tourists and businesspeople come and go against the backdrop of a grand central water fountain, and all he could think of was Tate Martin, trying to survive another night in Villa Marista. He hadn't bothered to wait for a response to his inquiry about the reason for Martin's transfer to maximum security. Instead, he had drafted a letter demanding Martin be sent back to a minimum security facility immediately. Landon had suggested he ask for a move to La Lima, which was still in Havana but had a good reputation. If Charlie didn't get a timely response, he would get Stewart involved.

His attention was drawn to a woman wearing a white eye patch — the second person Charlie had seen wearing a similar bandage in the past five minutes. As the woman crossed the lobby, he looked out through the main entrance at the last of a beautiful sunset, giving way to another warm Cuban evening. He checked his watch for the third time. He had missed Redden and Gray's arrival at the embassy because of a consular emergency, but had left word that he would pick them up at the hotel for dinner. Considering he hadn't slept that well the night before — after a hurried meal and a quick review of the inventory that confirmed nothing had been taken in the break-in — he didn't feel too bad. Between worrying about the break-in, the dissolved dope, and that Cuban detective, Charlie hadn't exactly spent a restful night. He was still thinking about Detective Viernes and politely waving the lobby bar waiter away when he caught sight of Jillian Gray making her way over from the elevators. He got up to meet her, and saw her smile as she spotted him.

"Welcome back," he said, unsure whether to extend his hand or go for the hug. She decided for him by leaning in for the two-cheek peck.

"Hi, Charlie."

"Where's Bruce?"

"Oh, he's not coming," she said, with a wave of her hand. "He called to say he's bagged and he's just going to get room service and crash."

Charlie hadn't planned for a one-on-one dinner with Gray, and was trying to decide whether he should be nervous or glad. Then again, he thought, he had enough real problems to worry about that dinner with a beautiful woman shouldn't count as one of them.

"I didn't make any reservations. I just thought we'd go somewhere nearby, or we could go into town, if you want."

"Nearby's fine."

"You like Italian? There's a little *paladar* just a few blocks from here."

"Sure."

Charlie led the way out through the entrance doors, into the warm evening air and to his car.

"So," he said as they got in, "how was the flight down?"

"Fine. It was pretty relaxing, actually, after twenty-four hours of madness trying to get out of the office."

"I'm sorry it was such short notice. We only found out on Tuesday about Ruiz leaving the country for a couple of weeks."

"Not your fault."

"I guess you're pretty busy." Charlie's eyes lingered in the rear-view mirror as she replied, and he was still preoccupied with the mirror when he realized the intersection with Fifth Avenue was coming up fast. He applied the brakes and they came to a stop at the red light with a little squeak of the tires.

"Sorry," he said, as Gray removed her hand from the dash. "I thought I recognized someone from work behind us," he added with a nervous smile. "I need to keep my eyes on the road ahead. You were saying things are busy back in Ottawa?"

"Yes, I'm involved in a half-dozen projects," she said, as the light changed and they crossed Fifth and took a right onto a little side street. "But this one's got priority right now."

"Well, that's good news for us." Charlie pulled the car over to the curb.

"Here already?" Gray was looking around. There was no obvious sign of a restaurant nearby.

"Just over there." Charlie pointed at a green house down the street with a barely noticeable sign out front in the shape of a pizza slice. Gray got out and followed him to the house, where Charlie opened the metal gate for her. As she walked through into the front yard, he shot a glance back down the street.

"Here?" Gray said, pointing to a little path leading around the side of the house.

"That's right," he said, opening the wooden gate by the side of what looked like an average residence. On the other side of the gate, the path led them to a large room with an enormous brick oven at the back and half a dozen tables, most of which were occupied. Charlie exchanged greetings with the proprietor, an enormous Cuban woman whose good nature was obvious, despite the barely comprehensible mix of Spanish and broken English. Charlie smiled as she rattled on for a few minutes before seating them at a table for two in a little alcove across from the oven.

"This is very cozy," Gray said as they sat.

"Yeah, it's pretty basic Italian food, but it's good."

After they had ordered and been served a complimentary mojito, they began to chat about the work plan for the next couple of days, beginning with the morning meeting with Gustavo Ruiz and his staff.

"The main problem is getting a meaningful appraisal to justify the price," Gray said, sipping her drink. Given the Cubans' well-known expertise in electronic surveillance — a legacy of the Russian presence here during the cold war — they had agreed not to discuss figures or strategy outside the secure spaces in the embassy.

"That's true," Charlie agreed. "Difficult to determine fair market value when there's no market."

"But as long as the price is fair," Gray said with a wink, "I'm sure we'll be able to work something out."

"Cheers to that," Charlie said, raising his glass to hers.

"And what about the short-listed developers? Are they all lined up for next week?"

"We're actually meeting with Société Immobilière on Friday. The rest are next week." Charlie was about to add something else when he noticed a face at one of the tables across the room that looked vaguely familiar. He was trying to settle the internal debate as to where he had seen it before, if he had at all, when he realized Gray was talking to him.

"I'm sorry?"

"Is everything all right, Charlie? You seem … preoccupied."

"No, it's nothing. I'm a little tired," he said with a smile. "I've been working late," he said, changing the subject. "So when's your return flight?" he asked, as the waitress arrived with several little plates of assorted appetizers.

"I left it open. I'm assuming we'll be working until next Friday, and I was thinking about staying for the weekend. You know, add a little pleasure to the business."

"Good idea. As for this weekend, you're all invited to my place for dinner," he added, remembering the promise he'd made on their last trip down.

The waitress interrupted to describe the contents of the various plates, then disappeared. Charlie had forgotten all about the man across the room, focused as he was on trying to figure out whether he should be picking up on subtle little clues Gray was implanting into her every word, or whether he was imagining the whole thing.

They had a leisurely meal together, with the conversation staying general and neither of them venturing anywhere near what had happened on the Malecón the last night of Gray's previous visit. In fact, by the time the cheque arrived, Charlie was no closer to knowing what Gray was thinking, but he had enjoyed her company anyway. It was about nine-thirty when he drove her back to the hotel and wished her a good night's sleep.

"So the meeting's at eleven?" she asked, leaning into the open car window.

"The driver will be here around eight-fifteen to bring you to the embassy. We'll go to the meeting from there."

"Good night then, Charlie."

As he drove back out toward Jaimanitas, Charlie's mind was buzzing, torn between worrying about whether he was being followed and whether there seemed at least a reasonable chance that whatever he was feeling about Jillian Gray was mutual.

# CHAPTER 23

The Canadian team, composed of Charlie, Gray, Redden, and a translator, sat in the meeting room on the top floor of the building that housed the Cuban state property program. Charlie had been there twice already since arriving in Cuba, and he had never felt comfortable. And whether his discomfort was by design or not, there was no denying that the four loveseats around a large glass coffee table wasn't your typical layout for a meeting room. Then again, as Charlie was beginning to realize, everything in Cuba was different.

They waited in silence, apart from their noisy positioning as they alternated between sitting back in the deep leather sofas — which seemed too informal, as though they were gathered around to watch a hockey game — or balancing on the edge, which was just plain uncomfortable. The exercise was cut short by the arrival of the Cuban delegation, led by Gustavo Ruiz, who greeted them with a broad grin, making his way around the room as Charlie introduced the members of the team. Though he knew Ruiz spoke excellent English, Charlie let the translator do his work for the benefit of Ruiz's three associates, who were introduced in turn. When they had all taken their seats — the Cubans reclining comfortably, the Canadians mostly perched — Charlie led off.

"First of all, let me thank you for accommodating us in your busy schedule. I understand you will be out of the country for a couple of weeks, and I hope you will agree that the presence of the Ottawa-based members of our team here today is an indication of just how serious we are about this site." Ruiz smiled and his associates nodded as the translator repeated Charlie's opening address in Spanish. "Our hope is that over the next two days we will come to an agreement on the major terms of the transaction, not just for the acquisition of the land, but for our ongoing partnership throughout the development of this important project," Charlie continued, mentally checking off the boxes of the items that they had all agreed upon at the morning's pre-meeting that he was to cover in his opening address.

He continued, with frequent interruptions to allow for translation, and after about ten minutes, it was Ruiz's turn to speak. He led off with similar platitudes about the desire to make the deal happen, and about the abundance of cooperation and goodwill at the table, to which everyone on the Canadian side of the table nodded and smiled. His next statement, which Ruiz chose to utter in English, took Charlie by surprise. "And before we move on to the main terms for agreement, I would like to say how sorry I was to hear of the unfortunate events at your residence the other night, and that we are working very hard with the diplomatic police service to get to the bottom of it."

"Thank you," Charlie said, as Gray and Redden looked on in surprise. He was wondering whether Ruiz was going to say more about the break-in when a woman arrived with a large tray of coffee and water.

As the cups were deposited in front of them, Ruiz pulled out a binder of photocopied documents and set it on the table. He began speaking in Spanish, and Charlie understood enough to know that he had moved back to the topic of the land. When Ruiz had finished, the translator took over, explaining that the documents were copies of the title report on the land, as requested by Gray. Charlie gave her the floor and she began talking about legal issues related to the land. Ruiz, in turn, deferred to his own counsel, and the two lawyers exchanged questions for a few minutes until they both seemed satisfied with the process that would be required before the deal could close.

As he sat there listening to the exchange and looking casually back and forth between Ruiz and his lawyer, Charlie noticed a little smile on Ruiz's face as Gray explained why an independent environmental assessment would also be necessary.

"We understand," Ruiz said, holding up a hand to his own lawyer and re-inserting himself into the conversation. "You need to be assured that there is nothing … how do you say … *unsavoury* on the grounds."

"Exactly," Gray said.

"Or under them," Ruiz added, looking at Charlie, who was frozen by the remark, though his face remained passive. "Like someone who buys a house, only to find something nasty buried underneath," he added, looking back at Gray and smiling.

Charlie looked at his hands and felt his chest constrict.

As the legal discussion continued, Charlie looked up expecting to find Ruiz staring at him, but instead the man was sipping his coffee and listening intently to Gray. When the title issues had been resolved, Ruiz broached the topic of price, and Charlie was glad that Redden was handling that one. He was barely listening as Ruiz and Redden put forward their respective positions to open the negotiations. He was too busy recalling all of the uncomfortable moments he had experienced over the past couple of days, from familiar cars in his rear-view to familiar faces in restaurants, and replaying them all in light of Ruiz's comment.

Charlie said his final goodbyes to the protocol officer and got into the embassy van. The driver had barely slid the back door shut, with Charlie still settling himself in his seat, when Gray spoke. "What was all that about your house?" she asked as the van pulled away from the curb.

Charlie turned to face her and noticed Redden was looking on with interest from the back row. "It's no big deal. Just a break-in. It happens."

"Don't you have guards?" Redden asked.

"Yeah. They're nice enough guys, but they're probably more interested in catnapping than watching my house."

"That must be a bit unsettling," Gray remarked, concern showing on her face where Charlie thought he had seen bare curiosity just a few seconds earlier.

"Yeah, especially with that business with the woman from the Indian embassy," Redden added from the back seat. "They don't think …"

"No, they don't think it's related in any way to Amirjit Saini," Charlie replied quickly, though, hearing the statement from his own mouth, it didn't sound very convincing.

"Did you have a lot of things stolen?" Gray asked.

Charlie tried to laugh it off. "If they were thinking the place would be loaded with valuables, they must have been pretty disappointed."

Gray didn't seem to be buying Charlie's nonchalance, but she didn't pursue it, perhaps sensing his true discomfort.

"So, pretty productive meeting, huh?" Charlie declared, changing the subject and looking at Redden to see if he would take the bait.

He didn't hesitate. "I'll get them down a few hundred thousand yet," he said confidently. Redden clearly fancied himself a deal-maker who never left much on the table, and though opinions varied as to whether this was actually true, he at least had a track record for getting projects done. "I'm just worried about whether we can get all the details worked out by the end of tomorrow. I don't like the idea of having to negotiate with Ruiz's underlings. I get the sense it'll be a waste of time."

"I agree," Gray said. "Ruiz is definitely the one calling the shots. We should try to present him with a draft first thing tomorrow and hopefully we'll have agreement in principle on the main points by the end of the day."

"Can we sign it tomorrow?" Charlie asked, looking at Redden, who deferred to Gray.

"No, but we could sign a letter of intent subject to some conditions — environmental and title searches, for example. We're going to need to get a hold of Sam Sanchez to help us with the drafting."

Charlie nodded, pulling out his BlackBerry and firing off a quick message to Sanchez. As Redden and Gray debated what should be in the letter of intent, Charlie's mind wandered to the expression on Ruiz's face when he had made his mysterious remark. He briefly entertained the idea of racing home to see if anyone had disturbed the flooring in his bedroom, but he knew he wouldn't have the chance. He had been hoping to forget about his personal problems for a while by throwing his energy into the property deal. But with Ruiz's remark, Charlie came to the very unsettling conclusion that more people than he cared to admit knew that something was fishy at his house.

The more he thought of it, the more it made sense that the state authority responsible for diplomatic properties would know the most about the houses in its portfolio — and Ruiz was pretty close to the top. But how could he have known there was dope buried under the floorboards? Could he be involved somehow?

Charlie found it hard to believe, though. Ruiz was a senior official in the government, for Christ's sake. But what did Charlie really know, and not know, about the underworld in Havana? He had heard there wasn't much of a drug trade, mostly because of the lack of hard currency to pay for it, not to mention the severe penalties involved. But even in Cuba, he was sure there was a clientele for someone willing to take the risk. It might be a smaller market, but the upside could still be high.

The sound of his name brought him back into the real-time discussion of how they were going to get a draft agreement ready in time for the meeting the next morning.

The van was almost back at the embassy when his hip vibrated.

"That's Sam now," he said, reading the incoming message. "He says he's available anytime after five. He's suggesting either his office or a conference room at the hotel. Any preference?"

"I don't care," Redden said. "As long as I get something to eat soon, before I pass out."

"I agree with that," Gray said.

Charlie looked at his watch, realizing that the meeting had been more than three hours long. "Why don't we go to the hotel and grab something to eat, and have Sam meet us as soon as he can?" Seeing the others shrugging their shoulders in unison, he typed out a message as the van rolled through the embassy gates. Getting out, Charlie had a quick word with the driver before turning to the others.

"I've got to make a run home first, if you want to check your emails upstairs. Hector here will take you out to the hotel in thirty minutes and I'll meet you there."

Charlie sat at the table in the backyard, munching on a hastily-assembled sandwich. He glanced at the pool and wondered whether there could be any remaining trace of whatever he had dropped in there. Surely it had been killed off by the chlorine, or evaporated, in the past week. He still worried about Teddy's exposure during his brief swim, but he had seen little of Stewart since his return from Panama, and the ambassador hadn't said anything about the dog, one way or the other. Charlie decided that was a good thing. Surely, if Teddy had gone home and pissed all over the inside of the official residence, Charlie would have heard all about it by now.

"I go now, Señor Charlie."

He turned to see Marta by the kitchen door and waved. Returning inside a few moments later, he watched the housekeeper chatting with one of the guards at the gate, and as soon as it closed behind her, Charlie headed straight for his room. He stood there for a moment, staring at the floor by the foot of his bed. He saw no evidence of any of the boards having been moved. If Ruiz's men had been in here, they had done a pretty good job of putting everything back in order. He glanced around the room, wondering whether they had a miniature camera hidden somewhere. He had been warned at his pre-posting briefing that the Cubans were experts at surveillance, and that while the house had been vetted by Gord Connors, there was no guarantee a bug or two hadn't been missed. But video was a stretch.

Charlie knelt down and tried to jiggle the boards loose, but they felt as solid as they looked. Could it be that Ruiz's remark had been mere coincidence, and that he knew nothing about Charlie's discovery?

Maybe he was just being paranoid. Charlie didn't know what to think, and he didn't have time to worry about it now. He was due out at the hotel.

# CHAPTER 24

Sam Sanchez took off his glasses and stopped writing. The four of them — Sanchez, Gray, Redden, and Charlie — had spent the last three hours trying to put together the draft purchase agreement, and they all knew there were still several hours of work left to do.

"Now, the import issue is a big one," Sanchez said, getting up for a stretch. "As you may know, the duties on foreign imports are considerable in Cuba."

"How considerable?" Redden asked. He had grown more and more irritated as the night wore on, as he learned of the growing number of obstacles that his construction project, which would be relatively straightforward anywhere else, would encounter in Cuba.

"On construction materials, it's about a hundred and fifty percent," he said, eliciting a bout of cursing from Redden. "But," he added, turning to Gray, "as long as you import it for the embassy, you'll be exempt from those duties, correct?"

Gray pulled her glasses down from their perch on top of her head. "That's right, but we can't pass our exemption on to our contractor, so we'll have to make sure that whatever deal we strike with the builder allows us to import the materials ourselves."

Charlie considered her answer from across the table, trying not to peek at the front of her white blouse, which he had noticed offered the occasional hint of cleavage, depending on her position at the table.

"That's going to be a nightmare," Redden said, also getting up. He already knew most of the construction materials would have to be imported, from bricks and nails to furniture and bathroom fixtures.

"Not if you do it right," Sanchez replied, picking up his pen again. "If we use ImCub as our customs agent, they're surprisingly efficient."

"Why do I think this is going to cost us?" Gray said as Sanchez smiled.

"They'll want their cut, but it won't be too bad, and nowhere near the delay costs and import duties you'll incur otherwise. The important thing is to include their role as import agent into the purchase agreement."

"So it will be built into the overall purchase price, instead of a separate cost?" Gray said, making a note.

"Exactly," Sanchez said. He read out the text of a proposed clause. Redden and Charlie nodded, while Gray frowned.

"I'm a little concerned about their role … as agent, I mean."

"Why?" Redden asked, his annoyance obvious.

Gray was unfazed. "Because we want to keep tight control of what's ordered, and what clears customs. I don't want our embassy project to fuel a black market in duty-free construction materials."

"Has that ever happened?" Charlie asked, intrigued.

"Not to us, as far as I know, but I have heard of unscrupulous contractors importing all sorts of things under diplomatic cover. Say," she continued, "you need a hundred sheets of Gyproc for a project. Your contractor imports a thousand, then sells the rest on the black market. It's one way to increase profit margins."

"And then there's the other stuff that gets shipped in," Sanchez said.

"Let's not even go there." Gray waved a hand. "We'll just have to make sure we specify that a Canadian has to be on hand for the opening of every container."

With everyone in agreement on the proposed course of action, Redden suggested a five-minute break. They were on the ground floor of the hotel, and everyone agreed it would be a good idea to go outside for some fresh air. They strolled out into the courtyard between the outdoor bar and the pool area. The ocean was close enough that they could hear the waves breaking, and the air was thick with the scent of salt water.

"Do you think we'll get this thing finished tonight?" Charlie asked, as Sanchez lit a cigarette.

"Absolutely," he replied. "We're through the worst of it already. Another hour, two at the most, and I'll have enough to put the first draft together. When's the meeting tomorrow?"

"Eleven," Charlie said, consulting his electronic calendar.

"Why don't I bring a draft to the embassy first thing, and then we can make final revisions before we take it to the Cubans."

"That works," Gray said, pointing at Sanchez' cigarette. "Can I bum one of those?"

"Of course." Sanchez offered her one from the pack and flicked open his lighter.

"So what have you got planned for the weekend?" Sanchez asked, after they had all agreed on the time for the morning meeting at the embassy.

"I'm heading out to Varadero," Redden said. "Some friends are there for a couple of weeks, so I'm going to hang with them for a couple of days."

"Sounds like a good plan," Charlie said, as Sanchez looked to Gray.

"Thought I'd putter around the market, maybe see the castle," she said.

"If I wasn't going to Mexico City tomorrow, I could have taken you out to the Bay of Pigs. It's a nice drive," Sanchez said.

"Oh, that is too bad," Gray said.

"I could take you out for dinner," Charlie heard himself say, realizing it sounded like he had just asked Gray out on a date … in front of the whole group. An awkward silence loomed as Gray took a long puff of her cigarette. Charlie's mind was churning to come up with a plausible and face-saving reply to her rejection when she blew out a long stream of smoke and smiled.

"Sure, why not."

# CHAPTER 25

Charlie drove around the same block for the third time, checking the map and the instructions Landon had given him over the phone. He had been disappointed to find the restaurant he had in mind was fully booked when he called first thing on Saturday for a reservation. But the alternate came highly recommended by one of Landon's friends, if only Charlie could find it.

"He said it was on this street, a building with a rooftop garden." He pointed through the windshield and began to wonder if he shouldn't just take his chances in town. Gray didn't seem worried.

"I'm sure it's here somewhere."

Charlie pulled over to get a better look at the instructions he had scribbled. "Wait a minute." He looked at the street sign and then checked the map, tracing the area with his finger. "We're on the wrong street. We're supposed to be on San Ignacio."

Gray leaned over to have a look, and put her finger a few inches from his. "There."

"You're right. Just a few streets up and to the left." As he started off again, Charlie caught the fragrant scent of Gray's perfume on the warm breeze coming in through the open car windows. She was wearing a blue linen dress with spaghetti straps that showed off the delicate bones of her shoulders. She had spent the morning at the outdoor market and her freckled cheeks bore a tinge of pink that gave her a healthy glow.

As they turned onto the next street, Charlie spotted it right away. It looked like an average six-storey apartment building, but unlike all of the others on the block, this building's top was covered in lush greenery that crept down the walls.

They parked and walked across the quiet street to the entrance, which gave no hint that there was a restaurant upstairs. Landon had conveyed the description he had been given of the place: "unique," and the food excellent. The only problem was that it had irregular hours, and Landon couldn't guarantee that it was actually open from one week to the next. There was no way to reserve either, so as they climbed the circular staircase, Charlie hoped they wouldn't be turned away. After five steep flights of stairs, they arrived at a metal gate blocking further progress.

"Are you sure this is the place?" Gray said as they stood catching their breath.

"Yeah. Drew mentioned this. We have to buzz up."

Charlie pressed the buzzer by the gate and waited. After a few seconds of silence, he pressed it again. He was about to call out when he heard a door opening somewhere above, followed by the appearance of a young man on the other side of the gate. Charlie asked for a table in the best Spanish he could manage, but the man shook his head, then rattled off what sounded like a denial. Undeterred, Charlie mentioned the proprietor's name, as instructed by Landon. The man paused, then disappeared.

"What'd he say?" Gray asked.

"I'm not entirely sure." Charlie was thinking of having to go back down all those stairs when he was surprised by a buzzing sound at the gate in front of him. He pulled it open and after a few more stairs, they were in what looked like someone's apartment. The young man reappeared and waved them to the right, down a hallway with impossibly low ceilings and little rooms off to each side. The first room held a single table, occupied by a young couple enjoying an intimate meal. The next seemed to be someone's bedroom, while the third was another, larger dining room with a half-dozen people sitting around a table laughing.

"Is this a restaurant or someone's apartment?" Gray whispered from behind him.

"I don't know, just watch your head," he replied as they came to another hallway with an even lower ceiling. The sides of the corridor were lined with lush plants, and the farther they went, the lower the ceiling seemed to get.

"Is that the sky up there?" Gray said, as Charlie parted the leaves of a plant so they could get by. Moving it to the side, he saw that she was right. They were looking up at the stars. They passed another little eating area to one side, where a foursome were sipping wine and smoking cigars, and a few seconds later they arrived at a little clearing with a table for two, surrounded by plants and open to the night sky but for a vine-covered pagoda overhead.

Their guide disappeared as they sat at the table and took in the unusual surroundings. It wasn't long before a woman appeared and introduced herself as the owner, switching to broken English when they told her where they were from. As the waiter returned to take their drinks order, the owner retreated and wished them an enjoyable evening, promising to check in on them from time to time.

"What a great place," Gray said as Charlie smiled back. Despite having seen other patrons on the way in, there was a strange intimacy in the quiet little clearing under the stars, surrounded by plants and soft music. It felt as though they had the place to themselves. Their reflections on the unusual setting led to a broader discussion of Havana's charms, and how different it was from Ottawa.

"So, do you miss it at all?" Gray asked.

"Ottawa? Not really." The truth was, Charlie didn't really know how he felt about the city that he had called home for the past twenty years. He generally didn't think about it much, no doubt due to its connection with Sharon and the flood of negative emotions she evoked. But with everything that had been going on lately, he had other things on his mind.

"Will you go back after your posting here is over?"

Another good question, for which Charlie had no answer. His plan had been to disappear to somewhere he wouldn't have to work too hard. Havana was undoubtedly a world away from Ottawa, but the cushy diplomatic lifestyle that he had imagined hadn't quite panned out. Not yet, anyway. Charlie had found himself working quite a bit harder than he had anticipated, though he also found himself enjoying the work. As he considered Gray's question, he couldn't think of a good reason not to pursue another posting rather than returning to Ottawa. There certainly wasn't anything, or anyone, waiting for him there that compelled him to return.

"I really don't know," he said, as the waiter arrived with a couple of mojitos and an assortment of little trays containing appetizers. "Lately I've been more focused on the present." He raised his glass before adding, "I guess I'm hoping the future will work itself out."

"That sounds like a good plan," Gray said, touching her glass off his and taking a sip of the cool rum concoction. She pointed at one of the dishes. "What do we have here?"

"Those are fried plantains." Charlie was confident he recognized the Cuban staple. "As for the rest, we're going to have to wing it."

Gray smiled at him across the table, the glow of candle-light catching the twinkle in her eyes. "Yes we are."

Charlie was rummaging through the back of his fridge, look-ing for a couple of cold Cristals he knew were back there somewhere, when he heard the splash. Spotting a glint of green, he pushed aside a yogurt container and pulled out the two bottles. Stopping by the laundry room to grab a pair of trunks that were hanging on a hook, he headed out to the pool deck just in time to see Gray swimming toward him. In the floodlit water of the pool, it was clear that she hadn't bothered with a bathing suit.

"Come on in, it's glorious."

"I'm coming," he said, tossing the trunks aside and setting down the beers. As she paddled off toward the middle of the pool, he stripped off his clothes and dove in, surfacing a few feet from her. He quickly closed the gap and she slipped into his arms, their torsos crushed against each other as their legs moved to stay afloat. They remained locked in an embrace as they gradually made their way back to the shallow end.

"Why don't you give me the upstairs tour," she said as she took him by the hand and led him toward the house.

# CHAPTER 26

They lay in the dim light provided by the moon outside the open window, Gray's head resting on Charlie's chest, rising and lowering in time with his breathing. After a while, she stirred and ran her hand across his stomach. "That was wonderful."

"Fantastic," Charlie agreed, realizing that the break in silence hadn't brought the magic of the moment to an end after all. He watched as she lifted her head and looked up at him, her cascading hair obscuring half of her face and the soft moonlight settling on the curve of her hip.

"I hope you don't think I do this on every trip," she said suddenly, cocking her head gently to one side.

Charlie laughed. "I should say the same. I had no idea a visit from HQ could be so, um … enjoyable."

"And if you tell Redden, I'll kill you." She slapped him playfully on the stomach. "He already hates me. All I need is for him to go back to Ottawa and start spreading exaggerated stories about me. How I seduced the MCO."

"Well …" he said, grinning.

"Very funny."

"Don't worry. I don't kiss and tell."

"Good," she said, pulling herself up onto one elbow and leaning over to kiss him. As they embraced, Charlie flinched at a sudden clinking sound coming from outside the open window.

"What was that?"

"I'm not sure," he said as Gray slid off him. He went over to the window and stepped out onto the little balcony over-looking the backyard.

"Do you see anything?" she asked from the bed.

"No, it's probably just the guard. They've actually been making the rounds lately."

"And here's me jumping into the pool in my birthday suit." She joined him at the window, sliding her arms around his waist and pressing herself up against him as she peered around him at the pool below. "I guess it must be a bit unset-tling, having someone break into your house."

"It's no big deal," he lied, reaching around to caress her hips. "Besides, they've doubled the guards. And they've told them to actually keep a lookout, instead of watching TV. So, there's nothing to worry about."

"It's such a beautiful night … so warm."

"We can go for another dip, if you like."

"You did interrupt my earlier swim," she said, biting him lightly on the neck.

Charlie went to the bathroom and came out with a couple of towels. He gave one to Gray and tucked one around his waist. "In case the guard walks by."

They made their way down to the pool and paddled around the warm water for a while before settling in the shallow end. With only the underwater lights on, the stars seemed espe-cially bright overhead as they stared up at them, submerged to their shoulders and leaning back against the pool steps. They chatted quietly about the funky rooftop restaurant and the new embassy deal. Eventually, Gray got around to the break-in.

"And they didn't take anything, huh?" she asked, looking up at the stars.

"No."

"But they trashed the place?"

"Hmm."

"Strange," she said, her tone matter-of-fact. "Almost as if they were looking for something." He said nothing as their eyes met for a moment, but Charlie felt compelled to tell her, though he wasn't sure why. Maybe he was just tired of carrying the burden of the secret alone. But he couldn't.

"What?" She searched his face for a reaction. Charlie glanced around, making sure they were alone before sliding closer to her. He was on the verge of saying something, then stopped.

"You can tell me, Charlie."

He wanted to, badly. Maybe it was the intimacy of the moment, but whatever the reason, it seemed the right time for truth.

"I found drugs," he whispered, "under the bedroom floor."

He saw her surprise and immediately regretted telling her. "You told Connors, right?" she said, after a brief pause, and in a voice that was barely audible.

Charlie looked back up to the stars.

"That's pretty serious business, Charlie, especially here. I don't have to tell you what could happen if …"

He was shaking his head. "I can't tell him now."

"Why not?"

"Because I don't have it anymore. I sort of … lost it."

"You *lost* it?"

"It fell in the pool."

"This pool?"

Charlie explained the tarantula, his resulting tumble into the pool, and Teddy knocking the illicit package into the deep end.

"Do you know what it was?" she whispered.

"Coke, I think. I'm not exactly an expert."

"How much?"

"A kilo or two?" He sketched the approximate size of the package in the air with his finger.

"My God," was all she said, and in the silence that followed, Charlie was wishing he had kept his mouth shut. What was he doing involving her? "So no one knows anything about it?"

"I think the Cuban cops know something."

"What? Why do you say that?"

"Things they said. The way they were looking at me. I don't know."

"You've got to tell someone, Charlie. Connors, or the ambassador," she said, putting her arm on his. "Especially if you think the local police might have an inkling; otherwise it'll be your word against theirs."

"It already is."

"It's a lot more convincing if the admission comes from you *before* you're behind bars, trust me," she said in a hushed whisper. "But I'd be more worried about the owner of the stuff. A package of that size, of that sort of commodity, doesn't just disappear without putting a major crimp in someone's bottom line."

Charlie's stomach tensed, hearing his own worst fear voiced. "But what am I supposed to do? Even if I knew who it was, I can't just call them up and say 'oops, I dropped your stuff in the pool. Sorry about that.'"

"You said you found it under the floorboards?"

Charlie nodded.

"Well, who had this place before you?"

"That's the first thing I asked after I moved in. It was my counterpart at the Venezuelan embassy. His posting came to an end and he went back to Caracas. I assume the stuff wasn't his, or he would have taken it with him."

Gray looked at him for a moment, but said nothing.

"What?"

"You said it was the first thing you thought of after you moved in. Did something else happen *before* you found the dope?"

"No … well, not really." Charlie could see she wasn't going to let him off that easily. "I did have a couple of strange visits, but …"

"What kind of visits?"

"A couple of working girls — at least, I think they were."

"Did they mention drugs?"

"No, they just wanted to know where Javier was, and they told me they wanted to party."

"Javier was the previous occupant? The Venezuelan MCO?"

"Javier Garcia, yes. Look, I'm sorry to unload all this on you. I don't know why I did. It's not your problem."

She shook her head. "I'm glad you did. I'm just worried about you, that's all."

"Well, don't be. I have no real reason to think anyone knows anything about it, and I haven't done anything wrong, anyway."

"I guess you haven't," she said, breaking into a grin.

"What's so funny?"

"I was just thinking, this probably wasn't what you had in mind when you moved to Havana."

"You mean swimming naked with you?" he said with a laugh. "I'd have come here a lot sooner."

"I wonder what Stewart would think," she said, a mischievous look on her face.

As he watched her swim off, what Stewart or anyone else thought was the last thing on Charlie's mind. He had spent too much of his life worrying about what other people thought. Maybe Havana had changed him already.

# CHAPTER 27

"So, what do you think?" Sam Sanchez turned toward Charlie and Redden. Gray was seated on Sanchez's other side at Société Immobilière's boardroom table, and their hosts had just left the room to arrange lunch at a nearby restaurant.

"I thought they sounded pretty good."

"They're good at telling us what we want to hear, that's for sure," Gray remarked.

"Yeah, I'm not sure their timelines are realistic, though, especially from what I've heard of projects in Cuba," Redden added.

"As long as we structure the agreement properly," Sanchez said. "We should be able to keep them to a reasonable schedule."

Charlie stole a glance at Gray. He found it odd to be sitting in the formal setting, separated by Sanchez, when just a few hours earlier he and Gray had awoken entangled together in Charlie's bed. They had agreed that discretion was the preferred option, but Charlie couldn't help wishing he didn't have to conceal his affection for her.

"What time's the meeting with the Cubans?" Redden was looking at his watch.

"Four," Charlie replied. "We're probably going to have to go straight from the restaurant. I should email the driver to let him know."

"I don't expect it will be a long meeting, with Ruiz out of town," Sanchez said. "If you don't have any plans this evening, I'd like to take you to La Guarida. It's one of the best restaurants in Havana."

Charlie noted a hint of a smile on Gray's face.

"I'm going to have to pass," Redden said. "My friends from Varadero are here and I made plans. Thanks for the offer, though."

"Next time," Sanchez replied with a smile. "Jillian? Charlie?"

"Sure, sounds great," Charlie said, as Gray nodded her agreement. As Sanchez described the location of the restaurant, Charlie leaned back to stretch his arms and neck, glancing out through the boardroom doors to the hallway in the process. He saw two men chatting at the end of the hall, and when the nearest one turned toward him, Charlie snapped his head back and found himself looking straight at Sanchez.

"You okay, Charlie?"

"Hmm?" He tried to appear calm as his eyes returned to their normal size, but his heart was racing. "Just strained my neck, I think," he added, making a show of turning his head from side to side.

"You look like you've seen a ghost." Sanchez looked past Charlie, out into the hallway. His face clouded with a frown and he seemed about to say something when SI president Daniel Leblanc returned to the boardroom.

"What is it?" Gray whispered.

"Nothing," Sanchez replied under his breath as Leblanc announced that their transportation to the restaurant was ready downstairs. As he stood up, Charlie felt the familiar buzz of his BlackBerry and slid it out of its holder to check the incoming message. He sighed as he scanned the email.

Gray stood next to him, packing up her satchel. "Everything okay?"

"That's the second consular case this morning. Must have been a rough weekend. I'm going to have to give the lunch a miss." Gray hung back as Redden and Sanchez left the room chatting about something.

"Do you feel weird?" she whispered.

"What do you mean?"

"You and I sitting here in a meeting, with Sam and Bruce completely oblivious."

He smiled. "I know what you mean."

"Can you make it to dinner?"

"You bet."

"And a moonlight swim after?" she added, leaning in and brushing up against him.

"Wouldn't miss it for the world," he whispered, following her out of the boardroom.

Charlie drove through the ill-lit streets of Havana, straining his eyes for the signs at every intersection. He knew he was close, but he had only driven by the restaurant once, and he couldn't remember its exact location. He noticed a pair of cabs across from a building with a sign that, by Havana standards, was pretty ornate. An enormous, smiling man was standing at the entrance, and when he greeted a couple who had just gotten out of one of the cabs, Charlie knew he had found La Guarida.

He pulled in behind a rusty Lada and the humid air smothered him the moment he stepped out of the air-conditioned interior of his car. He made his way over to the entrance and exchanged pleasantries with the doorman, slipping him a few pesos and asking if his car would be all right where it was.

"No problemo. You enjoy your meal, my friend."

"*Gracias.*"

Charlie stepped through the open doorway, noting the massive wooden door — it had to be at least twenty feet high — as he headed toward the spiral staircase. He walked across the creaking hardwood, past a row of clotheslines adorned with the laundry of the various inhabitants of the building's lower floors. He could see lights toward the rear of the building where the private apartments were, and the sound of laughter and Cuban music followed him up the crumbling stone steps that led to the next level. He could hear the soft echo of music and muffled voices on the other side of an ornately carved door, and as he opened it he was immediately assailed by the smells and sounds of a bustling little restaurant.

"*Buenas tardes, Señor,*" a smiling hostess said, closing the door behind him. Charlie mentioned Sanchez's name and was immediately led down a narrow and stifling corridor, past a cramped and hectic kitchen, and into the first dining room. They continued to another, much smaller, room where Sanchez and Gray sat by an open window, chatting over a glass of wine. The incoming breeze, although humid, was refreshing in comparison to the rest of the restaurant and it carried the familiar scent of Gray's perfume as she rose to peck him on the cheek.

"Glad you could join us," Sanchez said, shaking Charlie's hand as they took their seats.

"Me too," Charlie replied as the waitress hovered and he accepted a glass of white wine. "This is quite a building," he added, settling into his chair.

"As long as it doesn't pick tonight to fall down," Gray remarked. "I noticed some reinforcing rods on the second floor."

Sanchez laughed. "Don't worry. I acted for the engineering firm that did the structural assessment of this place. It's not falling down any time soon, despite appearances."

Their casual chat over drinks soon turned to the afternoon meeting that Charlie had missed with the Cubans, and Gray and Sanchez were quick to point out that, with the exception of some minor amendments, their draft agreement had been accepted.

"Any idea when we might see their changes?" Charlie asked, knowing that would be Stewart's first question in the morning.

"Well, this *is* Cuba," Sanchez hedged. "But we did get the sense that Ruiz had left them with instructions to speed things up."

"So, I'm right in thinking a couple of weeks?" Charlie guessed.

"Something like that, yeah," Sanchez agreed.

"So add in translation time, and review by good old Ottawa," Charlie added, winking at Gray, "and we could have a deal signed in a month."

"Cheers to that, then," Sanchez said as the waitress returned to take their orders. Sanchez asked for a little more time, as they hadn't even opened their menus.

"The fish is great here," he said, without bothering to look at the menu. "I highly recommend either the snapper or the dorado."

"I'm going to go with the snapper," Charlie said, turning to Gray.

"I'll try the dorado." She closed her menu and smiled at him.

After the waitress had taken their orders, Gray leaned over the table and looked at Sanchez. "So, what was it that you couldn't tell us this morning, at SI's offices?"

Charlie felt his stomach constrict as Sanchez looked first at him, before turning his attention to answering Gray's question.

"I recognized a guy in the hall," Sanchez began. "It's probably nothing, but let's just say he's somewhat of a well-known figure around Havana. A Colombian."

"Colombian?" Charlie heard himself ask. He had been hoping the conversation might quickly switch to another topic, but now his heart was racing.

"He's been associated with a certain element, if you know what I mean," Sanchez said, lowering his voice.

"I'm not sure I do," Charlie said, trying to conceal his growing alarm.

Sanchez frowned. "Let's just say there's a strong connection between Cuba and some of the South American countries. It's mostly Venezuela, but Colombia as well, to a lesser extent."

"I read something about the Venezuelan thing," Gray said. "How they ship oil to Cuba in exchange for medical services."

Sanchez nodded. "Yes, Cuba has an abundance of well-trained doctors. Many Venezuelans come here for treatment, especially eye surgeries."

"I noticed a bunch of people at the hotel were wearing eye patches," Charlie said, almost to himself.

"Me too," Gray said. "But what was this Colombian doing at SI's offices?"

Charlie sipped his wine and wished he had ordered something stronger. He didn't like the direction the conversation was going, especially in light of his recent visit with Tate Martin, who was still rotting in a Cuban jail.

"That, I don't know," Sanchez said.

"What's his name?" Gray asked, as an assortment of appetizers arrived.

Sanchez paused until the waitress had left before leaning in to whisper the name. "Diego Medina."

"I know it sounds sort of ignorant," Gray said, "but I can't help associating Colombia with the cartels."

"I don't think it's ignorant at all," Sanchez replied, taking a sip of wine.

"But what would the cartel be doing in Havana, anyway?" she continued, keeping her voice low. "I thought there wasn't a drug trade here."

"It's true that there are stiff penalties for traffickers in Cuba," Sanchez said. "And the drug trade doesn't exist to the same extent because of the scarcity of hard currency, but that's not to say it isn't around, just like gambling, prostitution, and the rest."

Charlie was growing more uncomfortable as the conversation continued on its course. He tried to focus on the food for a while, until a piece of fried potato got stuck in his throat and he gagged, taking a healthy gulp of water to dislodge it.

"Are you okay?" Sanchez asked, as Charlie coughed into his napkin and took another swig of water.

"Yes, yes, I'm fine," he said, avoiding Gray's eyes as she continued.

"I'm not sure I like the idea of this Medina guy being connected to SI if we end up in business with them," she said with a frown.

"Let me make some discreet inquiries at the office," Sanchez said. "His being there might be nothing more than sheer coincidence."

"It would be good if you could check," Gray said. "Don't you think, Charlie?"

He nodded quickly, glad to be moving away from the topic. But if he was hoping for a switch to tomorrow's weather forecast, he was soon disappointed.

"What do you know about Javier Garcia?" Gray asked, sipping her wine.

"Not sure I know the name," Sanchez said, putting down his fork and buttering a roll.

"He was Charlie's counterpart at the Venezuelan embassy until a few months ago," Gray paused before adding, "and the former occupant of his house."

Sanchez kept chewing as he looked from Gray to Charlie. "Are you thinking he may have had something to do with the break-in at your place?"

"God, no," Charlie sputtered, taking another sip of wine to conceal his discomfort. But neither the cold, dry liquid nor the breeze coming in through the open window could stop little beads of sweat from forming on his forehead.

"We're just curious," Gray said, the picture of calm.

"I don't really know much about the Venezuelans, and I'm not sure who handles their legal work. I could ask around if you like?"

Charlie waved a hand. "Don't bother, Sam. I'm sure the break-in was just some misguided thieves who thought they were going to roll the pad of a rich diplomat and ended up at my place instead."

"Well, it is a very impressive house. If I were looking for somewhere to rob, it would sure be on my list," Sanchez said.

"So, who's up tomorrow?" Charlie said, intent on keeping the conversation away from anything else he might have told Gray in post-coital confidence. He was beginning to wonder what else she would blurt out before the meal was over.

As they finished their appetizers, Sanchez excused himself to go to the men's room. He wasn't gone for more than a few seconds when Gray broke the silence.

"Is everything all right, Charlie? You're acting a little strange."

"*I'm* acting strange," he said, in an animated whisper. "I told you those things because … actually, I don't know why I told you those things, but I certainly didn't expect you to repeat them to every Tom, Dick, and Harry."

"Relax, it's only Sam. I'm just trying to help. Don't you want to know more about this Garcia guy…? And I saw your reaction today when you saw that Colombian. There's something you're not telling me."

"Look, I appreciate you're trying to help, but I really don't think—" He stopped talking when the waitress arrived to take their plates and an awkward silence descended over the table until she left.

"I think you're overreacting, Charlie."

He was about to respond when Sanchez reappeared.

"Now, Charlie," he said, taking his seat. "I'm very interested in your views on détente with the U.S. Does the embassy really think it's the first step in ending the embargo?"

"The political section is certainly taking the meeting seriously," Charlie began, glad to be onto a new topic of conversation, as Gray hid her expression in her wine glass.

# CHAPTER 28

Charlie navigated the car north through the darkened streets toward the Malecón. He and Gray had parted with Sanchez at the entrance to the restaurant after the meal, and the silence had been unbearable ever since. Finally, Gray broke it.

"Look, I don't know what the big deal is. I would have thought you'd be interested in finding out more about Garcia, given what you found under the floor of the house he used to live in."

Charlie continued driving, unsure of whether he was taking Gray back to her hotel or his place. He was thinking the former, and her tone only made that destination clearer.

"I was just surprised that you would have mentioned *any* of it to him, that's all."

"I was only trying to find out if there was an actual drug trade here. It's not like I told him you'd found a couple of keys of the stuff under your floor."

"It's my fault," he said, wondering whether he had over-reacted just a little, though he still felt annoyed. "I should never have involved you in the first place."

Silence reigned again as he drove west along the water-front, and Gray opened her window.

"I've got the AC on," he said.

"I prefer the breeze," she replied, looking out the window. He switched off the air conditioning and put his own window down, letting the muggy night air in. As they hit the underpass that led out to Miramar, Charlie realized he would soon have to make a decision about where to take her, but their continued silence decided for him.

"Where are you going?" she asked, as he turned off Fifth Avenue.

"To your hotel."

She looked out the window and he heard a little huff of disapproval. As he pulled up to the entrance to the hotel, she looked at him.

"I'm sorry. The last thing I wanted to do was pick a fight."

Charlie turned to face her and his annoyance melted away.

"I'm the one who should be apologizing," he said, as she unbuckled her seatbelt and reached for the door. "I don't know why I got so bent out of shape."

"You're probably just stressed, that's all. It's your place that was burglarized, not mine." They sat in silence for a moment, her hand on the door handle. "Can I buy you a nightcap at the hotel bar?" she said, a smile appearing on her delicate features.

They walked into the lobby of the hotel and were instantly hit by a wave of cool air and the sound of a live band performing something that was loud and fast enough to keep a dozen or so couples moving on the dance floor beside the lobby bar. Even from fifty feet away, the sound was earsplitting.

"Want to try the one by the pool?" she said, raising her voice so he could hear her over the music. He nodded and followed her downstairs and out into the open-air hallway that ran along by the pool and led to a smaller bar. There was music there as well, but it was recorded and much more subdued. They snagged a table at the edge of the pool with a view out to the ocean and took a seat. As he sat there looking at her, with the warm breeze blowing onshore, whatever irritation Charlie had felt earlier was long gone, replaced by a smile.

"What?" A grin of her own formed at the edges of her mouth.

"Nothing."

"Come on, out with it."

"I was just thinking …" Charlie said, looking around. The bar had only a dozen or so customers, and the waiter was on the far side, apparently engrossed in conversation with the bartender.

"We might get better service from your mini-bar."

She smiled. "You're pretty forward, aren't you Hillier? I only invited you for a nightcap. Nobody said it was going to be in my room."

They lay on the bed in the dark, a thin sheet covering them as he stroked her hair and watched the sheers over the open patio door fill like sails with each onshore gust, then fall again. Gray rolled off him and sat up on the edge of the bed.

"Why don't you see if you can find us a cold drink in the mini-bar?" she said, as she slid off the bed and padded across the tile floor to the bathroom. Charlie reached over and fumbled with the latch on the small fridge, finally springing it free and scanning the contents by the interior light. He pulled out a couple of beers and the two glasses from the nearby shelf, slipped his underwear on, and made his way out onto the balcony.

"There you are." Gray appeared in a white nightshirt and sat next to him, and the two of them sipped the cold beer and looked out over the water. The wind was creating little ridges of white near the shore, visible because of the powerful floodlights at the hotel's perimeter, just fifty feet from the waterline. "Another beautiful night in paradise."

"It's nice to have an ocean view," Charlie commented.

"I learned my lesson last time. My view was of that Russian embassy building. What a monstrosity."

"It's creepy, isn't it?" Charlie said, nodding. The compound's main feature was a large tower that, whether by design or not, resembled the handle of an enormous sword, thrust deep into Cuban soil. The twin red lights at the top of the structure lent it an even more sinister air at night, as though the beady eyes of some robotic monster were surveying everything below. "I suppose that was the point, right? Scare the crap out the locals."

Gray ran a hand through her hair. "Speaking of creepy, how *do* you know that Colombian guy that Sanchez was talking about — Diego Medina? You can't tell me you didn't recognize him from somewhere."

Charlie took a drink and looked out to sea. "He showed up at my house a week before the break-in."

"I thought you said your visitors were hookers."

"He was with them, the second time, driving. I caught a glimpse of him sitting out in the car."

"I guess he's not the kind of guy you easily confuse with anyone else."

"He's a scary-looking dude all right," Charlie agreed.

"So maybe he was the girls' pimp."

"Yeah, maybe."

They sat there for a while in silence, staring out over the water and up into the inky blackness above them, before Gray spoke again. "You think there's another reason he was there?"

"It's possible, but I'm trying not to think about it too much."

"You think he's—"

Charlie put his fingers to his lips and she stopped talking. She leaned into him and put her mouth next to his ear.

"You think he owns … *it*?" she whispered.

"That would be pretty much the worst-case scenario, don't you think?"

"But it's been almost a week since the break-in," she said, leaning in to whisper again. "From what Sanchez was saying, this guy doesn't seem like the patient type."

"That's the only reason I can sleep at night."

They stopped talking, each of them contemplating the dark waters beyond in silence.

"It's getting late," he said after a while, "and I should let you get some sleep. We've got another full day tomorrow."

He got dressed in the dim light of the hotel room, then she followed him to the door and kissed him goodbye. "I'm glad you came by tonight."

"Me too," he said, hugging her as he opened the door. "And we'll do the swim at my place later in the week. Maybe tomorrow night?"

"Sounds good."

He checked his watch as he made his way down the hall toward the elevator. It was almost one in the morning and he was feeling tired. He realized as another guest passed him by in the hall that he could have done with a quick look in the mirror before he left Gray's room, and by reflex he ran his fingers through his hair and began smoothing his shirt.

Waiting for the elevator, his reflection in the large mirror confirmed that he really did look as though he had just rolled out of bed. He was still smiling to himself as the doors slid open and he made to enter the elevator, oblivious to the man standing at the rear of the car, waiting to step off.

"Oh, sorry," he said, backing up without registering the other person's face.

"Charlie?"

His surprise at hearing his name turned to horror as he looked up and saw Bruce Redden standing there.

"Bruce…. Hi," he stammered. "What are you doing here?"

"My room's on this floor." Redden's tone suggested that the answer should have been obvious. "You?"

Suddenly realizing he had no plausible answer other than the truth, Charlie was hoping the doors would slam shut before he had a chance to speak, but Redden was casually leaning a hand against one side, keeping it open.

"Just meeting a friend," he said, unable to think of anything else. As Redden surveyed him coolly, Charlie began to fidget, which didn't make his cover any more credible, given his generally wrinkled and bed-headed appearance. In fact, he couldn't help thinking he looked exactly like someone who'd just had a roll in the hay, which would have been fine except that both men knew that the only person he would logically be seeing on this floor was Jillian Gray.

"Geez, what are the odds," Redden said, with a click of his tongue, "that your friend would be on the same floor as me, in this big old hotel?"

"Yeah, well …" Charlie's eyes darted away from Redden's. He was beginning to wish the elevator cable would snap and send him plunging eight floors to his death — anything to extricate him from this conversation. He was debating telling the truth and appealing for Redden's discretion when the latter removed his hand and the door began to slide shut.

"Anyway, you have a good one, Charlie," he said, giving him a sly grin.

# CHAPTER 29

Charlie was in the reception area, arguing with one of the cleaners about how often the floors were supposed to be washed, when he saw the embassy van pull up to the gates. He wasn't listening as the cleaner, a locally engaged woman who had been working at the embassy for the past ten years, rattled off a series of reasons why the floor shouldn't be cleaned more than once a week. He was watching Gray and Redden emerge from the van, and trying to get a read from their facial expressions. After his encounter with Redden the night before, Charlie had flirted with the idea of calling Gray's room to give her a heads up. He had decided against it, for reasons that at the time had seemed valid and convincing, but which now escaped him. He replayed the awkward elevator scene in his mind, seeing Redden's smirk as Charlie delivered his lame excuse, his rumpled shirt hanging out. He might as well have had Gray's lipstick smeared all over his cheek.

As he watched Redden and Gray head toward his office in the adjacent building, Charlie settled on absolute denial as his best course of action. But as he dismissed the cleaning woman and headed for the front door, it occurred to him that Gray and Redden had probably breakfasted together at the hotel. He froze inside the door as he imagined their morning conversation over bacon and eggs and fried plantains.

*By the way Jillian, I bumped into Charlie last night, just outside your room….*

Charlie swallowed hard. Perhaps he should have called to warn her, after all. He would have to find an opportunity to talk to her this morning.

"Good morning," he called out, stepping out onto the front steps just as Gray and Redden were rounding the corner.

"Oh, hi Charlie," Gray said with her usual smile.

*Nothing amiss there.*

"Hey, Charlie," Redden beamed. "You get home all right … after?" he added, in a lower voice, but not low enough that Gray didn't catch it. She gave Charlie a quizzical look as they made their way up the stairs. He wanted to give her a reassuring smile, but Redden seemed to be monitoring their reactions to his comment, so he thought it best to change the subject as quickly as possible.

"So, we've got twenty minutes before the driver takes us into town."

"Where's their office?" Gray asked as they reached the top of the stairs and Charlie keyed in his code.

"It's off the Prado," he said, remembering the email from the second of the three short-listed developers they were to meet this week.

"Oh good, we can grab something to eat in town before we come back here for the meeting with the Cubans," Redden said as they made their way down the hall, adding before he entered the spare office, "Unless you two have other plans, of course."

Gray stopped dead and looked at Charlie, who could only respond with a puzzled look. "What do you mean?" she said, taking a defiant pose in the doorway.

"Huh?" Redden looked up from the other side of the desk. "You know, like a meeting with Sanchez, or something."

Gray's spine returned to its normal curvature.

"Why, what did you think I meant?" Redden walked casually past, on his way to the coffee pot in the room next door.

"Whatever," Gray muttered, as she moved off toward her temporary office and Charlie retreated to his, making a mental note that he really would have to find a way to talk to her before the day was out.

Charlie sat at the far end of the conference room, pretending to listen to the presentation as he fiddled with his BlackBerry under the table. There was another message from the ambassador's assistant, the third this morning, asking whether Charlie knew where Teddy's rubber bone was. Charlie remembered the dog playing with it in the first couple of days of his stay, but he hadn't seen it since. As he read the text of the message from Stewart's assistant, his pulse quickened: "*Mrs. Stewart is desperate to find it, as she thinks it might have something to do with Teddy's recent incontinence.*" He stared at the email and imagined Teddy undergoing a battery of tests at the vet, and himself on the wrong end of some very awkward questions when the toxicology report came back.

"*Cocaine? Really? How odd …*"

Charlie was imagining the possible consequences — from a transfer to Burkina Faso to outright termination — when it occurred to him that maybe Katherine Stewart was right. Perhaps Teddy's soiling of the official carpets had nothing to do with his dip in Charlie's dope-infused pool, but, rather, to the loss of a favourite chew toy.

Charlie flashed back to his childhood, remembering a particular stuffed bear that made a little growl — it was more like a moo, actually — when he tipped it. Would Charlie have pissed the bed every night if Brownie had gone missing for a week? *Quite possibly*, he thought with a surge of hope. He fired off a response reminding the ambassador's assistant, politely, that he was in a meeting with one of the prospective builders of the new embassy building right now, but he would happily attend to the missing rubber bone at his earliest possible opportunity.

He knew he was going to have to go back to the embassy straight after the meeting, and dreaded the inevitable meeting with Stewart — official topic: work; actual topic: the official dog.

Charlie put the addictive little devil back in its holster and looked up, realizing he had missed the last ten minutes of what so far had been a less-than-inspiring presentation.

CubanaCan had looked respectable on paper, but it was quickly becoming apparent that they were a little light when it came to experience. Whereas Société Immobilière had furnished them with an elaborate brochure showcasing a dozen commercial projects that they had done in the past five years, to go along with the PowerPoint presentation, CubanaCan seemed a bit bush-league in comparison. Charlie had met the speaker, Doug Calvin, at a reception, and the way the ex-pat Calgarian had talked, he was responsible for building half of Havana. Now, as Charlie flipped through the poor-quality black-and-white three-pager that outlined the company's projects, it appeared that apart from one joint venture for the construction of a small office building, most of their projects were residential, and pretty small-scale. Charlie had to admire Calvin's ability to embellish, to the point that they almost sounded like contenders for the embassy project, but not quite.

And if Charlie was reading Redden's body language correctly, he was not overly impressed either. He started the same exercise with Gray, but soon found himself considering her in a rather more intimate light. She seemed to sense him looking and returned a quick smile. Sanchez was doing his best to look enthralled, but Charlie knew he was the least impressed of them all. In fact, Sanchez had warned them that CubanaCan might be in over their heads a little on a project of this size. Charlie felt his hip vibrating again and vowed not to answer the call. But when it started buzzing again a few minutes later, he couldn't resist snapping it out quietly and glancing at the little screen.

*Again with the goddamn rubber bone?*

Charlie and Sanchez stood on the front step outside CubanaCan's office. The sun had hidden itself behind a large, grey cloud, making the warm midday air quite comfortable.

"They could be a while," Sanchez said, lighting a cigarette and setting his briefcase down on a little brick wall. They had all spent fifteen minutes trapped in CubanaCan's lobby as the affable but long-winded Doug Calvin continued his pitch. Charlie and Sanchez had led a final push to leave, but Calvin had managed to hang on to Gray and Redden for the moment.

"So, what did you think?" Charlie asked.

"Pretty much as expected. Doug's a good guy, and CubanaCan's very reputable, but they don't really have the same track record as SI."

"No, that was pretty obvious. And they've got no previous experience building embassies."

"That reminds me," Sanchez said, pausing to suck on his Marlboro. "I made an interesting discovery this morning when I made a few inquiries about the former occupant of your house."

Charlie didn't remember asking Sanchez to make any such inquiries, and his surprise must have been obvious.

"I just happened to be talking to—" Sanchez stopped and seemed to reconsider what he was going to say. "Garcia's name came up, that's all."

"And?"

"Turns out more than his posting came to an end, if you know what I mean," Sanchez said, his voice lowered. He took a puff of his cigarette and exhaled the smoke as he waited for Charlie's response. When it didn't come, Sanchez continued. "He went back to Venezuela a couple of weeks before his posting here was due to end — to make arrangements for his permanent return to Caracas, I suppose — and never returned." He tossed the butt to the ground and crushed it under a loafer, edging closer to Charlie as he did so. "An accident. His car was incinerated, apparently. He was so close to the end of his posting that most people just assumed he had returned home a little early."

Charlie just stood there looking puzzled.

"For some reason," Sanchez continued, "the Venezuelan embassy seems quite happy to leave it at that."

"What do you mean?"

"Well, my source heard about this by chance, and when he tried to confirm it with the Venezuelans, they seemed pretty reluctant to discuss it."

Charlie's hip buzzed as he stood there, the colour draining out of his face. He plucked the BlackBerry distractedly from his hip and looked at the incoming message, noticing it was from Stewart's executive assistant.

*This had better not be about that fucking rubber bone again....*

He was about to put it away when he caught the word *police* in the subject line and opened the message. As he scrolled through it, he began to feel ill. Stewart wanted to

meet ASAP to discuss a call from the diplomatic police service. Charlie fired off a reply saying he was on his way back
to the embassy and then dialed the number for the driver,
who was nowhere to be found.

"Everything okay, Charlie?" Sanchez asked, just as Gray
and Redden emerged from CubanaCan's office looking tired.

"Yeah, but I have to head back to the embassy."

"Not going to join us for lunch?" Redden was patting his
stomach. "I'm starving."

"Can't. I'll leave the driver for you," he said, looking for
the nearest taxi. "I've got some consular stuff I have to deal
with," he lied, avoiding Gray's searching eyes and flagging
an approaching taxi. "I'll see you at the four o'clock meeting.
Have a good lunch."

# CHAPTER 30

Charlie sat in the waiting area outside the ambassador's office, fidgeting and trying to ignore the growls coming from his stomach. He had been there for almost fifteen minutes, time he could have spent doing something useful, like eating. He sighed and wondered why this always seemed to happen. First, Stewart's assistant would summon him with a call, but instead of being shown right in after the three minute walk from his office in the other building, Charlie would end up parked on the couch by the assistant's desk while she made a point of ignoring him. He could feel his blood pressure rising as his stomach growled again.

The assistant's phone buzzed, and a few seconds later she looked over to Charlie and gave him the nod.

"He'll see you now."

"Great," he said as he headed to the door, rapping gently before entering.

"Charlie, how are you?" Stewart was reading something on his computer and beckoned Charlie over to the sitting area. "Be right with you. Just reading this list of possible mission closures. I don't know what they're thinking in Ottawa."

"We're not on it, are we?" Charlie said, as he took a seat and glanced at the picture of Teddy.

"Don't laugh. You never know. And it's not like we'd get any warning, either. I'm not even supposed to have access to that list." Stewart shook his head as he took a seat opposite Charlie. "Minority governments. One decides it's going to shut down a dozen missions, and two years later the next one wants them all back up and running. It's the same old story. Tiresome, really." Stewart sighed.

"How was Panama, anyway?" Charlie asked. "I haven't had much of a chance to talk to you since you got back, what with the property visits, and ... other stuff."

"Productive. Very productive, indeed. I was wondering whether it was going to be a waste of time, frankly. But as it turned out, I gained some valuable insights into how some of our friends are running their Americas platforms."

Charlie nodded, not having the faintest idea what Stewart was talking about.

"Damn hot, though." Stewart frowned, as if at the memory of the unpleasantness of the climate. "But enough about that. I hear you had some trouble out at your house?"

Charlie nodded. "Yes, there was a break-in."

"I heard all about it from Gord ... after I got a call from the Cuban police, that is."

Charlie wondered whether Stewart was annoyed at not being briefed by his own staff first. But that was Connors's job, not his.

"I wasn't there at the time, and they didn't really take much," Charlie said, keen to minimize the significance of the break-in.

"And you were pulled over by someone posing as a Cuban cop?"

Stewart obviously knew all the details, and Charlie wondered what it was he was hoping Charlie might add.

"Yes, apparently in league with the thieves. Did the police

mention having any leads?" Charlie asked, trying to change the direction of the conversation.

"Oh, you know the Cubans." Stewart gave a snort and leaned back in his chair. "You never know what they're up to. If they did have a lead, they probably wouldn't say. They seemed puzzled by the fact that nothing was taken, though," he added, stroking his top lip with a manicured finger.

"I'm afraid my place doesn't have a lot to offer your average thief. Courtesy of my ex-wife." Charlie tried a chuckle, but it stuck in his throat just enough to sound forced.

Stewart smiled as Charlie's foot began to twitch.

"Yes, you mentioned your divorce. There but for the Grace of God, Charlie. That's what I always say." Stewart crossed his legs and flicked a piece of lint from the cuff of his pants before continuing. "Well, I'm assured they'll keep us up to date on their investigation, and I asked that Gord be briefed regularly."

"That's good."

"I suppose the whole thing must have been a bit unsettling. I hate to think what might have happened to Teddy if he'd still been there."

*Teddy's a fucking dog! What about me?*

"Speaking of which, I never did thank you properly for taking him while we were away."

"Oh, it was my pleasure," Charlie said, relieved to be changing topics.

"He didn't cause you any trouble, did he?"

"No. None," Charlie replied, a little too quickly. Stewart seemed very interested in his response.

"I only ask because he's been acting a little … off since we got back."

Charlie's pulse quickened.

*Fuck.*

"Really? How so?"

"Well, he's ruined Katherine's favourite rug for starters. You know the one in the sun room?" Stewart paused and looked at Charlie, then carried on. "She got it at a market in Damascus and, well … it doesn't matter now."

"How did he ruin it?" Charlie asked, wondering how many favourite rugs Katherine Stewart had collected over the years.

Stewart ignored the question. "You did take him out for his regular bathroom breaks, didn't you?"

"Yes, of course."

"And you didn't have any problems?"

Charlie paused for a split second. He had to be careful here. His housekeeper knew the cook at the official residence, and Stewart's wife wasn't beyond submitting them both to a polygraph.

"Well," he said, deciding on a version that was part fact and part ass-covering. "He did have a couple of accidents at first, but I made sure I took him out regularly. I'm sure it's only temporary," Charlie assured him, trying another tack. "He probably just missed you."

Stewart grunted and shifted his weight in the chair, eyeing Charlie with what could only be interpreted as suspicion. Charlie reminded himself that he hadn't lied to Stewart, exactly. He *had* failed to mention the cocaine-infused doggie-paddle and the fact that it coincided with Teddy's loss of bladder control, but that didn't change the fact that Charlie had been treading in the official mutt's massive crap piles since day one. He used this knowledge to reach down for some genuine outrage.

"I assure you, I did my best to look after him."

"Of course you did," Stewart said, with a flash of his charming smile. "And Katherine and I are very grateful. Which reminds me," he said, slapping his knee and getting up. He pulled something out of his desk drawer and returned to the sitting area, handing Charlie a brightly wrapped parcel about the shape and size of a rolled-up magazine.

"What's this?"

"A token of our thanks."

Charlie sat there staring at it.

"Well, aren't you going to open it?"

Charlie nodded and gently tore away the wrapping, puzzled to find what looked like a cloth fajita.

"Don't look so surprised Charlie. It's a hat."

He unrolled it to confirm Stewart's statement. "A Panama hat?"

"Always retains its shape," Stewart said, grinning. "The perfect item for the traveller. I got one myself."

Charlie shook it loose and was surprised to see that it did, in fact, instantly morph from fajita into hat. "You didn't have to bring me anything," he said, feeling a surge of guilt.

"Thank you, Charlie," Stewart said, repositioning himself on the chair and signalling the imminent end of the meeting. "And I'll keep you posted on this investigation," he added, getting up.

"I'd appreciate that."

"By the way, I understand they've given you extra guards. I hope you still feel comfortable there?"

"Yes, it's fine." The truth was, the news that the former occupant of his house had ended up dead had made him feel distinctly uncomfortable, but telling Stewart about it wasn't going to help, so he rolled up his hat and headed for the door.

"Oh, and Charlie?"

"Yes?" He stopped at the door.

"Do have a look for that rubber bone will you? Katherine's convinced that it's the only thing that will salvage the rest of the flooring."

Charlie was returning from the front entrance, having just escorted the Cuban property delegation out when he saw Sanchez and Gray seated at a table by the pool.

"You want a coffee?" Gray asked, heading toward the little cantina.

"Sure," he said, taking a seat opposite Sanchez. "Where's Bruce?"

"Gone to do some emails."

"So, that went very well," Sanchez commented as he lit a cigarette.

"Yeah," Charlie agreed. The Cubans had requested a couple of minor drafting changes, but were otherwise ready to sign the legal documents as soon as Ruiz returned, in a week's time. "I just hope it's not too good to be true."

"What do you mean?" Sanchez said, as Gray emerged from the cantina delicately balancing three espresso cups.

"Thanks," Charlie said, getting up to relieve her of his coffee before continuing. "Just that, from what I've heard, things aren't supposed to go so smoothly in Cuba."

"That's true," Sanchez said, "but they do seem genuinely motivated to do this deal."

"Have a little faith, Charlie," Gray said, smiling.

"You're right."

"And take some credit," Sanchez added, patting him on the shoulder. "You've accomplished in a few weeks what several of your predecessors couldn't manage in an entire posting."

"That's why they pay me the big bucks," Charlie joked as they drank their coffees.

"Sam told me about Javier Garcia," Gray said, changing the subject.

"You left before I could tell you everything," Sanchez said. Charlie was instantly curious. Suddenly, everything about Javier Garcia had become required knowledge.

"I'm all ears."

"He was quite a ladies' man, apparently. I don't know if that explains why no one at the embassy wanted to discuss him."

"What do you mean?" Charlie sipped his coffee.

"Maybe he was fooling around with the wrong women," Sanchez said. "It wouldn't be the first time — this is Havana after all." Charlie was thinking back to the odd visits just after he had moved into his house and that they now made more sense. "A few years back," Sanchez continued, as Gray leaned over and took one of his cigarettes, "there was a Swedish diplomat who was recalled suddenly … and I mean *suddenly*. It turns out he had been sleeping with the wife of a government official who had made it known that he wanted the guy at the bottom of Havana Bay."

Charlie's mind was flooded with uncomfortable images of Sharon and the Swedish Meatball in that broom closet. If it hadn't been winter, he might have considered tossing Lars Whatshisface into the Rideau Canal himself. He looked up and caught Gray's eye. She said nothing, but seemed to sense his discomfort, though she couldn't know its cause. Perhaps she was thinking, as he had when he first heard of Javier Garcia's sudden death, that it was somehow related to the drugs found under his floor.

"Then again, I've been to Venezuela, and the roads really are lethal. It probably was just an accident," Sanchez said, tapping his cigarette in the ashtray and gathering his bag. "What time shall we meet in the morning?"

"The next presentation is here at eleven. I don't think we need any prep."

"All right, I'll be here."

"Thanks, Sam," Charlie said as the lawyer made his way toward the front gate. Gray sat there for a moment, looking at him.

"You look like you could use some cheering up."

He saw her smile, and suddenly the troubling thoughts that had been cluttering his mind all day disappeared.

"I feel better already."

# CHAPTER 31

Charlie lay in bed with Gray, his breathing still laboured, and their bodies stuck together by a film of sweat.

"*Mmmm,*" Gray moaned softly, sliding off him and rolling onto her back, running a hand through her hair while her other arm fell against Charlie's torso. "What is that music?"

"Hmm?" He put his arms over his head and adjusted the pillow. "Someone local. She was singing at a restaurant the first week I was here. You know how they go around afterward with the donation basket and a couple of copies of their CD."

"And there you were, fresh off the boat." She nudged him in the ribs and he laughed.

"Off the plane, actually, but yeah … she wasn't going anywhere until I bought one."

"She's good."

They lay together in silence for a while, listening, until Gray rolled over and pulled herself onto her elbows.

"I'm going to miss these nights," she said, looking up at him. He had been trying not to think of it — the fact that none of this was meant to last. He knew Havana itself was only for a few years, and he was fine with that. It was exactly what he had wanted. But Gray wasn't part of his plan, and what had started as a fling seemed to be turning into something else. The only problem was, her time in

Havana was limited to a couple more days, after which she would return to her life in Ottawa. As much as he told himself that becoming involved with another woman was the last thing he wanted, Charlie couldn't help himself, and he was beginning to dread how he would feel after she had gone.

"How long can you stay?" he said, looking out the window as the wind picked up. Soon, it would be hurricane season. Even with most of his meals either prepared for him or eaten in *paladares*, Charlie already felt as though he had consumed a lifetime supply of chicken and beans, and the shortages at the grocery store hadn't even started.

"I've got to be back in the office on Monday, so I guess I'll have to leave Sunday afternoon. I've already changed my flight and my room's available for the weekend."

"Why pay for a hotel room when you can stay here?"

"I don't know. It's bad enough Redden knows about us, without me staying at your place. I'm sure he'll be blabbing it all over the office on Monday. Asshole. I wouldn't be surprised if he's told everyone around here, too."

"Who cares?"

"Easy for you to say, you're in the land of mojitos and salsa. This is what you're supposed to be doing."

They were sharing a laugh when a loud bang at the window jolted them.

"It's the shutters again." Charlie got up and secured them to the side of the house, and closed the window halfway. "Boy, it's really getting wild out there," he said, hopping back onto the bed. "I hope the weather's okay for the weekend. We should do something special for your last couple of days."

"Don't go to any trouble."

"Hey, maybe your flight will be cancelled and you'll be trapped here until after the hurricane season's over."

"Sounds nice," she said, laying her head across his chest. "Say, Charlie?"

"Yeah?"

"About Javier Garcia. I didn't know Sam was going to go digging up information. I certainly didn't ask him to."

"It's fine," he said, running his hand down her spine, feeling the little notches as he went.

"I'm glad he did though, aren't you?" She looked up at him. "I mean, it sounds like his death was an accident, but if it wasn't, it was most likely a jealous husband who got to him, not …"

"Not some drug dealer he stiffed out of a couple of kilos of coke?"

"You don't sound convinced," she said, as he continued to stroke her hair. When he didn't answer, Gray pressed on. "You have another theory?"

"Remember the discussion we had about importing construction materials for the project, when we were drafting the purchase agreement?"

"Yeah." She leaned onto her side, propped up on one elbow.

"You said you'd heard of projects where other stuff came in under diplomatic cover, right?"

"You think what you found under your bed came in under—" She stopped at the sight of Charlie's finger over his mouth, or maybe it was the way he had straightened up when she had spoken those words. He couldn't blame her. He had brought it up, without really thinking that someone could be listening to their every word. He got up and walked over to the CD player and hit the play button. As the music resumed, he lay back on the bed, leaning in close to Gray.

"It would be a good way for it to come in, wouldn't it?" he whispered. "And it would explain why I saw that Medina guy at SI's offices."

Gray put her mouth right to his ear before speaking again, in a whisper so low he could barely make it out. "You think Medina used Garcia to import dope in the shipments of construction materials for the Venezuelan embassy?" She pulled back to see him nod, and then it was his turn to lean in to her.

"What if Garcia got greedy, and decided to keep some of Medina's stuff for himself?"

They both lay there, contemplating their whispered exchange in the darkness for a while, neither one saying what they were both thinking — that with every passing second, their theory was sounding more plausible than the one Sanchez had offered this afternoon. And a lot more ominous for Charlie.

Charlie drove back along Fifth Avenue, his being the only car on the road apart from the occasional taxi near the hotel. The dashboard clock read 2:00 a.m., and as he put the window down a strong gust of warm wind blew in, shaking the car on its shocks. He wondered when the first storm would hit, and what his first hurricane season held in store to welcome him to Cuba. The previous year had apparently been relatively calm, but he remembered at least two storms, both beginning with the letter *F*, making the news in Ottawa in the past five years or so. Glancing in the rear-view mirror, he thought he saw the glint of headlights far behind him, but when he looked again they were gone. He felt suddenly exposed out on the deserted avenue in the middle of the night. What would he do if someone tried to pull him over now? Hit the gas pedal, most likely, and hope he didn't end up in the slammer as a result. As he turned onto his quiet street, he felt a wave of relief at the sight of the hut outside his house, with one of the guards sitting inside and another standing out front smoking a cigarette. Safe. For tonight anyways.

Charlie waved as the guard tossed his cigarette aside and opened the gate for him.

"*Gracias,*" he said, getting out of the car and walking toward the front door.

"*Buenas noches, Señor.*"

"*Buenas noches.*"

Charlie locked the front door behind him and tossed his keys on the hall table. He kicked off his sandals and walked to the kitchen for a glass of water. He was parched. As he stood there in the dim fluorescent light drinking his water, all he could think of was Gray. He missed the warmth of her smile and touch already. As he caught sight of the bowl he had used for Teddy's water, still sitting on the floor in the corner of the kitchen, he even found himself missing the stupid dog.

He put the glass in the sink and headed upstairs to bed. Thank God the first meeting wasn't until eleven. As he hit the upstairs landing, he decided he would make a point of sleeping in a little in the morning, and then he caught sight of the rumpled bedsheets and felt another pang of loneliness. They had agreed it would be best not to risk having Redden see him dropping her off early in the morning at the hotel. Redden was leaving on the afternoon flight, and then they would be free to be together as much as they wanted until Gray had to leave on Sunday. Charlie planned to make the most of it, and he was thinking of where he might take her on Saturday when he noticed something that made him freeze in his tracks.

The baseboard below his bed was crooked.

He just stood there staring at it for a moment — as if to confirm that it was out of place — before turning his mind to possible explanations. He hadn't noticed anything before he left to drop Gray off at her hotel; but then again, he hadn't really been looking, either. After all, in the half-light of the room, it would easily go unnoticed. But it had struck him like a bolt of lightning the moment he had turned his eyes to the floor.

He scolded himself for being paranoid, but he couldn't rationalize it, as hard as he tried. The strip of baseboard was definitely out of place. Had someone been in here in the last thirty minutes? He felt a shiver of fear run down his spine as he looked toward the open door of his closet. He knelt down and fumbled under the bed for the nine-iron he had been keeping there since the night of the break-in. Gripping the handle of the club tightly in his left hand, he made his way to the closet, reached in, and flicked the switch. He waited a split second, then jumped in front of the doorway, the club raised and ready to go.

*Nothing.*

Charlie spun around at the flapping of the curtains. He switched on the bedside lamp on his way over to the open window. The wind was bending the tops of the trees and whipping the bushes at the perimeter of the yard back and forth, sending a shower of little leaves and twigs into the pool below. Rain was beginning to spit in through the window, so he pushed it shut and engaged the latch. He turned to look at the floor by the head of the bed and got his pocketknife out of the drawer in his bedside table. Kneeling by the wall, he wedged the knife blade under the baseboard and pried it up. A minute later, he had pulled up the floorboards. He moved his flashlight over the hole where he had uncovered the illicit cache and found it empty. As he replaced the boards and tapped the baseboard gently into place, Charlie glanced up at the rumpled sheets on the bed where he and Gray had been chatting just an hour earlier.

*What had she said exactly?*

He pictured her lying there in his mind's eye, and her exact words returned to him, as clear as when she had first uttered them: *"You think what you found under your bed came in under ..."*

There was no getting around it, Charlie thought as he sat on the floor looking at the lamps on either side of the bed, the ceiling fan, the light switches — all places where surveillance microphones could be easily concealed. Someone had been listening to their conversation. How else, in the brief window of opportunity afforded by Charlie's dropping Gray at her hotel, could someone have entered his house and known which couple of square feet to search out of a couple of thousand? Or had the baseboard always been crooked? Was he going crazy?

Charlie got up and went downstairs, creeping into the darkened living room and peering out through the rain at the guard hut. He could see cigarette smoke coming from the window, where the two men would be sheltering from the weather. Gord Connors had told Charlie before leaving the embassy that they had scaled back to two guards again, and Charlie had thought nothing of it. Now, as he looked out at the hut, he knew the guards had to be in on it.

Somewhere, he realized, someone had been listening to Charlie and Gray from the moment they had walked in the door. Charlie felt unsettled at the thought of this person eavesdropping on their entire evening, from conversation to more intimate acts, just waiting for some tidbit of information. And it had come, and initiated an organized break-in on very short notice. It was even creepier to think that they were still listening. Could they be watching as well?

He returned to the bedroom, washed his face, and lay on the bed. The wind raged outside and the room felt hot. What should he do? Tell Connors first thing tomorrow?

Tell him what? He lay there for a good hour, trying to make sense of what had happened. No one could have gained such easy access, and on such short notice, if the guards weren't in on it. In fact, it might very well have been one of the guards who came in to do the quick search, replacing the baseboard imperfectly in his haste to get out.

Then again, the more Charlie thought about it, the more the night's events just went to show the Cubans were as clueless as he was as to the floorboard cache. Why else would they need to eavesdrop on Charlie and Gray's conversation just to find out there might be something worth checking out under his bedroom floor?

As he lay there in the dark, with his mind whirling and the possibility of sleep becoming more remote with each passing hour, Charlie looked at the clock on his night table: 3:00 a.m. So much for the good night's sleep he was counting on. Even if he did sleep in, he was still going to feel like shit in the morning when he went in. Thinking of the office, it occurred to him that he still hadn't found Teddy's rubber bone. He sighed and looked at the clock again. Searching the house for a stupid rubber chew toy at three in the morning did not really appeal to him, but neither did another day of ducking calls from Stewart's assistant, or worse, his wife.

Charlie groaned and got out of bed. After a brief stop at the fridge for a drink of cold water, he was about to check behind the furniture in the living room when he realized he hadn't checked the basement yet. He opened the door and cautiously descended the darkened stairway. At the bottom, he reached around the corner and flicked the switch and felt a surge of pride at the way the room filled with the light from the bulb he had wired up himself.

After a cursory search of the floor revealed no sign of the rubber bone, Charlie looked around the room, unfurnished apart from some shelving in the rear corner and a heavy wooden storage chest near the crawlspace under the stairs. He pulled open the doors of the chest, in the unlikely event that Marta had put the chew toy in there. As far as he knew, she never ventured into the basement. He pulled out the only drawer and saw it was empty, apart from a collection of dust balls and long-dead and dried-up insects. He tried to move the unit out from the wall, but realized with one tug that it wasn't going anywhere. He gave it another yank for good measure, but it didn't budge. No wonder it had come with the house — it would take a small army to get it up over the stairs. He shone the flashlight down the back of the unit, and after he was satisfied that Teddy's bone wasn't wedged there, he leaned up against it and looked at the open space under the stairs.

Charlie shone the flashlight into the corners underneath the stairs and smiled as he caught sight of the end of the blue rubber bone sticking out of the corner where Teddy had stashed it. Charlie had to get down on his hands and knees to reach it, and he tugged it out and retreated hurriedly, for fear of encountering God only knew what kind of creature that might inhabit a dingy Cuban basement. But in his haste to back out and straighten up at the same time, he forgot that he had left the drawer to the unit open, an error that he would soon regret as the back of his head crashed against the heavy wood. For a split second everything went black and he could have sworn he saw stars.

He collapsed back onto his knees with a loud curse and, rather than trying to stand up again, waited for his head to clear. He ran his hand over the back of his skull and was relieved, and not a little surprised, to find it free of blood. He could already feel the outline of what was going to be one hell of a bump, though. He felt something flutter past his ear and swatted at it instinctively. But instead of some creepy-crawly, Charlie watched as a sheet of paper fluttered by and came to rest on the floor in front of him. Picking it up, he saw that it was a handwritten note addressed to "Javier." The flowery stationary, and the pronounced curl of the letters, was distinctly female. Charlie read the text and, though he didn't get all of the Spanish, he knew he was reading a love letter, and he felt instantly intrigued and guilty all at the same time. The writer was expressing her love for Javier, who Charlie assumed could only be Javier Garcia, and the note was signed "QS."

Looking up from where he sat on the floor, Charlie saw the end of an envelope taped to the bottom of the drawer, and what looked like another similar note sticking out. He removed the drawer, careful not to rip the envelope or its contents, and flipped it over onto the top of the unit. He detached the envelope and opened it up. Inside he found a half-dozen notes, all on the same stationary. They were all addressed either to "Javier" or simply to "J," and all were signed at the end with the same initials in the same ornate handwriting: "QS."

Charlie forgot all about the throbbing in the back of his skull and pored over the notes, reading them one after the other. The more he read, the more interesting the notes became, and though he wasn't a hundred percent sure of his translation, he could tell what he was reading was pretty steamy.

*"You've lit the flame of passion deep within me ..."*

*"I burn for you ..."*

*"I'll follow you to the ends of the earth ..."*

Charlie sat there, looking at the collection of notes, with a new respect for the former occupant of his house. To have elicited such passion was impressive. He looked at his watch and recoiled at the time — it was after three-thirty. He had to get some sleep. He gathered up the letters and stuffed them in his pocket, put the drawer back in the unit, and was about to turn off the overhead light by pulling the chain, but decided against it. Better to turn it off at the switch, or next time he would be fumbling around in the dark trying to feel for the chain. He grabbed the rubber bone and made his way back upstairs, just as the pain began to return to his head.

Charlie lay in bed, rubbing the ever-growing bump on the back of his head. It had been twenty minutes since he had downed a couple of Tylenol, and he thought the pain had begun to dull a little. Whereas before he had been pre-occupied with who might have disturbed his floorboards, his mind was now alternating between two entirely different topics. The first was the love letters, and who the mysterious QS might be. According to Sanchez, it could have been any-one, but Charlie couldn't help wondering whether QS was the wife of someone who had discovered her extracurricular activities with Garcia and brought them, and perhaps Garcia himself, to an end. Or maybe it was just one of a number of women that Garcia was romancing, all at once, at the time of his death. The letters were undated, so there was no way to know whether they had been stuck to the bottom of that drawer for a month or a year. Charlie couldn't help being intrigued by the fact that such a renowned ladies man had felt they were special enough to keep secreted away. Maybe he had felt the same way about the mysterious QS.

As the Tylenol kicked in and his eyes began to grow heavy with sleep, Charlie's thoughts turned to Gray. Did she feel any of the same passion for him, he wondered? Or would she return to Ottawa without a second thought for him? One thing was for sure. He was going to miss her when she was gone.

# CHAPTER 32

Charlie heard the sound of the security door slamming shut down the hall, followed by Bruce Redden's familiar voice. A moment later, Redden walked by and gave a wave.

"Morning, Charlie."

"Bruce, Antoine," Charlie replied, as Lefebvre appeared behind Redden.

"Is Jillian already here?" Redden asked, as Lefebvre looked at his feet. Charlie could only imagine how Redden might have embellished his late night encounter with Charlie at the hotel.

*We were standing there at the elevator door and Gray's panties fell right out of his pocket....*

"She didn't come in on the morning run with you?"

Redden and Lefebvre exchanged looks.

"No. She didn't show up," Redden said. "We waited around for an extra five minutes. We just figured, you know ..."

*No, I don't fucking know.*

"... she made her own way in," Redden completed his thought and searched Charlie's face for something that would confirm what he had obviously been thinking.

"Did you call her room? Maybe she slept in," Charlie said, calling out to his assistant, who appeared a few seconds later between the two men at his door.

"Alena, could you call the Meliá Habana and see if Ms. Gray is in? She missed the morning run with Hector and we think she must have slept in."

She nodded and disappeared to make the call, while Charlie checked his emails again, just to make sure Gray hadn't sent him a message saying where she was. Seeing nothing, he rattled off a quick message in the hope that she had her BlackBerry turned on: *Meeting's about to start. Everything ok? Let me know if you need a ride.*

Redden looked at his watch. "The meeting's supposed to start in five minutes."

"I don't suppose she met Sanchez first," Charlie said, as his phone began ringing. He felt a sigh of relief as he saw the number on the handset display. "That's the front gate — it's probably her now." He snatched up the phone as Redden and Lefebvre stayed in the doorway. "Yes, oh it's them? I'll be right there. Señor Sanchez as well? Good. Any sign of Ms. Gray, the lawyer from Ott— No? All right." He hung up the phone, his disappointment obvious.

"She's not with him?" Redden's mischievous look was gone, replaced with one of concern, most likely for the potential delay to the project's progress if she missed the important meeting.

Charlie shook his head and was about to say something when Alena appeared at his door.

"She's not answering at the hotel."

"Well, they're waiting for me at the gate," Charlie said, getting up out of his chair. "Why don't you guys head over to the conference room. We'll have to get by without her. Alena, can you keep trying her room?"

"What's going on?" Landon poked his head in the door-way.

"Oh, hi Drew," Charlie said, reaching for his jacket. "It's

Jillian. She didn't make Hector's morning run from the hotel and there's no answer in her room."

"When's your meeting?"

"Now. Well, in a few minutes."

Landon looked at his watch. "I've got to be back here for noon, but I could take a run over to the hotel and see if I can track her down, if you like?"

Charlie nodded as he slipped into his jacket. "If you wouldn't mind, that would be great. I've got to go down to the gate."

"I'll come down with you," Landon said as they made their way past Redden and Lefebvre.

"We'll meet you in the conference room," Redden called out as Charlie and Landon went through the security door at the end of the hall.

"Is everything okay, Charlie?" Landon asked, once they were on the other side of the door.

"I don't know. It's really odd for her just not to show up like this."

"When did you see her last?" When Charlie didn't respond immediately, he added: "I just meant ..."

"I saw her last night," Charlie said quickly. He sensed Landon knew, and was confident of his discretion. "I dropped her off at the hotel around one."

"I'm sure she just slept in."

"Yeah, me too," Charlie said distractedly as they reached the bottom of the stairs.

The meeting with the Cuban property delegation had been uneventful, and the final form of the documents had been agreed upon, subject to comments from Gray, whose absence Charlie had attributed to a sleep-in or a sudden but minor illness. He was shaking hands with Gustavo Ruiz's second-in-command at the front gate, and promising to be in touch to arrange the signing, when he spotted Landon hovering near the embassy's front steps.

"Any sign of her?" Charlie asked, after he had finished seeing the Cubans off.

Landon shook his head. "I spent ten minutes knocking on her room door."

"You sure it was the right room?"

"I got housekeeping to let me in. It was her room all right, but no sign of her."

"That's odd." Charlie rubbed his chin.

"Yeah," Landon continued. "I talked to the girl at the executive counter on the ninth floor. She said she thinks she saw Jillian leave early this morning with some guy. She said he wasn't Cuban, more like South American … and she said he had his arm around her." Charlie's concern must have been obvious. "I'm sure there's a good explanation."

"Really? Our lawyer doesn't show up for a meeting, doesn't leave any kind of message whatsoever, and the front desk sees her being walked out of the hotel with some stranger."

Landon said nothing.

"I'm sorry Drew. I didn't mean to snap at you. I'm just worried about her, that's all. There's something not right about this."

"You're not thinking this has something to do with Amirjit Saini are you?"

Charlie stared at him for a moment. "Why do you say that?"

"I don't know. Two women, both connected to diplomatic missions, both—"

"Jesus, don't even say that!"

They both stood there, Charlie rubbing his finger over his top lip.

"I'm sure it's nothing like that," Landon backpedalled, but Charlie had stopped listening. Something had occurred to him that set his feet in motion toward the front gate.

"Where are you going?"

"I ... I gotta go. I'll be right back," Charlie muttered, heading out the gate and crossing the street toward the parking lot.

# CHAPTER 33

Charlie drummed his fingers impatiently on the steering wheel as he waited for the line of cars to edge forward to the corner. Reaching it, he squealed the tires as he took the right turn off Fifth Avenue toward home. His mind was whirring, flooded with images of Gray, in his arms on the Malecón, swimming in his pool, lying in his bed ... and being escorted out of her hotel by God only knew who. He gave a curt blast of the horn as he neared the entrance to his house. The guard shuffled over, annoyed at having his cigarette break interrupted.

*"Gracias,"* Charlie muttered as he jumped out of the car and raced up the front steps. He took them two at a time, and once inside he bolted up to the bedroom, pulling open his top dresser drawer and retrieving the bundle of love notes he had found in the basement the night before. He stared at the first one and felt his legs give out under him as he backed up and sat on the edge of the bed. He just sat there for a moment, staring at the two letters at the end of the note. It wasn't *QS*, as he had mistakenly thought the night before. It had taken Landon's mention of her name to make him see the flowery script in a different light — as *AS*, for Amirjit Saini. Garcia had been seeing Amirjit Saini.

Charlie re-read the letters, one after another, with a new focus on their content. She was saying she would follow him anywhere. Did that mean back to Venezuela? She said she didn't care about her job, that she just wanted to be with him. Charlie checked again in vain for a date on any of the notes. Were they from months or years ago, or was it a matter of days before Garcia had ended up incinerated in his car in Caracas? Either way, it would only have been about a week or two after Garcia's death that Saini disappeared. He recalled the night he had met her at the ambassador's reception, and her mention of South America, when he had asked her about her plans after her Havana posting was up. She had changed the subject quickly, and there was that unmistakable sadness in her eyes. As he sat there on the bed, tying together everything that had been in the back of his mind on the drive over — things he had been too afraid to actually consider as real possibilities — a clear picture emerged. Saini had gone missing because she was connected to Garcia. The dope had been under Garcia's floorboards. Garcia had overseen the diplomatic shipments of building materials for the Venezuelan embassy. Société Immobilière had built it, and SI had connections to the one person Charlie feared the most in Havana: Diego Medina.

Sanchez had warned him about the risk of something other than building materials coming in under diplomatic cover for the Canadian project. And Gray had said she had heard of it happening elsewhere. Apparently, it had happened *here* already, but instead of black-market building materials, Garcia and Medina must have worked out a deal to bring in something far more rare, and valuable, in Havana: drugs. Had Garcia gotten greedy? Had he decided to skim some of the shipment for himself? Charlie remembered that Saini's house had been ransacked before she was taken. Charlie's had too, but not before someone, likely Medina, had tried a more subtle approach by means of the lovely Maria Aguirre.

Charlie could no longer pretend that his post-coital memory loss wasn't the result of some sedative that she had slipped into his beer, giving her ample opportunity to look through the house while he dozed. He could only assume that Garcia had refused to give up the hiding place, even if it cost him his life, not to mention Saini's.

Charlie froze as a thought occurred to him. Could it have been Medina, or one of his goons, who had escorted Gray out of the hotel this very morning, his arm around her in an apparently casual gesture, while a knife or a gun in his belt prevented her from making any attempt to flee? But why had they taken her and not him?

What had he gotten her into?

He tried not to think of where Gray was at that very moment, preferring to focus on a plan to get her back to safety. It was simple enough: trade the dope for Gray. Which would be great if he hadn't dropped it in the pool….

With nothing to exchange, Charlie decided he had no choice but to go back to the embassy and tell Gord Connors everything, right away. Surely, he would realize that Charlie was no dope dealer. The riskiest thing he had done in his twenty years as a bureaucrat was to partake in an unregulated lottery at the office by buying fifty-fifty tickets. Who would believe he was capable of importing a couple of kilos of cocaine with the intent to distribute it around Havana? He jumped up off the bed as another thought occurred to him. Maybe they could test the pool water for traces of the stuff that would support his outlandish story. Either way, he didn't care anymore. He stuffed the letters in his pocket and raced down the stairs. He was almost at the front door when he heard the doorbell and whipped the door open to find the guard standing there, his finger still on the button and a look of surprise on his weathered features.

"What is it?"

"For you, Señor. Delivered earlier this morning."

Charlie took the envelope from the guard's outstretched hand. "Delivered…? By whom?"

The guard shrugged. "It was in my hut when I come back from my rounds."

Charlie looked at him to see if he was telling the truth. The man's usual bored expression showed no sign of duress. "*Gracias,*" he said, swinging the door shut as the guard turned to leave.

Standing there in the vestibule, he tore open the envelope. The note inside, typed and in English, was short and to the point. It read: *You have 24 hours to return our property, or the woman dies. If you say anything to the police or anyone else, the woman dies. We will contact you again soon.*

Charlie read the note three times over as his mind swam. He couldn't go to Connors now, and without the coke to exchange…. Just then his BlackBerry started ringing, and jolted him out of his waking nightmare.

"Charlie, where are you?" Landon's voice was a harried whisper.

"I'm … on my way back. What's wrong?"

"Connors is looking for you. He seems pissed off, and he was asking me about … well, you'd better hurry up."

# CHAPTER 34

Charlie sat in the chair in front of Gord Connors's desk, trying to get his story straight in his own head as the security officer spoke to someone on the phone. He had come straight over upon his return to the embassy, and by the look on Connors's face when Charlie had poked his head around the door, it was not going to be a pleasant meeting.

"All right," Connors said into the handset. "I'll let you know the minute I do." He hung up the phone and looked across the desk at Charlie. "Shut the door."

Connors's tone betrayed his mood and Charlie felt his knees wobble a bit as he got up to close the door.

"That," Connors said, before Charlie had regained his seat, "was Jillian Gray's boss. She's *not* a happy camper."

"I … I guess not," Charlie said, settling back in his seat and trying to find something on the desk to look at. He could feel Connors staring at him.

"When was the last time you saw Jillian Gray?" he asked suddenly.

Charlie looked up. "Um, I guess it was last night. After our meetings had wrapped up, we went to dinner with Sanchez."

"And what time did dinner end?"

"I don't know, maybe ten, ten-thirty."

"Did she get a cab back to her hotel?"

"No, I had my car, so I took her," Charlie said, trying to avoid as many outright lies as possible. He could tell Connors wanted more specific answers. "I mean, I dropped her off."

"And you didn't see her again last night?"

Charlie shook his head.

"You haven't seen her since, then?"

"No," Charlie repeated, trying to infuse a twinge of protest in his response. Connors seemed unconvinced, and looked ready to put the screws to Charlie when his phone rang again. He sighed as he looked at the displayed number.

"Shit, that's the diplomatic police."

"You want to take that in private?" Charlie offered, trying not to sound too eager.

Connors sighed. "Don't leave the premises. I need to take a statement."

"A statement? What for?"

Connors glared at him as he picked up the phone and put his hand over the receiver. "Just don't go anywhere."

Charlie returned to his office, and was only at his desk for a couple of seconds when Landon appeared at the door.

"Got a minute?"

"Sure, Drew, come on in," he said, as Landon shut the door behind him and sat down.

"Connors knows."

"Knows what?"

"About you and Gray. That you've been ... well, you know."

"Shit, I knew it." Charlie slumped into his chair and ran a hand through his hair.

"I didn't say a word, I swear," Landon said.

"It's all right, Drew," Charlie said with a sigh, as he imagined how he was going to explain himself to Connors now. "I ran into Redden at the hotel late the other night, coming from her room. He must have blabbed."

"This is serious, Charlie."

"We're both adults, for God's sake. Besides, you'd think he'd be more concerned about her whereabouts right now, instead of her love life."

"I don't think you understand."

"What?" Charlie stared at Landon for a moment as his brain assorted the possibilities, then selected the worst-case scenario. "He doesn't think—" he began to say, then stopped himself. "You can't be serious."

"I overheard Redden talking to the architect earlier," Landon said. "Saying Connors was thinking about taking you into custody."

"*What*?"

"I know you didn't … I mean, I know it has nothing to do with your relationship with her, but is there something you're not telling me?"

Charlie looked at him for the split second needed to plant a seed of doubt in Landon's mind. He badly wanted to spill the beans to someone, anyone, but all he could think of was the note, and it paralyzed him with fear.

"Come on, Drew. This is me, Charlie. You know I wouldn't hurt a flea, especially not her."

Landon seemed to be about to say something else when there was a loud rap on the door, and Connors appeared in the doorway.

"Head of mission wants to see us both. *Now*."

Charlie and Connors were shown into the ambassador's office as soon as they arrived, which was a first for Charlie, and a regrettable one at that, since he was hoping to have a few minutes to collect himself before facing Stewart. He felt flushed and dizzy as they entered Stewart's office.

"Come in, sit down," Stewart said, shutting the door behind them as they took a seat around the coffee table. Stewart sat on the same side as Connors, and Charlie felt instantly outnumbered.

"You all right, Charlie? You look a little ... *off*."

"I wouldn't mind a glass of water."

"Water please, Martine," Stewart said curtly, waiting by the open door while his assistant fetched a couple of glasses and some bottled water.

"Now," he said, returning to his seat. "What's all this about our legal counsel going missing? I just got a call from an assistant deputy minister from Justice, all hot under the collar and wanting to know how we lost one of his lawyers down here."

"She didn't show up for a meeting this morning, sir," Charlie began, filling the glass with water and pausing to gulp down a mouthful. "So Drew went over to the hotel and checked her room. She wasn't there."

"When was the last time anyone saw her?" Stewart asked.

"Last night." Connors looked at Charlie as he replied. "Charlie and Sam Sanchez had dinner with her, then dropped her off at her hotel around ... when was it, Charlie?"

"Ten or ten-thirty."

"And you tried her BlackBerry?" Stewart said.

"Yes, sir. She's not responding to messages," Charlie replied.

Stewart stroked his chin with a finger. "Could she be sick? Where did you eat?"

"La Guarida," Charlie said. "Sam had the same entrée and he's fine."

"Hmm," Stewart looked at Connors. "Have you been in touch with the Cubans about this?"

"Yes, sir. They're aware of the situation and have offered their help, although technically it's too early to file a missing person's report."

"Well, how does Justice know she's missing, then?"

"I think one of her colleagues on the property team might have said something to someone in Ottawa, and word got around," Connors said. Charlie stared at his feet.

*Redden....*

"Bad news travels fast, I guess. So, what do we do?" Stewart seemed troubled by the news.

"There's not much we can do, other than what we've already done," Connors said. "The Cuban police are on notice, and if she hasn't turned up by tomorrow morning, we'll file a formal request for assistance. In the meantime, we keep trying to get in touch with her."

"The Cubans don't think this is related to that awful business with that poor Saini woman, do they?" Stewart asked.

"There's no reason to connect the two events," Connors said, turning to Charlie. "Right?"

"No. No reason," Charlie said, managing to sound convincing and determined to survive this meeting so he could work out a plan.

"When was she due to leave?" Stewart was looking at his watch.

"This afternoon, originally, with the rest of the property team," Connors said. "But she changed her flight to Sunday. Isn't that right, Charlie?"

"I think she mentioned sticking around for a bit of R&R, yes," he replied.

"Well, I'm sure she'll turn up." Stewart looked at Charlie for a moment, then back at Connors. "Are you in contact with Justice on this, Gord?"

"Yes, I spoke to Gray's boss and promised to keep her briefed."

"Good. Let's just hope she turns up by the end of the day. I'll need an update this evening if she hasn't."

"Yes, sir."

Stewart sighed as he glanced at Charlie. "That's all."

Charlie stood up and waited for Connors to join him, but Stewart waved him off. "I need a minute with Gord ... *alone*."

"Of course. I'll catch up with you later," Charlie said, looking at Connors and making his way quickly to the door. He returned to his office and fell heavily into his chair, his mind spinning as he tried to figure out his next move. He glanced at his computer and noticed a couple of new emails, one of which featured Tate Martin's name in the subject line. Ever since his visit to Villa Marista, Charlie had been making daily phone calls to various people in the Cuban government, asking for Martin's immediate transfer to a more suitable facility.

He clicked on the message and was pleasantly surprised to see that his efforts had not gone unrewarded. Martin had been transferred to La Lima, a minimum security prison in Havana. The message was short and lacked any explanation as to why Martin had been sent to Villa Marista in the first place, but Charlie wasn't going to quibble — he had gotten the result he wanted. At least something positive had happened, he thought, imagining Martin's relief at the transfer. But the reprieve was short-lived, as Charlie's thoughts returned to Gray and how he was going to get her back safely. Suddenly, something occurred to him, and he was out of his chair and hurrying down the hall, hoping he could make it to the front gate without Connors stopping him.

# CHAPTER 35

Charlie sat in the interview room at La Lima prison, wondering how much longer they were going to make him wait, or whether they were going to let him talk to Martin at all. Usually, consular visits were arranged well in advance, and the Cubans were sticklers for procedure. It had taken a fair bit of persuasion on Charlie's part to get this far, but he still wasn't sure he would get a meeting. He glanced at his watch, worrying that the longer he was out of the embassy, the longer Connors might think he was trying to give him the slip.

He heard footsteps outside in the hall and a few seconds later the door swung open and Martin appeared with a guard. He was sporting a fresh uniform and a shave and looked much better than the last time Charlie had seen him. He stood as Martin approached and realized that, unlike the previous visits, Martin wasn't shackled. The guard allowed Charlie to shake his hand and then left, closing the door behind him.

"You look good," Charlie said, as they took their seats.

"I don't know how you did it, but all I can say is thanks, man." Martin shook his head, and Charlie saw a brief smile appear on his face for the first time.

"I told you not to give up."

"What's up with you though?" Martin said, his features clouding. "You look terrible."

Charlie was struck by the irony of his own situation being worse than the prisoner he was visiting, but decided to get to the point. "I was hoping you might be able to help me, actually."

"Anything," Martin replied with a shrug.

"Last time we met, you mentioned the investors in the new hotel you were going to be competing with were Colombian."

Martin nodded, his face taking on a puzzled frown.

"Do you know who's building it?"

"I think it's a Spanish contractor."

"It's not Société Immobilière, is it?"

Martin shook his head. "No, it's not them. It's definitely a Spanish company. I can't remember the name."

Charlie nodded. "What about Diego Medina," he said, lowering his voice, "have you ever heard of him?"

Martin looked blank. "No. Who's he?"

"I know he's Colombian, and I thought maybe he was connected to the hotel project, but I could be wrong."

"What's going on, Charlie?"

He looked at Martin and shook his head. "I can't really get into it right now. I was just looking for general info ..."

"What does this Medina look like?"

Charlie shrugged. "Big guy, dark features and a brush cut. He's got a fairly distinctive scar here," he said, pointing to his cheek. He noticed Martin's eyes had widened visibly at the mention of the scar. "What is it?"

Martin leaned forward across the table, prompting Charlie to do the same. His voice, when he spoke, was barely more than a whisper. "The man you're describing ... I've only heard of him by his nickname, and if it's him, whatever you do, you want to stay the hell away from him, Charlie."

Charlie felt himself swallow hard.

"Why? Who is he?"

"There are some dangerous people in Havana, but this is the one guy you want to steer clear of, you know what I'm saying?"

Charlie could tell by Martin's expression and the barely audible whisper that he was scared, and that even if he did know more, he was unlikely to share it here, where their conversation might very well be recorded.

"You said he had a nickname?" he whispered.

Martin nodded, before inching even closer to speak it, with a gravity the sent a chill down Charlie's spine.

"They call him *La Muerte.*"

Charlie swallowed hard, then took a deep breath as the two men sat in silence.

"It seems this place is a bit better than the Villa Marista," Charlie said, changing the subject in an attempt not to let his growing fear get the better of him.

"It's night and day," Martin said. "I can't believe you managed to pull it off. What the hell did you do, anyway?"

Charlie shrugged. "I guess they got sick of my letters, emails, and phone calls. I didn't even ramp it up to getting the ambassador involved."

"Do you think there's a chance you could get me *out* of here?" Martin's plaintive expression told Charlie that the transfer from Villa Marista had given the hotelier hope. The last thing he wanted to do was crush it. It also occurred to him that any doubts he had had as to Martin's innocence had waned with each visit.

"I'll get you out, Tate," he heard himself say, although he had no idea if he really could. "If it's the last thing I do."

# CHAPTER 36

Charlie pulled up to his house and nodded to the guard as the gate closed behind him. He felt as though he were functioning on autopilot — driving the car, walking to the front door — all of these things were taking place, but he didn't notice them, he was so consumed with trying to figure out what he was going to do when Diego Medina contacted him next.

After returning from his visit to Martin, Charlie had spent his time trying to avoid Connors, but in the end he had been forced to give a statement, a false statement at that, given that he had refrained from mentioning that he had, in fact, seen Jillian Gray much later than the ten-thirty time he had decided to stick with for official purposes. He had also neglected to mention that he had been seduced and drugged while his house was searched a few weeks ago, or that days before that he had discovered enough dope under his bedroom floor to put him behind bars as a trafficker in most jurisdictions, before promptly dumping it all into his pool....

*What the fuck were you thinking!?*

He felt drained as he put the key in the front door, but despite his mental exhaustion, he was no further ahead in formulating a plan. These sorts of situations always arose in the movies, and the hero always had a foolproof plan that would outwit the bad guy at the last minute. But hours after receiving that fateful note, Charlie had come up with precisely nothing.

Tossing his keys on the hall table as the door swung shut behind him, Charlie took a few steps before he registered the fact that the hallway was dark. He reached for the light switch and realized it was already in the on position. He flicked it back and forth a couple of times before it dawned on him that the power was out.

*Perfect.*

He sighed and continued on toward the kitchen, immediately re-immersed in the mental struggle of trying to figure out what to do next. The sound of his own footsteps on the tiled floor took on an otherworldly echo as he paused near the entrance to the living room, darkened even more by the trees outside the front window. He resisted the temptation to reach for the light switch, and as he stood in the doorway to the room, unable to make out more than rough outlines of furniture, he felt a chill descend his spine, just before the deep voice came from somewhere within the gloom.

*"Señor Hillier."*

He was too frozen by fear to move or call out, unable to do anything other than watch as an imposing figure rose from a chair to his right.

"I believe you have something belonging to me."

Charlie's heart pounded as he stared up at the broad-shouldered man standing a few feet from him, the distinctive scar across his right cheek suddenly visible as he turned his face into what dim light there was coming through the windows. If the idea was to be represented by a terrifying figure, the cartel, or whoever the man worked for, had chosen well. Just to look at Diego Medina had a paralyzing effect, and he couldn't help thinking the nickname *La Muerta* was just as apt.

"What?" he heard himself say.

"You heard me. Where is it?"

"You sent me the note?"

"I said *where is it?*"

"Where is *she*?" Charlie heard himself ask.

"Safe, for the moment," Medina said, producing a grainy Polaroid of Jillian Gray holding up a copy of *Granma* — the Communist party's official paper. Charlie squinted in the low light but thought he recognized the cover page from the office and was sure it was today's edition. She was alive, and in relatively good shape from what he could see. "But I'm losing patience." Medina withdrew the photo. "I don't think you realize what you got yourself into when you pulled up those floorboards," he said, with a rough laugh. "Garcia hid it well, but not well enough. You must have been quite surprised at your discovery."

"You could say that."

"But the time for games is over," Medina said, his hand going to his belt. "And I want what Garcia thought he could take from me."

Charlie watched the glint of a long steel blade emerge as Medina drew his hand back from his waist, and he took an instinctive step backwards.

"I'll ask you one more time. Where is it?"

"You get nothing until I see her," Charlie said. Though he could feel himself shaking, he had managed to sound quite calm, and in that moment of terror, one thing became clear to him — Medina would have killed him already if he didn't think Charlie could lead him to the drugs. He summoned what was left of his failing courage to add: "If you've done anything to her, I swear I'll never tell you where it is."

Medina let out a sharp breath, then approached slowly as Charlie just stood there, immobilized by fear. He could smell the stench of the Colombian's cologne — he must have bathed in it, it was so strong — as Medina's face hovered within inches of his own and the blade of the knife slowly rose between them, its tip touching Charlie's cheek with just enough pressure to sting, but not to draw blood.

"I think you will," Medina said, as Charlie fought to keep his fear under control. The big Colombian was still staring into his eyes when Charlie felt the air go out of his stomach. The shove that followed the surprise body blow sent Charlie flying back into the wing chair near the entrance to the living room. Doubled over and gasping for air, Charlie didn't resist as Medina grabbed his arms and pulled them around the back of the chair. He heard the sound of packing tape and his hands were quickly bound. Helpless as he sat there, Charlie wondered what was next, and thought he knew when Medina approached him again with the knife, pressing it into the flesh of his cheek, below his right eye. With a lightning-fast flick of the Colombian's wrist, Charlie felt the knife tear into his skin, followed by the unmistakable sensation of blood running down his face. He tried to shield himself out of instinct, but his hands were held firmly behind the chair, and he could only sit there, waiting for the end. Instead, the Colombian straightened up and tucked the knife into his belt, laughing as he did so. He allowed himself a few moments to savour Charlie's terror and confusion before he spoke again.

"Midnight tomorrow, at the Alameda de Paula. You will bring what is mine, and we will make an exchange. The woman for the *coca*, and then you will leave Havana and never return. Is that clear?"

Charlie managed a hurried nod.

"And if you try to involve anyone else in our arrangement, I will gut you like a fish and toss you in the bay, along with your girlfriend."

Charlie was too terrified, not to mention surprised he was still alive, to react to the blow to his temple that seemed to come out of nowhere and plunged him into darkness.

When Charlie came to, he was slumped in the chair and Medina was gone.

He strained against the tape that bound his wrists, and noticed drops of blood from his face on the floor in front of him. After a few minutes of exertion, he managed to stretch the tape and separate his hands. Bolting out of the chair, he noticed a smear of blood on the floor to the left of the entrance to the living room, leading toward the kitchen, and he ran to the patio door and looked out over the garden. The sliding door was unlocked, but there was no sign of anyone outside. As he surveyed the yard, the lights inside the house came back on and, putting his hand to his face, he went to the bathroom. The first glance in the mirror, and the sight of a considerable amount of blood smeared on his face shocked him. But after wiping it away with cold water, he was relieved to see the cut was not deep, and after a few minutes of pressure the bleeding stopped.

As he sat at the kitchen table, Charlie realized he was still shaking. He tried to pull himself together with a couple of fingers of Scotch, but he could barely bring the glass to his lips, his hand was trembling so much.

All he could think of was tomorrow night. What the hell was he going to do?

# CHAPTER 37

"What happened to your face?" Landon asked as he stood at the door to Charlie's office.

"Ran into a door, would you believe," he replied, in his best aw-shucks impression.

"Still no word on Gray?"

"No," Charlie replied. He had made a point of inquiring with Connors first thing, though he knew only too well that there would be nothing to report.

"That's awful," Landon said. "But they can file a missing persons report now, at least." He was obviously trying to be upbeat, but they both knew such a filing with the Cuban police would mean nothing.

"What do you make of this hurricane?"

Charlie looked up from his computer. "What hurricane?"

Landon's eyebrows shot up. "The first one of the season's on its way," he said, walking over to the window and looking out. "You didn't notice the sky?"

"Come to think of it, it did seem kind of dark on the way in this morning," Charlie said, though he was so preoccupied this morning that he might not have noticed if a plague of locusts had swarmed the island. He got up and joined Landon at the window. "Is it supposed to be a bad one?"

"Depends on what sort of shape it's in when it hits here," Landon said with a shrug. "Could be pretty wild. You might want to move your patio stuff inside."

Charlie nodded and looked out at the clouds, which seemed to have gotten darker even in the few seconds he had been standing at the window. He had seen a few major summer storms in Ottawa, but nothing like a hurricane. He might even be worried, if not for everything else that was going on right now. An impending hurricane seemed the least of his problems.

"Hey Drew," Charlie said, just as Landon was starting for the door.

"Yeah?"

"Do you remember whose property borders mine at the rear?"

Landon shrugged his shoulders. "I thought it was some government compound or something. Why do you ask?"

"I know the cops said it was government property when they were investigating the break-in. I was just curious which department."

"There's no house on it, is there?"

"It's hard to see with that big hedge and all the greenery on the other side, but I don't think so."

"If it's government, it's probably under the control of our good friend Gustavo Ruiz."

"What do you mean?" Charlie was taken off guard by the response.

"Well, whatever department is using it, if any, Ruiz's shop is probably in control of it."

"I thought he was only responsible for foreign governments."

"No, ImCub's responsible for the works, as far as I know. I can check if you want."

"No, don't bother," Charlie said, waving the offer off.

"Coffee later?"

"Sure," Charlie said, managing a half-hearted smile as Landon left, and betraying no sign of the breakneck speed at which his mind was replaying his memory of his last meeting with Gustavo Ruiz, and the strange comments he had made. What was it he had said when they were talking about environmental liabilities? *You need to be assured that there is nothing unsavoury on the grounds … or under them.*

Charlie had thought it an unsettling remark at the time, but he saw it in an even more ominous light now, especially after a sleepless night of replaying and dissecting every statement and piece of information that came to mind in an attempt to figure out what to do at the fast-approaching midnight meeting.

His mind returned to where he had begun after his terrifying encounter the night before — with Medina's presence in his living room, which he had initially attributed to his diplomatic guards being involved. Why then, had Medina left through the back of the house? The one smudge of blood on the hallway floor, which could only have been left by Medina's shoe, clearly showed he had exited from the back, not the front, of the house. It occurred to him that the guards might not be involved after all, in which case the people who had torn his house apart on the night of the break-in would have taken the same route. He had gone out in the yard with a flashlight the night before and found nothing but a chain-link fence behind the large hedge at the rear of his property, complete with razor wire at the top. How, then, had it been so apparently easy for Medina and whoever had broken in to get in and out? He had gone the length of the fence and seen no obvious point of entry, but it had been dark, and who knows what he had missed. Besides, uncovering their escape route wasn't helping with the more urgent problem of what he was going to do tonight. He was deep in thought when Connors appeared at his door.

"The Cubans want to talk to me about Jillian Gray. I think you should come."

Charlie sensed this was more of an order than a request, so he nodded his agreement. "The meeting's at their headquarters in the old town at noon. I'll meet you there. You know where it is?"

"Yeah, sure."

"And the ambassador wants a debrief this afternoon, around four, after he gets back from his own meeting at the Ministry of Foreign Affairs."

Charlie nodded and sighed. What else could he do?

Charlie drove up out of the underpass from Miramar and felt the car lurch to one side as an onshore gust bore down on him, bringing enough sea spray with it to obscure his vision for a couple of seconds before his wipers cleared the windshield. The sky had gone from a dark blue-grey to downright black, and the wind had been gradually picking up all morning, chasing even the hardiest of anglers from the seawall. The ominous weather was consistent with the turmoil going on inside Charlie's head as he made his way toward Old Havana.

Noticing a long line of cars waiting ahead, and a roadwork crew blocking the westbound lanes of the Malecón, desperately trying to pack up their equipment before it was blown or washed away, Charlie took a right by the Meliá Cohiba and began working his way east through side streets. He was still working on what was so far a hopeless plan when he caught sight of a familiar car in his rear-view mirror. Keeping his head facing directly forward, he carefully checked the other car's position as he made a couple of turns that eventually brought him out onto the Linea, heading east again. Checking the mirror, he saw that the car was still there. It was far enough back that it was hard to make out the model, but it looked relatively new. Maybe a Peugeot? Like Gord Connors drove …

Charlie decided that it was normal for Connors to be headed in the same direction, since they were both due at the same place in a few minutes. But why would he be taking precisely the same convoluted route? And why wouldn't they have gone together if they were both coming from Miramar? It occurred to him that despite what Landon had said about the likelihood that Redden had shot his mouth off about Charlie's liaison with Gray, Connors had not pressed him on the point. Did he really think Charlie might have something to do with her disappearance? He scanned the mirror for other cars, wondering whether the Cubans might also be following him as part of a joint surveillance exercise with Connors.

And then it hit him. A plan.

If Connors really was following him, all Charlie had to do was lead him to the meet tonight, and wait for him, and probably the Cubans, too, to bust things up. He would just have to stall Medina long enough — maybe with a bag of flour wrapped in cellophane — to hold the fort until the cavalry came to the rescue. Perhaps not the greatest plan on earth, but it was better than what he had two minutes before.

Arriving outside the police station, Charlie parked and got out of the car just as a turbulent blast of wind caught the open door, almost wrenching it off its hinges. Fat raindrops had begun to fall, and he had to shield his eyes from the leaves and little twigs whipped up by the buffeting winds as he made his way across the street.

He was not at all surprised to have arrived ahead of Connors, and he tried to act naturally when the former showed up five minutes behind him, shaking the rain from his clothes and muttering something about having come from a nearby meeting. As they went through the motions of filing a formal missing persons report with the Cubans, Charlie wondered whether the two cops sitting opposite them at the table had him under surveillance as well. He hoped so, and for the first time since receiving the note from Medina, he felt there was a chance, if only a slim one, that both he and Gray might survive the night.

# CHAPTER 38

Charlie flinched as a tree branch slammed into his wind-shield and he fought the wheel to keep his car straight against a vicious gust of wind as he made his way along Fifth Avenue. The briefing he and Gord Connors had been scheduled to give the ambassador at four had been cut short. There was no news on Jillian Gray, and nothing much they could do for now. The weather had deteriorated to the point where Stewart had decided to close the embassy, and he had become caught up in issuing emergency orders to ensure staff and equipment were safely tucked away before the storm hit. Charlie slammed his foot on the accelerator and sped along through a calm patch, eager to get back to his house before he was blown off the road. He was no meteorologist, but he could tell by the gusting winds, and the way they were bending even the biggest trees, that this was serious. He wondered what the conditions would be like later, when he was supposed to meet Medina in the old port. He had heard that the Malecón had been shut down, so he would have to find an alternate route if it hadn't been re-opened by midnight.

Charlie had spent the whole day trying to refine his plan and had slipped home at lunch to prepare the package of flour that he hoped to fool Medina with for long enough that he and Gray might be spared. As evening approached, Charlie began to fear that he would blow it when it came time for the meeting. He had to be convincing enough with Medina that keeping him and Gray alive for as long as it took Connors and company to arrive would lead the Colombian to his precious dope. If he wasn't, *La Muerte* might just kill them both on the spot. The fake brick of cocaine had been much trickier than he could ever have imagined, and he had looked like the Pillsbury doughboy by the time he was done. But the plastic-wrapped bundle, bound with masking tape, looked enough like what he had found under his floorboards that it just might just buy him some valuable time.

As he turned onto his street and the guard hurried out from his shelter to open the gate, Charlie felt a rush of relief at having made it home. But when he turned off the car and closed his eyes, all he saw was Gray's frightened face staring back at him from the grainy photo. What was she going through right now? Surely if there was a God, he wouldn't let her suffer the same fate as Amirjit Saini, whose only crime was to fall in love with a man who was willing to take risks of which she was probably completely unaware.

Charlie ran through the torrential rain to his front door and fumbled with the key, just as the sky lit up with a blinding flash of lightning, followed a couple of seconds later by an earsplitting bang that displaced the air around him. Once inside, he slammed the door and looked around at the darkened interior of his house. He flicked the nearest switch and realized the power was out again.

*Shit!*

He made his way upstairs and fumbled in the dim light of his bedroom for some dry clothes. He was throwing on a T-shirt when the room was flooded with the silver glow from another lightning strike, followed by an even louder eruption of thunder. A few seconds later, the light in the ceiling fan over his bed flickered for a moment, and rather than the return to darkness Charlie expected, the light continued to burn brightly. He breathed a sigh of relief and stepped out of the bedroom, oblivious to the fist hurtling toward his midsection that took his breath away and left him in a crumpled heap at the top of the stairs. He looked up to see Diego Medina's fearsome bulk hovering over him.

"Get up."

"What … what are you doing here?" Charlie said, trying to ignore the dull throbbing in his midsection.

"I said get up."

"But … you said midnight."

"Change of plans. Get the fuck up!"

The urgency of the command got Charlie upright, just in time for Medina to bark another one.

"Where is it?"

Charlie's mind was racing. He willed himself to stay calm. He had to stick to the plan, to the extent possible.

"Where's Gray?"

"Waiting for you, but I have to warn you that your reunion will be very short-lived unless you give me what I want. Come on."

Medina grabbed him by the shirt and shoved him down the stairs, then yanked him toward the dining room. Charlie understood when he stepped into the room and saw Jillian Gray sitting at his dining room table, her mouth covered in duct tape and her hands bound behind her back.

"Are you all right?" he said, rushing toward her until another man, wielding a gun, stepped into his path and pushed him roughly into a chair at the head of the table. Gray's eyes were wide with fear, but she seemed otherwise unharmed. Charlie looked around and noticed the drapes had been closed, so no one could see into the room. A flash of lightning outside lit up the edges of the curtains, and this time the roll of thunder was delayed by a few seconds. The storm was moving away from them.

"Now you see her. Now I want my package." Medina kicked Charlie's chair, causing him to jump.

"I … I have to go get it. It's nearby. Not here."

"You don't mean this, do you?" Medina said, tossing Charlie's carefully packaged flour onto the table. The side had been cut open and a cloud of flour dust shot up as it hit the centre of the table. Charlie just sat there staring at it.

"Doing some baking?" Medina said, and his associate at the side of the table chuckled. "We searched the place while you were out," he said, approaching him, and leaning down to talk. "You weren't going to try and fool us with that were you?"

"No … of course not."

"You have about three seconds to tell me where the coca is, or you're both going to die."

All Charlie could think of was Connors, possibly sitting in his car down the street, munching on plantain chips and waiting for Charlie to make a move. He was going to die in here and Connors would never know. He had to think of something, anything.

"You'll have to take me to it," he said, not looking up. "It's buried."

"Where's it buried?" Medina said, grabbing Charlie by the front of his shirt and staring into his eyes.

"Near the hotel, the Meliá Habana, under some rocks."

Medina continued to glare at him for several moments, and Charlie began to sweat.

"You want me to drive you to Meliá Habana in a fucking hurricane?" Medina yelled, his face so close to Charlie's that spittle flicked into his eyes.

"I'll make him talk, boss," the other man said, starting to move toward them, but Medina just stared at Charlie, his dark eyes boring into him.

"You don't have it, do you?"

"I do. It's buried."

"I don't think you do. I've been following you since last night, and I get the feeling you're just stalling."

Charlie shook his head. "I'm telling you, it's buried."

"Well, I'm going to get the truth out of you, whatever it is. Come on," Medina said, grabbing Charlie by the shirt again, yanking him back out into the hallway and toward the basement stairs, as the other man followed with Gray. "I tried to do this the easy way, but you force my hand," Medina said, as they descended the stairs, with only the light from the hallway above to guide them.

"Please, I'm telling you the truth. A five-minute drive, and we'll be there."

"Enough!" Medina yelled, as they reached the bottom of the stairs. "The time for you to talk is over. Now, you'll see what happens when you lie to me."

Medina dragged him to toward the centre of the room and sat him roughly in the only chair in the otherwise empty basement. Charlie could barely make out the other man, forcing Gray to sit on the floor by the bottom of the stairs.

"Tie him up," Medina ordered.

As Charlie's hands were bound behind the chair, he tried to think of something to slow things down, his time running out. "How did you get in here, anyway?"

The Colombian looked at him and laughed. "I'll bet you didn't know the head of Batista's secret police used to live in this house." Medina paused long enough to enjoy Charlie's surprise. "I guess I'm better informed than you."

"What do you mean?" Charlie was even more puzzled by the cryptic answer.

Medina shook his head. "Enough questions," he said abruptly, walking over to the other man and pointing at his gun.

"Give me that," he said, taking the 9 mm. "And turn on the light. It's too fucking dark down here."

As the other man searched for the light switch by the bottom of the stairs, Medina returned to Charlie and waved the gun at him. "The knife will be what kills you in the end, my friend, but I'm going to have some fun with this first," he said, as Charlie tried to imagine what he had in mind. Whatever it was, it wasn't good, and for a moment, all he could think of was what an utter waste his life had been; to have blown fifteen years on a marriage to an unfaithful wife, and to have sacrificed his career in the process. If he could have just one of those years back now…. But this bastard was going to kill him, and then he was going to kill Gray, and there was nothing he could do about it.

With that realization came a sudden rage. "Fuck you, Medina," he said, without noticing he had spoken the words aloud.

"What did you say?"

"I told you to go fuck yourself, same goes for your friend over …"

Charlie never saw the punch coming, but it jolted his head sideways with such a force that for a moment everything went black. He waited for the immediate pain to pass, before spitting blood back at his tormentor. "And your dope? You're never going to find it, because I threw it in the pool. I hope it was worth a fucking fortune!"

Medina looked at him, and his eyes narrowed in anger. "You threw ten kilos of high-grade cocaine *into your pool*?"

"Yes, so why don't you go drown yourself in it …" Charlie said, before registering Medina's words. Had he said *ten* kilos? He was trying to figure out how that one package could have weighed so much when he heard the click as Medina slid the safety off the gun, then turned to the other man by the foot of the stairs.

"Where's that fucking light? I want to see him die."

"I can't find a switch, boss."

"Forget it," Medina said, spotting the chain dangling from the overhead fixture in the dim light from the stairs. He reached up for it, his other arm rising in the process as well and, as he pulled the chain, an arc of light lit up the basement for a split second before plunging it into a darkness that was immediately interrupted by another flash of light from the end of Medina's arm, accompanied by a deafening bang.

Charlie felt the gunshot, or thought he did, but the screams weren't his.

Whatever light had come from the hallway above was gone now, and it took a couple of seconds for his eyes to adjust to the inky blackness, and to make out two figures lying on the ground before him. Medina lay motionless on the floor at his feet, while the other man was writhing in pain, clutching what Charlie thought was his upper thigh.

Charlie began wriggling furiously, tugging with all his might at the ropes holding his arms together, and he was surprised to see Gray standing over him, turning her own bound hands back on to meet his, and undoing the rope a few seconds later. Charlie had wrenched the gun out of Medina's rigid hand by the time the other man had stopped shouting and realized that the tables had turned, though he seemed to have no idea why his boss had suddenly decided to shoot him in the ass.

As Charlie stood there holding the gun and wondering what to do next, the clatter of footsteps on the floor above made them all look up. A few seconds later, Connors stood at the bottom of the stairs, followed by two Cuban cops, flashlights and weapons drawn.

"Are you all right?" Connors said breathlessly, looking first at Charlie, then noticing Gray, and finally the two Colombians on the floor, one of them still writhing in pain. "What the hell happened? The whole block lost power, and we heard a gunshot."

Charlie stood there, staring at the scene of confusion before glancing up at the fixture above his head. The bulb was gone, and so was the chain that Medina had grabbed onto in an attempt to turn it on. He turned to look first at Medina's lifeless stare and then the little chain still clutched tightly in his other hand.

"I guess I'm not much of an electrician," he said, looking at an uncomprehending Connors.

# EPILOGUE

Charlie and Landon sat on the balcony of the restaurant, looking out over Havana Bay, and El Morro beyond. They had been driving by, noticed the multicoloured lights strung along the balcony, and guessed it was a *paladar*. Neither had high expectations for the quality of the cuisine, but the view was fabulous, and it was a beautiful night.

"*Salud,*" Landon said as their beers arrived.

"Thanks, Drew. It's good to get out." Charlie took a sip of the cold beer and looked out at the Sunday evening strollers on the Malecón and the tranquil waters of the bay. For the first time in weeks, he felt he could finally relax.

And the past few days had been interesting, to say the least.

After the dust had settled and he and Gray had been whisked out of his basement on Friday night, the missing pieces of the puzzle Charlie had been trying to assemble since moving into his house gradually fell into place. It was clear that they weren't going to get much out of Medina, who was confirmed dead within minutes of the Cuban cops' arrival — his heart having exploded when he had touched that metal chain and closed the circuit on the little electrical deathtrap that Charlie had unwittingly created weeks ago, under Teddy's watchful eye. Any remorse he felt for Medina evaporated when he thought of what he had done to Amirjit Saini, and what the Colombian might have done to Gray, not to mention him. It sent a chill down his spine to think that he could easily have fried his own heart any number of times by touching that chain. The embassy had gotten the electrician in — he had come on short notice, for once — and he had apparently crossed himself a few times before referring to whoever had rigged up the light as *loco*.

But it wasn't until the electrician pulled the disconnected fixture out that things really got strange. Hidden in the ceiling around the fixture hole were another four packages of similar size and shape to the one Charlie had found under the bedroom floor, each containing two kilos of pure cocaine. Charlie had since heard varying estimates of the street value of such a find, but the bottom line was that it was in the millions.

Armed with this cache, the Cuban police had conducted numerous inquiries into the activities of Diego Medina over the past eighteen months, and come up with some interesting information. First, they discovered immigration stamps in his passport that confirmed he had made a half-dozen trips to Bogotá in the last six months, as well as one excursion to Caracas. The timing of Medina's Venezuelan trip, around about the time Charlie had moved into his house in Jaimanitas, also coincided with the "accidental" death of Javier Garcia on a remote mountain road outside Caracas, and left little doubt that it was no accident at all.

Medina's partner in crime, who had been much more fortunate than his boss — the wound to his derriere having been patched up the same night — was also placed under the microscope by the Cuban authorities, and was soon identified as a Venezuelan national named Oscar Suarez. Their inquiries also apparently revealed that Suarez had connections to drug smugglers in Santo Domingo and Miami, all of which led them to the conclusion that Havana was just the importation point, and that most of the drugs were destined for more profitable streets further afield. Oscar Suarez had also made several trips to Venezuela in the past few months.

And while Charlie had been pleased that the whole business appeared to have been solved, he was surprised to learn that Suarez had been shipped back to his native Venezuela within twenty-four hours of the shooting. While they had been happy to provide information about the now-defunct drug operation in the aftermath of the events at Charlie's house, by way of regular updates to Gord Connors, the Cubans had been rather tight-lipped about the rapid deportation, other than to say they were confident that Suarez had nothing to do with the death of either Amirjit Saini or Javier Garcia.

In the end, Charlie supposed it didn't matter. Gray was safe, as was he, and the Cubans appeared pleased to be permanently rid of Medina, whom no one doubted was responsible for Amirjit Saini's death. As for Suarez's rapid exit, Charlie should not have been surprised, given the close political ties between Cuba and Venezuela. He did wonder how long the Cubans had been watching Medina, since they seemed to have pieced together an awful lot of information in a very short period of time. He couldn't help thinking that he had probably also been under surveillance, possibly from the beginning, and, while he wasn't about to ask for confirmation, he had a feeling Maria Aguirre might have been sent not by Medina, but by the Cubans. It didn't seem to matter now.

The last piece of the puzzle — how Medina had accessed Charlie's house undetected at least twice — fell into place when Gord Connors's inspection of Charlie's basement in the aftermath of the shooting revealed a hole in the floor under the stairs. A series of wooden steps led down into a tunnel that ended at the ruins of a house some hundred metres away on the government-owned property behind Charlie's. He had confirmed Medina's assertion that Charlie's house had once been occupied by Batista's head of security, but the real surprise came when he discovered that the last official use of the government building behind him was by the KGB. They still didn't know whether the tunnel had been dug by the Russians, or if it had been there since the fifties. Either way, it was clear that Medina had become aware of it somehow. There were even rumours that Medina may have had connections to organized crime in Russia, perhaps even the FSB, but that was just speculation. Still …

"So," Landon said, bringing Charlie back to real time. "Are you gonna keep in touch with Jillian?"

Now there was a question.

"Yeah, I think we'll be in touch." Charlie nodded, sipping his beer. The truth was, he didn't know where they stood. He could still picture her standing there at the airport, looking fragile but beautiful. He could hardly blame her for wanting to leave on the next available flight after what she'd been through. She had called a few days later, to thank him, of all things.

*Thanks for almost getting me killed.*

Charlie would be going back to Ottawa for some training in the fall and he would have a weekend there. Maybe he would look her up. Or maybe she would always associate him with what happened to Amirjit Saini, and what had very nearly happened to her.

"You sure you're ready to go back to the office tomorrow?" Landon asked him as their meals arrived — beef kebabs that looked about as tender as shoe leather. At least the place had a nice view, and the beers were cold.

"I'm ready," he lied. While both Connors, the ambassador, and the Cubans had cleared Charlie of any wrongdoing in the whole affair, he still felt embarrassed by it all, and he wasn't sure how he felt about returning to work. Stewart had actually praised Charlie for his courage, although he had written that off to the ambassador's good humour at Teddy's sudden recovery of full bladder control now that his toy bone had been returned.

There had been one other positive result of the whole mess. Charlie had made a point of mentioning his suspicion that Diego Medina might have been trying to insinuate himself into the construction of a new hotel on José Martí Square, and that he may have had an active role in orchestrating the incarceration of a competitor in the hotel business, as a gesture of good faith. He had pressed for a full investigation into Tate Martin's case. It seemed that the investigation was a non-starter, but less than forty-eight hours after Charlie's debrief with the Cubans, he learned that Martin had been released.

As he and Landon sat there in the warm evening breeze, chewing their kebabs and recounting the events of the past weeks, even managing a laugh or two, Charlie came to a realization. Havana had turned out much differently than he had imagined, but his experiences here so far had changed his outlook on life forever. While he felt some sadness over Gray's departure, he wasn't convinced their story was at an end, and having come so close to death, it was difficult not to embrace life now. And Tate Martin's release had given Charlie renewed hope that maybe he was capable of doing something meaningful with his life, after all.

# ACKNOWLEDGEMENTS

Thanks to Kirk Howard and the team at Dundurn for all your hard work, and especially to my editor, Allison Hirst, for going to bat for the series. David Jacques, Pat Marshall, and Oriana Trombetti all read versions of the manuscript and provided valuable feedback, and Tara Snell helped me decipher copyright and related issues. Thanks also to everyone at the Bureau (you know which one!).

Special thanks to Tanya, for letting me explore my fictional world by keeping things on track in the real one.

## MOSCOW CODE
### Nick Wilkshire

**As Charlie Hillier discovers, in Moscow,
the truth can be a dangerous commodity.**

Ottawa bureaucrat-turned-diplomat Charlie Hillier is back. Having barely survived his first posting in Havana, he is eager to put what he learned there to good use. And it isn't long before he's working a fresh case: a technical writer from Canada has been jailed on dubious drug charges.

But Charlie has barely put a dent in the brick wall that is the Russian legal system when the jailed man dies — the official explanation: suicide. And just when evidence to the contrary is discovered, the body is "accidentally" cremated.

Undeterred by bureaucratic stonewalling, and assisted by the victim's sister and a journalist friend, Charlie follows the sparse clues available. What they uncover brings them all way too close to powers more dangerous than they could have imagined. Suddenly, the truth is less important than getting out of Russia alive.